RIDER OF THE RIFLE ROCK

RIDER
OF THE
RIFLE ROCK

BENNETT FOSTER

Sagebrush
Large Print Westerns

First published in the United States by Morrow

First published in Great Britain by Harrap

Published in Large Print 2005 by ISIS Publishing Ltd,
7 Centremead, Osney Mead, Oxford OX2 0ES,
United Kingdom
by arrangement with
Golden West Literary Agency

British Library Cataloguing in Publication Data
Foster, Bennett
    Rider of the Rifle Rock. – Large print ed. –
    (Sagebrush western series)
    1. Western stories
    2. Large type books
    I. Title
    813.5'2 [F]

ISBN 0–7531–7288–7 (hb)

Printed and bound by Antony Rowe, Chippenham

This book
is affectionately dedicated to
O. E. FOSTER

CAST OF CHARACTERS

CHET MINOR had been beaten, doublecrossed, sold out. There was only one way for him to come back — fighting.

POWELL OVERMAN meant to stay on top — even if it meant killing.

BEN REVILLA played with both sides — but it was his own game.

OTTO HAHN was Chet's friend once, but now he was scared.

BARNEY LOVELESS ran a "cull" ranch, but he could tell a man when he saw one.

JOE FRENCH worked for Barney. He licked Chet — for a reason.

DOC LAIRD was too honest for his own good.

SALLY LAIRD could be wrong about a man — but not about another woman.

NORVILLE KIRKPATRICK had a deal in mind.

MAIDA OVERMAN knew what she wanted — and how to get it.

ED AMES was a killer — sometimes for more than money.

CHAPTER
ONE

All the trees along Montana Street were green when Chet Minor came limping along the board sidewalk; and to the west the light green of the aspen in the draws striped the dark color of the nearest mesa's side. The lawns in front of the houses were green with the bright colors of fall flowers marking the borders. A woman looked curiously from a window as Chet passed by, and another, sweeping her front porch, paused in her work and watched him. Chet, turning in at a gate in a white picket fence, went up the path from gate to house, climbed the steps to the porch and stopped before the door. He lifted his hand to knock, then hesitated. He had come back to Rifle Rock and he should have been sure of his welcome. He was not.

The indecision passed and Chet's knock sounded sharply. Answering his summons, a pleasant-faced native woman opened the door and asked a question with her eyes.

"I'd like to see Mr. Scotia," Chet said.

The woman nodded and retired, leaving the door open, and Chet looked into the familiar hallway. Presently the maid returned, nodded to Chet and invited him in, her Spanish soft and courteous. Chet

1

followed her down the hall and, as she stood aside, looked through a door and saw Mark Scotia sitting in the sunlight that came streaming through a bay window. Scotia had a book in his hand, his finger marking a place, and his eyes were on the door. Chet stepped past the woman and went into the room, his hat in his hands.

A year had changed Mark Scotia. His face, in the sunlight, was gray, and the heavy lines that marked it had grown into crevasses in the flesh. His eyes held no recognition as he looked at his visitor and his voice was uncertain and a little high as he spoke.

"Yes?" Scotia said. "You wanted to see me?"

Chet advanced another step, closing the distance between himself and the man in the chair. "I've come back, Mr. Scotia," he said. "Chet Minor. Do you remember me?"

It seemed as though Mark Scotia searched his mind before he answered. "Minor?" he said questioningly. "Chet Minor?"

"I worked at the ranch," Chet explained, anxiety coming to his voice now. "I ran the wagon for Mr. Druerson."

Scotia nodded. "Oh yes," he said. "You come from the ranch."

"No," Chet explained, "I got hurt, Mr. Scotia. I've been gone."

Mark Scotia was silent for a full minute. His eyes had strayed from Chet to the pattern of sunlight on the floor. Then he looked up. "I remember," he said. "You were hurt. Eades told me about it. You're all right now?"

Chet nodded eagerly. "I came back," he said. "I wanted to see you about a job at the Triangle. I'm all right now . . ."

Mark Scotia leaned back in his chair, the interest gone from his eyes. He did not look at Chet. "You can see Powell Overman," he said. "I . . . I don't go to the ranch any more. I'm sick. You can see Powell."

"I thought . . ." Chet began, and stopped. Mark Scotia had opened the book and was looking at the page his finger had marked. Chet waited, waited for Scotia to look up again. When the man in the chair turned a page, Chet stepped back into the hall.

When he reached the street again Chet paused and then, making up his mind went on to the cross street, Vermont Avenue. He walked the short block east on Vermont and at the corner paused again. This was Idaho Street, the principal thoroughfare of Rifle Rock.

There was activity on Idaho Street and for that reason Chet had avoided it when he left the depot. Now he looked up and down its length. There were horses tied to the hitchrails that lined the street, cow ponies that slumped on three legs and dozed in the sun, teams hitched to wagons, the horses languidly switching their tails at late flies.

A big man coming hurriedly out of Wolfbarger's store, walked to a buckboard tied to the hitchrail immediately at Chet's right. Chet stepped forward.

"Hello, Mr. Mitchell," he greeted.

3

Royce Mitchell, the man at the buckboard, looked around to see who had spoken. Seeing Chet he left the side of the vehicle and stepped up on the sidewalk. He came toward Chet, his hand extended. "Chet Minor!" Mitchell exclaimed. "When did you get back?"

The smile was warm on Chet's face as he took Mitchell's hand. "About half an hour ago," he said. "I came in on the noon train. How are you, Mr. Mitchell?"

"Fine!" Royce Mitchell boomed, releasing Chet's hand. "And you, Chet?"

"I'm all right now," Chet said. "I came back to go to work."

Mitchell's eyes narrowed. "For the Triangle?" he asked.

"I went to see Mr. Scotia," Chet said, not directly answering the question.

"Mark has been sick." Mitchell was studying Chet. "Overman is foreman at the Triangle now."

"Mr. Scotia told me," Chet answered. "Have you got a full crew at the Gunhammer, Mr. Mitchell?"

"Well now . . ." Mitchell moved back toward the buckboard as he spoke, and Chet took limping steps to follow. "I'll tell you." Royce Mitchell's eyes were fixed on Chet's leg, his short right leg. "I've got a pretty full crew, Chet. I need a man to start some horses but . . ."

"I can start broncs," Chet interrupted eagerly. "You know I can, Mr. Mitchell."

"Sure," Mitchell's deep voice was smooth. "You were a master hand with a bronc, Chet. But I've got a man in mind . . . half way promised him the job."

4

Chet said, "Oh," and then, after a moment, "sure, Mr. Mitchell."

"Couldn't go back on my word," Mitchell said heartily. "You come out and see us, Chet. Ride grubline an' stay a while." He turned, busying himself with a package in the buckboard. "I'm glad I saw you," Mitchell completed.

Still Chet waited. Mitchell got the string off the parcel and took out a blanket. He tossed it over his arm and stepped back up on the walk, hurrying along toward Wolfbarger's entrance. Chet watched him go into the store. Wolfbarger's door closed. Slowly Chet stepped down from the walk and, limping, the dust thick about his boots, crossed the street.

Otto Hahn's Staghorn Saloon was dim when Chet entered and he paused a moment just inside the door. The sight of Otto Hahn reading the paper at a table in the rear of the room made Chet, for an instant, oddly homesick. Otto had always picked the darkest place in the room to do his reading. Hahn, looking up over the paper, not recognizing his visitor, laid the paper aside and got awkwardly to his feet, moving toward the bar. Chet said, "Otto," and the big man paused and stared and then, slowly, a smile wreathed his face.

"Chet!" he exclaimed and, lumberingly, advanced, drying one big red hand on his apron and holding it out. "By golly, Chet!" Otto exclaimed as Chet took the extended hand. "By golly!"

He drew Chet back toward the table he had quitted, kicked out a chair, shoved Chet toward it, and stood, hands on his fat hips as Chet sat down. "By golly!"

5

Otto said once more and then: "When did you get back, Chet?"

"This afternoon." Chet took the chair, looking up at Otto. "I'm mighty glad to get back, Otto. What's new in Rifle Rock?"

Otto shook his head. His Dutch mind was methodical and things came in their proper order. "First we take a drink," Otto announced, "then we talk." He moved toward the bar, throwing words back over his shoulder as he moved, questions for Chet Minor to answer.

"Did you get well, Chet? Did they fix you up in El Paso?"

"Pretty good." Chet's eyes followed the big man. "I've got one short leg, Otto. It don't hurt me any!" Chet's voice was quick as he spoke the last words. Otto was measuring liquor into two small glasses. Carrying them, he came back to the table.

"Tell me, Chet." Otto put the glasses on the table. "Tell me what happened. I was gone when you were hurt an' when I come back they say that you have been hurt an' that the Triangle shipped you to El Paso to get well or die, they don't know which."

Chet's face softened. The concern in Otto's voice was so evident and so sincere that it touched him.

"There's not a whole lot to it, Otto," he said. "Powell Overman an' me had gone out to doctor a bull. Powell had found one of the shorthorns with a bad shoulder an' he wanted me to help him with it. I put a rope on the bull an' got jerked down. I was ridin' a green horse. That's what happened."

6

"An' so they sent you to El Paso."

Chet nodded. "Eades Druerson had me sent there," he said. "The saddle caught me when the horse went over an' I was banged up pretty bad. They worked on me down in El Paso an' a month ago they turned me loose. I stayed around for a while an' then I came on back."

"So!" Otto picked up his glass, raising it toward Chet. Chet, smiling, imitated the other. They drank and put their glasses down again.

"An' now what do you do?" asked Otto Hahn.

"Get a job," Chet answered. "I talked to Scotia an' he told me that Powell was the boss at the ranch, now that Eades is gone. Then I hit Royce Mitchell for a job. He said he was full-handed. Do you know of anything, Otto? Any kind of ridin' job? I'm not much good afoot. Never was."

Otto did not answer the question but rather, asked one. "Who paid the bills, Chet? For you, I mean."

"Why," Chet answered, "I paid them, Otto. It was me that was hurt."

Otto Hahn grunted. "And now you have come back to get a job," he said.

Chet smiled ruefully. "I'm broke," he announced. "Doctors and hospitals don't come cheap."

"I . . ." Otto said and hesitated, then, "You were working for the Triangle when you got hurt. I think . . ."

"It was my fault I got hurt," Chet said quickly. "I want to get a job, Otto. I thought the Triangle would have a place for me but with Powell for foreman I don't know. Do you know of anything, Otto?"

"I think," Otto answered. "Maybe I think of something."

"What's new in Rifle Rock since I've been gone?" Chet knew that Otto Hahn was not to be hurried. "Have any more nesters come in?"

The saloon keeper nodded slowly. "There are families all along Willow Creek," he answered. "The railroad has been sending out advertising an' they have brought in people. There are maybe a hundred new homesteads in this county, Chet, and the railroad sold some land."

Chet whistled a low, long note. "An' the cowmen don't like that," he surmised.

"There is some talk," Otto admitted. "Royce Mitchell says that the nesters steal Gunhammer cattle. Alec Crow over at the AC run a family off the Tarheel spring where they had settled. Some people went into the JAK vega an' built a house an' it was burned down an' they left for another place. Me, I say, let them come. Some year we will have a dry time an' they will leave again. I have seen it happen."

Chet nodded. "But they put up fences an' shacks an' they plow range an' it goes into weeds," he said. "They ruin a country, Otto."

Otto Hahn wrinkled his forehead. "When I come here," he commented, "old Windy Krueger was alive. Windy had trapped in this country when it was only Indians that lived here. Windy said that the cowmen ruined the country."

8

Chet laughed. "I reckon they did for Windy," he said. "I remember him. Anythin' else besides the nesters, Otto?"

"You have another drink, Chet?" Otto answered. "I got some Sunnybrook. You always liked Sunnybrook."

"I don't need a drink. Tell me what else has been goin' on." Chet knew Otto Hahn. Otto, when he wished to hide a thing, always attempted to change the subject. He tried now.

"I just been thinkin'," Otto said. "There is a man on the Tramparas, Clyde Stevens, that comes in sometimes, an' I think his rider has quit him. If you go to the Tramparas . . ."

"What is it, Otto?" Chet's voice was quiet.

Otto squirmed uneasily. "This man on the Tramparas . . ." he evaded.

"Tell me!" Chet was insistent. "What is it, Otto?"

Otto Hahn got up. "We had a wedding, Chet," he said. "A big wedding. Powell Overman is manager for Scotia now. He runs the Triangle."

"Well?" Chet's voice had dropped a tone.

"Well." Otto looked around as though to seek an avenue of escape. "Powell was married. He . . . That is good Sunnybrook, Chet."

"You're tryin' to tell me he married Maida Scotia," Chet said quietly.

"You knew it then?" There was concern in Otto's voice.

Chet shook his head. "No," he answered. "I didn't know. I guessed."

9

The Staghorn's door opened and men came in. Otto Hahn left Chet to attend his customers, and Chet, his back to the door, sat quietly at the table. He had made the wrong move in returning to Rifle Rock, he thought. A mistake. There was bitterness in his mind, and uncertainty. Mark Scotia was childish now, and Eades Druerson was gone. Chet had wondered why Eades, stopping off in El Paso, had been so insistent that Chet join him when he was able. Now Chet knew. Eades had known about Maida Scotia and Powell Overman, and he had known, too, that Powell was Chet's successor on the Triangle. Eades had tried to help Chet Minor. Chet shook his head as a man does to clear his brain following a blow. Powell Overman, manager of the Triangle. Maida Overman . . . Maida Overman . . . Not Maida Scotia any more. Her lips had been sweet and her hands caressing there in the dark shadows of Mark Scotia's porch. Chet had thought . . . He had thought . . .

Up at the bar Royce Mitchell's deep voice boomed. "He hit me for a job," Mitchell said. "Had the nerve to ask for a job startin' broncs. Why didn't he stay in the hospital where he belongs? Think I'm goin' to hire a cripple at the Gunhammer?"

Otto Hahn's voice came swift and low, too low for Chet to hear the words. Then Mitchell said, "Oh, I didn't know . . ."

Chet did not stir. He heard the glasses clink on the bar as Royce Mitchell and whoever accompanied him set them down. Then the door opened and closed, and Otto Hahn came back to the table.

"Is that what they think?" Chet asked quietly. "That I'm a cripple an' no account any more?"

Otto Hahn could not answer. He could see the pain deep in Chet's eyes and, beyond the pain, fright. Chet got up. "I'll be back," he said to Otto Hahn. "Thanks, Otto."

It had been a mistake for Chet Minor to come back to Rifle Rock. A year ago Chet had been at the top of the heap, second in command to Eades Druerson on the Triangle, the biggest ranch in the Rifle Rock country, on his way up to fill Druerson's shoes, a top hand, a cowman par excellence, unexcelled at the things by which the Rifle Rock measured a man's worth. He had been proud and sure then and, sometimes, in his pride and his sureness, he had spoken abruptly, given a needless judgment, made enemies. Now he was back, a little shabby, limping, something in his eyes that spoke of the uncertainty in his mind. Men are cruel. Let a man lift up, rising toward the top, and there are certain to be those who envy him, sure to be those who would pull him down if they could, inevitably men who would gloat over his misfortune. The Rifle Rock was no exception to the rule.

On Idaho Street Chet met friends and acquaintances and enemies. His limping gait, his pallor, made him conspicuous. Men with whom he had ridden greeted him, welcomed him, bought him liquor, patted him on the back. To Chet Minor it seemed that their eyes pitied him even as they made him welcome. The pity hurt, hurt more than the little triumphant look that came

11

into the eyes of other men who spoke to him. Pride was all that Chet Minor had left, a haughty, stiff-necked pride that would not bend. He returned the greetings, he took the drinks and bought drinks himself. By mid-afternoon his face was flushed and his limping gait had become more unsteady.

It was unfortunate that young Tom Neil, but recently entered into his heritage of the Rocking Chair, should have been in Rifle Rock that Saturday. Tom Neil and Chet Minor had worked together, Neil acting as representative for his father's brand when Chet was in charge of the Triangle wagon crew. There had been differences of opinion between Tom Neil and Chet Minor then, and Chet, as wagon boss, had overridden the son of the neighboring rancher.

Tom Neil had been drinking and he had been hearing things. He had taken a drink with Royce Mitchell, and Mitchell had spoken of Chet Minor. Tom Neil had listened and grunted. Tom Neil had talked with Alec Crow, shortly after that wrinkled misanthrope had refused Chet a job. There was a desire for revenge in Neil's mind and the liquor made him bold when he saw Chet limping toward him. Walt Kadey, the Rocking Chair foreman, was with Neil as Chet approached, but that wise old hand had no chance to interfere.

It was on the corner of Vermont Avenue and Idaho Street that Chet met Neil and the youngster from the Rocking Chair called to Chet.

"Hi, Minor, come over here!"

Minor limped across the street, expecting the usual greetings and inquiries concerning his health. In place

12

of that Tom Neil asked a question. "I hear yo're lookin' for a job," Neil said. "Is that right?"

Chet's eyes were eager. "I sure am," he answered.

"I got a job you might fill," Neil continued, grinning maliciously at Chet. "I've got a big crew at the Rockin' Chair now. What kind of work did you want to do?"

"'Most any kind," Chet answered honestly. "I . . ."

Neil broke in. "Got a Chink cook," he said. "Keeps him busy cookin' for the crew. Come out an' I'll give you the job of helpin' him. It's all a cripple's good for."

The sheer cruelty of the words kept Chet silent for a moment. Then his temper flared.

"Cripple or not," he snarled, "I'm a better man than you'll ever be!" With that his hand lashed out and Tom Neil reeled back under the impact of the blow.

Recovering himself before Kadey could interfere Neil attacked, swift and sudden, the attack of a man who is strong against one who had been weakened by months abed. Chet Minor went down under the fury of Neil's blows, his lips split and bleeding, a raking cut along his cheek. Walt Kadey caught Tom Neil's arms and pulled him off, and other men, running to the corner, lifted Chet up and half-carried him away, almost crying with his rage and impotence.

The men with Chet took him to the back room of the Staghorn. There Otto Hahn got a basin of water and a clean bar towel and made repairs on Chet's face while the men who had brought him in demanded to know what had happened and why Tom Neil had hit him. Chet did not answer their inquiries and they left him, their curiosity unsatisfied. Hahn put the towel on an empty beer barrel and looked sorrowfully at Chet.

"What happened, Chet?" he asked.

"I got knocked down," Chet said bitterly. "I got told that I was a cripple an' good for nothin'. I took a swing at Neil an' he showed me he was right."

"Listen, Chet," Otto said anxiously, "you stay here now for a while, mebbe. You ain't feelin' so good. You stay here this afternoon an' you stay around town for a while. Somethin' will turn up that you can do . . ."

"You too, huh?" Chet Minor grunted.

"What do you mean?" Otto asked.

The bitterness in Chet spilled over then. "You're like all the rest of 'em," he said. "You think I'm a cripple an' that I'm no damned good. By God, I'll show you! I'll show all of you!"

The wildness in Chet's eyes frightened Otto. He tried to restrain his friend. Chet pushed him away. Limping, lurching a little in his stride, he shoved past Otto, on into the front room of the Staghorn, through the men there, and out the door.

The clerk at the Parker House, Rifle Rock's one hotel, gave Chet a room. The man at the bar at the hotel sold Chet Minor a quart of whisky. The Parker House Bar was unoccupied at the moment and the bartender would have engaged his customer in talk, but Chet, paying for the bottle, stamped out of the place.

Upstairs in his room on the second and highest floor of the hotel, he uncorked the bottle and took a drink. He sat down then on the edge of the bed, cradling the whisky in his hands. All the things that Royce Mitchell

14

had said, not knowing that Chet could hear him; the short, "I don't need hands," of Alec Crow; the insult of Tom Neil; they burned in Chet. And yet, while those things hurt, there was a deeper wound. Powell Overman had married Maida. Powell Overman had the job that he, Chet Minor, should now hold. The bottle had been lifted and lowered as Chet sat there thinking. The whisky burned hotly in his mouth and throat but not so hotly as his thoughts. All the long and weary time he had lain abed, Chet Minor had been sustained by anticipation, by the thought of the things that he would do when he was home again. And now the last prop had been kicked out from under him. He was through, done, finished.

There was a dance in the K. P. Hall in Rifle Rock that night. It was Saturday night and the first of the month and the riders of the Rifle Rock country had come to town. Festivities were in order. Over against the far wall Maida Overman was holding court, handsome, dark-haired, proud-faced. Powell Overman was beside her, tall, blond, gray-eyed. There was achievement in the way Powell Overman stood beside his wife, achievement and, perhaps, arrogance. He had married Mark Scotia's daughter, hadn't he? He had carried away the prettiest woman in the country and he was manager of the biggest ranch. And six months ago he had been a puncher, a forty-dollar hand. Powell Overman stood beside his wife, his hand on her shoulder and his lips smiling while the cowmen of the Rifle Rock came up to do Maida homage and to ask her to dance. Maida laughed and shook her head. She had promised Powell, she said. She was dancing all the waltzes with him and she wasn't dancing any of the two-steps or the schottisches.

On the other side of Maida Overman sat Mrs. Royce Mitchell, full and ample, with black lace mitts on her hands. Beyond Mrs. Mitchell was Tom Neil's young wife, and beyond her Grandmother Crow, wrinkled and looking as though she would enjoy the pipe which, rumor said, she smoked in the privacy of her bedroom. The aristocracy of the Rifle Rock was in the K. P. Hall for, besides their wives, there were Royce Mitchell of the Gunhammer, and Tom Neil of the Rocking Chair, and Alec Crow of the AC. Only old Barney Loveless who ran the Screwplate away up north along the Tramparas, and Bob Jumper, the owner of the JAK, were absent, and they were bachelors and did not count anyway.

Across the hall, near the door, the riders of the Rifle Rock were congregated. There, with clerks from Wolfbarger's and the Bon Ton, with the blacksmith, with a railroad man or two, with the lesser lights, they had taken their place and brought their partners. One or two of the punchers were with nester girls, believing that feminine company of any sort was better than none at all, and these, somewhat defiantly, glanced now and then toward their owners. But from those lower ranks none came to ask for a dance with Mrs. Tom Neil or Maida Overman or ample Mrs. Mitchell. The democracy of the range country did not transcend to quite that stature. When a girl was young and unmarried, even though she was the boss's daughter, then the cowboy might aspire. But when she became the boss's wife . . . that was quite another matter.

Puce Clark at the fiddle, Alfy Little with his accordion, Jiggs Maples with his guitar, were ensconced on a platform raised at the center of the right wall, and they were playing a schottische. The fiddle whined and the accordion wheezed, for Alfy had had an accident and patched the spot with court plaster. Under that the guitar beat out a solid rhythm and the dancers skipped around the floor, boot heels thumping and slippers twinkling. Powell Overman kept his hand on his wife's shoulder but his eyes followed the dancers. There was a good-looking nester girl with Pete McGrath. A mighty good-looking girl if she were better fed. Powell Overman considered. After six months of married life he was conscious of a certain monotony. Perhaps he could vary that. A discreet inquiry of Pete, who rode for the Triangle; a quarter of beef, taken on a saddle bow and given free: what better introduction could a man ask?

The music stopped. Grinning, bronzed, laughing youngsters took their partners to the benches along the wall. Some retired to the doorway. A match flamed and cigarette smoke eddied and voices mingled with laughter and the whine of the fiddle as Puce tuned it.

"Are you having a good time, dear?" Powell Overman asked. "Would you mind if I went out a minute?"

Maida Overman smiled up at her husband. "Of course not," she answered.

Powell, with a final finger pressure on the shoulder beneath his hand, started across the floor and then stopped short. There was a disturbance at the door. The group of men gave way and a man emerged from it. Chet Minor!

Chet's face was very white and his eyes were wide and glassy, seeming to catch and reflect light. It was plain that Chet was drunk, very drunk. He did not stagger as he came limping out onto the dance floor but rather wavered and, when he stopped in the center of the floor, it was plain that he could go no further.

Still, catching sight of Maida, white-faced there upon the bench, Chet bowed. He went too far forward in the gesture and catching himself with an effort, straightened. From the group through which he had pushed his way, men started forward. They did not quite reach Chet Minor.

Weaving on his feet, his voice thick and flat and hoarse, Chet Minor addressed Powell Overman.

"Hello, Powell," he said. "Hello, Powell . . . you sneak!"

Powell Overman took another step toward the man who stood weaving there in the center of the room. Chet's flat voice went on. "You sneaked my girl," he said. "You sneaked my job. I came to tell you," by a miracle he retained his equilibrium, "I came to tell you that you're welcome to 'em."

Chet Minor fell forward, crashing down upon his face.

Behind Powell Overman, Maida spoke sharply. "Get your hat, Powell," she ordered. "We're going home."

CHAPTER
TWO

Powell Overman got his hat. Two men had already reached Chet Minor, lifted him up and half-carried him out of the K. P. Hall. When Powell returned to the bench Maida was ready, her wrap gathered about her shoulders, and the two, man and wife, left the dance. When they reached the bottom of the stairs they turned and went along Utah Street, rounding a corner and going on toward Montana. Although Powell and Maida Overman lived at the Triangle ranch they were stopping at Mark Scotia's big house in town that night.

"Well," Powell said awkwardly as they came to the quiet street, "well . . ."

"You stood there like an idiot," Maida snapped. "Why didn't you do something?"

"What was there to do?" Powell demanded. "I couldn't go out there . . ."

"You needn't have stood and stared!" Maida's voice was sharp. In the six months they had been married Powell had learned that tone and was wary of it.

"But what could I do, Maida?" he asked. "I didn't know Chet Minor was in town. I . . ."

Maida stopped short on the walk. "You didn't know he was in town," she mimicked. "I suppose if you'd known, we wouldn't have gone to the dance. We would have stayed at the ranch so you wouldn't see him. I never thought that I would marry a coward. And I saw you looking at that girl with Pete McGrath. Don't deny it! I saw you! If you ever try to play fast and loose with me, Powell Overman, you'll be sorry. You'll wish you hadn't!"

Powell Overman averted his head and let the storm of his wife's words rage about his ears. He was manager of the Triangle through virtue of being Maida's husband. He knew how he had gotten the job, knew the lengths to which he had gone to get it. There were times when he was sorry, times when he believed that he had earned the position.

"Come on home, Maida," Overman begged. "Come on home. Somebody will hear you."

"I don't care if they do!" Maida flared. But she allowed Powell to lead her on down the street.

There were repercussions other than that between Powell Overman and his wife that arose from the dance in the K. P. Hall. Pearl Suplan and Jeffry Sears took Chet to his room in the Parker House and undressed him and put him to bed. They listened to Chet's mumbling while they stripped off his clothes and then they left him. Pearl was all right, a good, tight-mouthed boy who rode for Alec Crow; but Sears was given to gossip. Chet's mumbling talk had not been good and Sears retailed some of it, adding a few ideas of his own.

Chet emerged from the Parker House sometime after noon on Sunday. He had a headache, his eyes were bloodshot and he carried upon him that filthy feeling a man has on his hide after a big drunk. Unfortunately the first man he met was Wolfbarger.

Chet had bought many a bill of goods from Wolfbarger in the days when he had been foreman under Eades Druerson. He went across the street to speak to the merchant. Wolfbarger avoided him. Two women, coming toward Chet, crossed the street, ostentatiously turning their faces away. Chet went on. He wished, how devoutly he wished, that there were someone he could talk to, someone that would be casual and act as though nothing had happened. He met no one. The thought of food revolted him and the saloons were closed for Sunday. The town, on that Sunday afternoon, was barren of people. In Rifle Rock, as in most towns on Sunday, men and women ate a big dinner and then somnolently retired, almost hibernating, for the balance of the day.

Chet left Idaho Street and traversed the short block to Montana. He strolled along that thoroughfare, paying no heed to where he went, simply walking. There were a number of small boys playing ball on a vacant lot on Idaho. Chet passed them and then turned back to watch the game. At least it would be something to do. He turned, took a step and stopped. Three of those youngsters, cruel with the cruelty of youth, were imitating his limp. Chet turned back and, hurrying as best he could, went toward the railroad tracks. He knew a place. In that part of town called "Chihuahua", across the tracks, Juan Salas kept a cantina. Juan Salas paid no attention to closing laws, or to other laws for that matter. Chet Minor headed for the cantina.

Tequila on an empty belly and a whisky foundation has a cutting edge. Two quick drinks and a little time for them to work, and Chet felt better physically and worse mentally. He had made an ass of himself, knew it, could do nothing about it, and so he took another drink. It was at this point that Ben Revilla came in.

Ben Revilla was one of Rifle Rock's bad boys. He was a thin little man with quick, beady eyes and — when he would work — a good cow hand. The trouble with Ben Revilla was that he would not work, not constantly nor steadily. There was Anglo blood in Ben and, because of his connections, he usually could get a job when there was a press of work at one of the neighboring ranches. At other times he lived alone in an adobe shack in Chihuahua, one of his three good-looking sisters occasionally coming in to keep the place somewhat in order.

Ben had been at the Triangle when Chet was hurt, had been one of the men who came from the ranch with a wagon to bring Chet in, and, in his own peculiar way, was fond of Chet. When Ben Revilla appeared in Juan Salas' cantina, Chet Minor brightened. Here, at last, was one of the breed, a man who knew the feel of leather clamped between his knees; and while Chet, like most cowboys, did not consider anyone with native blood his equal, he was glad to see Ben.

The gladness carried over into buying Ben a drink. Chet had a little money, not much but a little. Ben Revilla saw that and attached himself. The one drink called for another. By six o'clock Chet was roaring drunk again and when a party of young natives invaded the cantina he took umbrage where none was meant and before Salas could stop the trouble a fight was raging: Chet Minor against the world with Ben Revilla as Chet's second.

Vance Murray, city marshal and deputy sheriff in Rifle Rock, broke up the battle and, save that Vance was sorry for him, Chet would have spent the night in jail. As it was he slept with Ben Revilla in the adobe shack, only to awaken on Monday and start the whole proceeding over again.

For three days Chet Minor staged a big, drunken party, never happy, always surly, his leg aching, his tongue thick, his eyes red and combative, the beard sprouting into an unkempt stubble on his face. Ben Revilla stayed right with him, the only difference being that liquor made Ben happy and tuneful.

The night of the third day, with a half-gallon jug of tequila between them, Chet Minor and Revilla were in the adobe shack. Ben was trying to hum *El Rancho Grande* and Chet, morosely sitting on a bench, was nursing a tin cup half full of the colorless liquid. Giving up his attempt at song Revilla assayed the rôle of missionary.

"Yo're draunk, Chet," Ben stated.

Chet grunted, "Uhhuh," and raised the cup.

Ben searched his mind for the proper words to voice the thing he wanted to say, and found some of them. "It makes no difference with me," he said. "*No le hace*. I'm not amounteeng to a damn anyhow. But you should not be draunk."

"Why not?" Chet demanded combatively.

"Bicause," Ben hiccoughed and looked around to see if anyone had heard, "me, I'm supposed to be draunk. Yo're not. Yo're nice fallo, Chet."

"I'm a damn' cripple," Chet answered. "I can't get a job an' I've made a fool of myself."

Ben Revilla caught the word cripple. The missionary spirit departed and the detective entered Ben's mind. "You sabe for why yo're cripple?" he demanded, with an intent look.

"Horse was jerked down," Chet answered surlily, downing the tequila in his cup and reaching for the jug, "an' damn you, don't you say he throwed me!" There was still the rider's pride in Chet.

"Sure," Ben comforted. "*Seguro*. Theese horse is jerked down. He was a green horse, Chet."

"I c'n make any horse do what I want him to," Chet boasted. "Green or not."

"*Seguro, seguro*," Ben hastened to agree. "But theese green horse an' theese big bull are too mooch. *No bueno*, Chet. *No bueno por nada*."

"Powell come in to get me to help him doctor the bull," Chet recounted past events, sipping from the cup. "We went out together an' I told Powell I'd catch the bull around the neck an' stop him, an' he could get his heels an' we'd stretch him out. I dabbed down on the bull an' Powell was right behind me, swingin' his rope. I yelled to him he was too close an' right then my horse jumped an' the bull jerked him down."

Ben nodded sympathetically. "Theese horse get the rope across hees romp," Ben contributed. "I was bring

24

heem in an' I see where the rope come cross behin' the saddle. That spook the horse an' . . . ."

"He never neither," Chet interrupted. "The rope was right out to his side. I was standin' off in the stirrup to help the horse when the jolt come. I reckon I ought to know!"

"But the rope is made a mark across the horse's romp," Ben argued. "I seen it. Just like somebody hit the horse with a rope an' leave a mark on hees skin. I say to myself, '*Mira*, Ben. Theese horse ees spook by a rope behin' the saddle,' I say . . . ."

"Hell, forget it an' have a drink," Chet interrupted. "I'm crippled. Ain't that enough?"

The last thing Ben Revilla wanted was trouble and something in Chet's voice told him it was coming. He fell silent and took the drink.

On the morning of the fourth day Chet woke up fairly sober. Lying there on a tangle of dirty bedding in Ben Revilla's shack, he stared up at the cobwebbed ceiling and told himself what a fool he had been. He would brace up, he thought. He had to brace up. The thing he needed to do was take a grip on himself. Carefully he sat up in the bed, looked across to where Ben Revilla still snored, and then got out of bed and dressed.

There was a coffee pot on the stove. Chet made a fire and manufactured coffee from the grounds in the pot and a little fresh coffee that he found in a sack. It was hot and bitter when he drank it. He shaved with a hand that shook, using Ben's razor and a piece of broken mirror. Then, leaving Ben Revilla still asleep, he went toward the railroad, crossed the tracks and on to Utah Street. He was looking for a job, just any kind of job.

He met with a cold reception. At Wolfbarger's they did not need a clerk nor a warehouse man, nor did they know of any work to be found in Rifle Rock. Chet, his jaw a little squarer, left Wolfbarger's and went on down the street. It was the same story at the Bon Ton store, at Carver's, at Bacharach's. Systematically Chet canvassed the businesses of Rifle Rock and, wherever he went, he was turned down. The livery barn did not need a hostler, the blacksmith grunted and looked at Chet's short leg, there was no work at the meat market. By noon, Chet, his eyes bleak and the skin tight around his jaws, knew that there was nothing for him to do in Rifle Rock. He went into Otto Hahn's Staghorn Saloon and stood at the bar. Slowly Otto came along the length of the counter.

"Hello, Chet," Otto said quietly.

"Hello," Chet answered.

"Somethin'?" Otto asked.

"You said that there was a ridin' job on the Tramparas," Chet said. "Stevens, you said, had a job open. Is it still open, Otto, or do you know?"

Otto Hahn shook his head sorrowfully. "I think not," he said.

"Who got it?" Chet asked.

Otto shrugged. "Nobody that I know," he answered.

"Then . . ." Chet began. "There ain't a job in town, Otto. I've been around and asked. What's the matter with the ridin' job?"

"I tell you, Chet," Otto said slowly, "you made a fool of yourself. You know that?"

"Any man can go on a drunk," Chet said defiantly.

Again Otto shrugged his fat shoulders. "Sure," he agreed, "sure, but . . ."

"But what?"

"You can't buck the cowmen," Otto said. "You can't buck Powell Overman."

"What's Overman done?" Chet demanded.

"He's blackballed you, Chet," Otto answered, and turning away, began to rearrange the stacked glasses on the back bar.

Chet was quiet for a moment, then, "I see," he said slowly. "Thanks for tellin' me, Otto."

Otto Hahn did not turn around when the door closed.

Chet Minor, walking back toward the railroad tracks, kept his eyes on the ground. He was blackballed. That meant that he was finished in the Rifle Rock country. A man can stay and fight a blackball but usually it does him no good. Cowmen will not give a blackballed rider a job. To do so means that they are going against the word and judgment of a fellow rancher. And in town the stores and the places of business will not hire a blackballed man. The stores want the cowman's trade. Chet knew that he was finished. He was all alone. Powell Overman had passed the word around and that was the finish. When Chet walked into Ben Revilla's adobe shack Ben was just getting up. Ben looked cheerful in spite of the way he must have felt.

"Hello, Chet," Ben greeted. "We have a dreenk before breakfast, no?"

"Why not?" Chet Minor grated.

There was still a little money left. Tequila is cheap and mescal is cheaper. A man doesn't need much money for food when he is drinking. A man doesn't need to pay for a room in the hotel when he can tumble into dirty bedding in an adobe. Liquor warms a man when the fall nights are cold and liquor keeps a man's brain befuddled and cuts the sharp, poignant agony of self pity, dulls it, wears it down. Liquor, something to drink! A man will steal for it, go out and search for junk to sell for it, pawn his clothing, get his new, sacked saddle from the depot and sell it, bargain and whine, and finally, beg.

Chet Minor was in Ben Revilla's shack, a bewhiskered, dazed Chet Minor on a day three weeks after his return to Rifle Rock. To him there came the Reverend John Bradshaw, a young man, an earnest man, a man with a mission and with but little experience.

"Hello," Chet Minor said.

John Bradshaw cleared his throat. The day would come when John Bradshaw, wise and experienced, would be presiding elder of the district. That day was in the future. Now, "You are Mr. Minor?" the minister asked.

Chet nodded.

"I have come to reason with you, brother," John Bradshaw said. "I have come to pray with you. You are drinking your life away. You . . ."

"Have you ever been drunk?" asked Chet Minor.

John Bradshaw looked shocked.

"Have you got a job you can give me?" Chet demanded.

John Bradshaw shook his head.

"Then get to hell out of here!" Chet Minor shouted, rising. "Get out! Get out! Get out!"

CHAPTER
THREE

It was not often that Barney Loveless and Joe French, his foreman, came to Rifle Rock. Loveless's Screwplate lay north, on the upper reaches of Tramparas creek and the old man came to town only when there was a reason. The fleshpots of Rifle Rock offered no inducements to black-bearded Joe French. It was so with the three Screwplate hands, Jesse Lauder, Earl Keelin, and a grizzled oldster who, in the Rifle Rock country, had no other name than Laramie.

The Screwplate was a cull outfit. Barney Loveless willed it so, and so it was. Headquarters on the Screwplate looked like the devil. The house was of logs from Tramparas Mesa, weatherbeaten and shoddy. The corrals always seemed to be ready to fall apart. The barn roof had a sag in the middle. So far as the riders of the Rifle Rock were concerned, the Screwplate was just *no bueno*. Always had been. Barney Loveless's men rode old horses, they were old men, and the cattle they handled were the culls and the cutbacks of the Rifle Rock range.

When a man had gummers to sell, Barney Loveless would buy them. Dogies, pot-bellied calves that had lost their mammies, found a ready buyer at the

Screwplate. Old cows, old bulls, lump jaws and cripples, all went north to the Screwplate. No one thought much of the Screwplate, its crew or its owner, no one except Stevens Claypool, the banker in Rifle Rock, and Stevens Claypool treated old Barney Loveless as a banker is apt to treat his best customer and principal stockholder.

No, Rifle Rock had a low opinion of the cull outfit up on the Tramparas, not knowing about the warm tight comfort of the old log house, or the ease that the dilapidated corrals imparted to handling cattle and horses, or how tight that sagged-roof barn really was. The Rifle Rock could not see the skill and care with which those aging riders worked cattle, nor just how good the old horses were. It is doubtful if the Rifle Rock would have known the wisdom of handling cull cattle as though they were the finest of purebreds. No one in the Rifle Rock could see those things, excepting only Banker Claypool, and he had the bank account of Barney Loveless.

Barney and Joe French came to town in a dilapidated buckboard. It took six hours to come from the Screwplate to Rifle Rock by buckboard, but Barney and Joe, having broken their journey at the Rocking Chair the night before, arrived early in the morning and intended to be home before midnight.

Joe tied the team to a hitchrail and hung gunnysack morrales on the long heads of the team, and the two men separated, Barney to go into Wolfbarger's and bargain shrewdly for supplies, and Joe to go to the post office for the mail.

The mail consisted of a letter or two and some catalogs, a few magazines and papers. Joe got the bundle from the postmaster and left the office. He had headed back toward Wolfbarger's when he saw a limping, disheveled man come from the saddle shop and, dangling a pair of spurs, go up the street. Joe French went into the saddle shop.

"Wasn't that Chet Minor in here?" Joe French asked Wayt Higlow when Wayt came out from the back room.

Wayt nodded. A grizzled, taciturn man, Wayt, who had supplied the Rifle Rock country with saddles and gear for fifteen years. "That was him," Wayt said crustily.

"Looked kind of bad," Joe French commented.

Wayt grunted. "Wanted to sell me his spurs," Wayt said. "Guess he's out of money."

The story of Chet Minor, the scene at the dance, and the way Chet Minor had gone to hell was prevalent over the Rifle Rock range. Joe French had heard it.

"Wanted to sell his spurs?" Joe said.

"All he's got left," Wayt said shortly. "I wouldn't buy 'em. He'd just get drunk again."

"Where's he livin', Wayt?" French asked.

The saddlemaker shrugged. "With Ben Revilla, over in Chihuahua," he answered. "Did you want anythin', Joe?"

"A new curb strap," Joe French answered, and while Wayt got the desired bit of leather, stood looking at the display of saddle hardware in the showcase.

French paid for the strap and went out, walking on down the street toward Wolfbarger's. At the store Sears

32

Lawson told the black-bearded man that Barney Loveless had gone to the depot, and so, leaving the mail and the curb strap in the buckboard, Joe followed his boss.

Old Barney was standing against the depot's red wall, his hands on his hips and the shoulders of his old sheepskin coat pressed against the boards, when Joe found him. There were three immigrant cars on the depot siding and four men, three of them middle-aged and one young, were unloading one of the cars. There was a woman with five tow-headed youngsters in the car that was being unloaded and her voice was shrill as she gave directions for the disposal of her household goods in the old spring wagon. Barney spat darkly when Joe came to stand beside him and, for the moment, made no comment. Joe French spread his broad shoulders beside the narrow back of his boss as he too leaned against the depot wall.

"There you are," Barney Loveless said finally, in his harsh, cracked voice. "It's comin' fall. Winter will be down on us before we know it. They'll take them kids out to some shack that's got cracks in the floor big enough to drop a dawg through. They won't have nothin' but some side meat an' corn meal. They had about enough money to git here an' that's all. They won't make it."

Joe said nothing and Barney, spitting again, continued his discourse. "Pore damned fools," he said. "The railroad company sells 'em transportation an' turns 'em loose. I reckon they think this is the Promised Land."

"An' they don't know how tough it can be," Joe French concluded in his deep voice. "Poor fools."

"Freeze out, dry out, or starve out," Barney Loveless stated. "But before they go they'll plow up some good range."

To that French had nothing more to offer and Barney, with a heave, pulled his shoulders from the wall. "An' they'll kill a little beef," he said, "just to keep from starvin'. An' some of 'em will maybe rustle a cow or so. An' they'll pick land that the cowman wants an' pretty soon . . ."

"Yeah?" Joe French said.

"Pretty soon there'll be hell to pay," old Barney Loveless concluded. "When I come in here the Triangle owned the whole country. The Triangle an' the Diamond Dot. I crowded in an' they gave me room. There was other brands. A man with a good horse an' a big loop could start a cow outfit. The Diamond Dot an' the Triangle fought us an' we fought back. We made a place for ourselves but there was some killed an' the Diamond Dot don't run cattle here no more. It's the history of the country, Joe. Only now we got a sheriff an' courts an' in them days a man packed his reasons in a saddle scabbard."

"That's time gone," Joe French said.

"It could come back," Barney Loveless commented. "What you got on yore mind, Joe?"

Joe French started guiltily. There was no hiding anything from this keen-eyed old hellion. He might as well blurt it out. "Chet Minor," Joe answered.

Barney Loveless's yellow eyes were keen as he stared at his foreman. "Old man Minor was pretty good to you," he said.

"Yeah," Joe French agreed.

Barney Loveless looked away toward the immigrant car where now the woman was directing the unloading of a stove. "I never seen a woman yet that didn't know more about a stove than a man did," he commented. "Well, what about Chet, Joe?"

"He's makin' a damned fool of himself," Joe French said.

"I'd heard," Loveless agreed dryly.

"He looks like hell," Joe added.

"I'd heard that too."

"He made a damned fool of himself at the dance last month," Joe French went on. "He's crippled an' Powell Overman has blackballed him."

Barney Loveless turned fiercely upon his foreman. "Who in hell do you think I am?" he demanded. "Santa Claus?"

"Chet's clear down an' out," said Joe French. "He ain't worth a damn."

"You said that Powell blackballed him?"

"Uhhuh."

The old yellow eyes were fierce. "Powell would!" Barney Loveless said. "Powell's that kind."

"But folks think highly of Powell," Joe French said, and smiled slyly beneath his black beard. "You've done right well handlin' cull cattle, Barney."

"I treat 'em right," Barney Loveless answered.

35

"Laramie," French's voice was guileless, "killed a man up in Wyomin'. Had to take it on the run."

Loveless grunted.

"Jesse ain't got but half a left hand," Joe French said. "Chet is livin' over in Chihuahua with Ben Revilla."

Barney Loveless shifted his chew. "All right, damn it!" he snapped. "All right! Every cockeyed sick kitten in the country. I get 'em all. I'll drive over in the buckboard after a while, Joe."

The grin split Joe French's black beard through the middle and white teeth showed. "Blackball an' all, huh?" he asked.

"Who gives a damn for a blackball?" snarled Barney Loveless. "Powell Overman is just a thirty-a-month hand. Runnin' the Triangle! Huh!"

Big Joe French took a last look at the immigrant car, where now the stove was unloaded. He pushed his broad shoulders from against the wall and nodding to his boss, strode off. Old Barney Loveless watched his foreman depart, with something strangely like affection in his fierce yellow eyes. "Regular damned reformatory!" snapped Barney Loveless. "That's what I'm runnin'!"

Chet Minor was in Ben Revilla's shack when Joe French, without the courtesy of a knock, pushed open the door. Chet's belly, his whole body, every fiber and nerve of it, were clamoring for alcohol. He had not had a drink for twenty hours. He was broke and his credit at Salas' cantina was exhausted. He stared at his visitor with bleary, redrimmed eyes.

"Hello," Joe French said, and then looking around the shack, "Where's Ben?"

Ben Revilla, now that the money was gone, had pulled out. Chet did not know where Ben was. He shrugged. "I dunno," he answered.

Joe walked over, shifted the coffee pot on the cold stove, glanced at the empty coffee box that served for a cupboard, and said: "I wanted to see him. Had a job that maybe he could do."

"Job?" said Chet.

"Nothin' much," Joe's voice passed over the matter lightly. "Damned if you don't look like hell, Chet."

For three weeks Chet Minor had lived on whisky and self pity. Right at the moment he was feeling mighty sorry for Chet Minor. "I know it," he said. "I feel like hell. I came back here, crippled. I thought I could make a go of it in my own country, but what happened? Everyone turned me down. Wouldn't give me a job. Overman blackballed me. I . . ."

"You sat aroun' an' cried in yore milk," Joe French said caustically. "You never was much good anyhow, Chet."

Chet looked up and some of the uncertainty left his bloodshot eyes. "I was a top hand before I got crippled," he stated, "an' you know it!"

"You let a horse throw you," Joe French jibed. "Top hand, hell!" The big man was eyeing his victim narrowly. If there was still fight in Chet . . . Joe French surely hoped that there was still fight in Chet Minor.

"He never throwed me!" Chet snapped. "I didn't ask you to come in here, French. You can pull your freight just any time."

"You wouldn't be puttin' me out, would you?" French drawled sarcastically. "After all I come to see Revilla about a job. You wouldn't be interested in a job, would you? All you want to do is lie around an' soak up whisky an' feel sorry for yourself."

"That's a damned lie!" Chet came to his feet. "Get out, French!"

"Well," French taunted, "so the whisky bum is orderin' me out. If I thought you was worth a damn I'd give you a job, blamed if I wouldn't!"

Chet's fists clenched. "You came in here to ride me," he snarled. "You haven't got any job to give. Now damn you, get out or I'll put you out."

Relief surged up in Joe French. The fight was still there. The thing that made a man had not been burned out of Chet Minor. That was the thing Joe French had set out to discover. The thing he must of necessity know. "Put me out then," French snapped. "Go on an' put me out if you can!"

A crazy, fighting strength welled in Chet. Something was happening here, something that had not happened since his return to Rifle Rock. Men had looked with compassion upon him. Men had felt sorry for him. Men had said things behind his back, things that were a mixture of pity and contempt. But here was a man that challenged him, that said nothing of his being a cripple, that took him on an equal footing. Chet Minor clenched his fists and with a wild spring, attacked.

38

Joe French — who could handle any man in the Rifle Rock, not excepting the blacksmith, and could handle them with ease — ducked that first wild flurry of blows. He took a hard hand on one big shoulder and he let Chet's flailing left fist hit him in the belly. Joe French almost chuckled. Then, his eyes narrowing a little, he stepped back a pace and, measuring his man with his left hand, struck once, hard and true to the angle of the jaw. Chet Minor flopped down and lay limply sprawling. Joe French stood there and let Chet Minor lie where he had fallen.

Presently a buckboard came to a rattling stop outside Ben Revilla's adobe shack and a testy voice called "Whoa!" Barney Loveless made his appearance at the door, surveying the scene.

"So he'll still fight, will he?" Loveless asked.

Joe French nodded slowly. "I made him," he admitted. "I wanted to know if he would."

"Wouldn't be worth a damn if he wouldn't," Barney Loveless snapped. "Well, load him in an' we'll be goin'. It's a long ways home."

Grinning, Joe French stooped and, picking up Chet Minor as he might have handled a sack of feed, carried him out of the door and dumped him down in the bed of the buckboard.

"I reckon that's all," he said to Loveless. "There's nothin' else to go, is there?"

"No," snapped Barney. "Git in an' we'll start for the kindergarten!"

★　★　★

The buckboard was well along its way north before Chet Minor sat up. Ahead of him, on the seat, loomed the big shoulders of Joe French and the humped back of Barney Loveless. Barney was driving and the buckboard rattled right along. There were supplies loaded in around Chet and, as he moved, the hard corner of a box dug into his ribs. He squirmed around, and French, apprised of his movement by the little lurch of the buckboard, turned his head.

"Woke up, did you?" French asked casually.

"What am I doin' here?" Chet demanded.

"You said you wanted a job," French stated. "Mr. Loveless here said that he could use an extra hand for a while."

Chet thought that over. "You aren't takin' me out because you feel sorry for me?" he asked, and there was something in his voice that made Joe French avoid his eyes. "It ain't that?"

Old Barney Loveless answered the question when French did not. Barney could put a harsh crackle into his voice. He had been the best trail boss of Goodnight's drivers and a man doesn't get that reputation by being soft.

"I got a job," Barney snarled. "I was lookin' for a man to do it. If you don't want the job . . ."

"I want it," Chet said eagerly.

"Well then, don't figure that you won't earn yore money," Loveless snapped. "Thirty a month an' yore chuck, an' if you don't earn it you can walk back to town."

40

"But . . ." Chet Minor said, "I've got no outfit. I've got no saddle or . . ."

"Hell," snarled Barney Loveless, "you don't need a saddle to make hay. You ride a mower."

Chet Minor leaned back, content. He had forgotten that, of all the outfits in the Rifle Rock, the Screwplate was the only one that put up a lot of hay. Other ranches might be content with enough hay for the horses and to feed the hospital bunch, but not the Screwplate. On the Screwplate they put up enough hay to feed all the cull cattle.

"An' you'll work on a stack too," Loveless growled over his shoulder. "Don't think you won't!"

Chet relaxed against the hard corner of the box. He was not thinking that this was late September and that the hay was usually all in the stacks by now. He was not thinking that, at the most, the haying could last but a few weeks, nor was he thinking of the hard work in the hay vega. Somewhere in Chet Minor's mind there was a little warm glow that would not die. He had a job, he was a man again; and the warmth in his mind stifled the clamoring of his nerves for whisky.

CHAPTER
FOUR

Barney Loveless put Chet to work on a meadow he had not intended to cut that year. The vega had dried and Barney's plans were to let it go and graze cattle on it when winter shut down. Revising those plans he started Chet on a mower and Amador Fernandez, the native roust-about, on a rake. Amador's wife, Rufina, did the cooking for the Screwplate and occupied a room in the ranch house with Amador. Joe French and Barney Loveless also dwelt in the big house, but the hands occupied a cabin to themselves.

Chet Minor was eager enough to work and the eagerness washed out the resentment he harbored against Joe French. Chet had a job and that was the main thing, but he found that a year spent in hospitals, part of the time flat on his back with a weight fastened to his leg, and a three-weeks' drunk were not good training for the hay field. Still, he tried. He rode the mower. Amador bunched the cut grass with the rake, and, when it was cured, bucked it to the stacker while Chet climbed up on the stack with a fork. They needed another man to drive the stacker team but they got along, albeit slowly.

In the bunkhouse Chet did not do so well. Laramie, Jess Lauder, and Earl Keelin were taciturn men and they were riders. Chet had once been a rider and high-hatted the hay hands. Now he came in for some of that himself. A week of work soaked the liquor out of him and he began to harden. Also a week saw the little vega just about finished.

Chet had no outfit at all. He was sleeping on borrowed blankets and he had no clothing other than what he wore. It was filthy and Chet was distressed. When Sunday came he borrowed a cake of soap from Rufina and went to the creek. There, despite the crisp weather, he took a bath and washed his clothes, even including in that washing the worn trousers of the suit he had bought in El Paso. Wrapped in a blanket and sheltered under the creek bank, he waited for the clothing to dry. He was there when Laramie and Earl arrived on the bank above him.

Laramie and Earl were taking a busman's holiday. There was no particular work to do this Sunday and so, naturally, Laramie and his companion had saddled horses and ridden out from the ranch. Either of them would have saddled a horse to go across the street, for they were riders, not footmen. Chet could hear the Texas drawl of Earl's voice and the crisper accents of the northern man as they talked.

"Goin' to cramp us not havin' that vega for pasture," Earl announced. "We needed it. The old man always rests one vega every year. Wonder why he decided to cut this one."

"Because," Laramie was very explicit, "we got this fellow Minor on our hands. He was goin' to hell in a hand basket an' they had to give him a job. Joe an' the ol' man are always nursin' some kind of dogie."

Earl said, "Uhhuh," with no enthusiasm and made further comment. "He's just about as useful as a hip pocket on an undershirt," Earl said, referring to Chet. "He can't do a day's work an' Amador is gettin' sore as hell. This ain't no time of year to cut hay an' Amador knows it. He ought to be out gettin' the fences in shape an' such. Instead we do that an' Amador gets hay down his neck."

"Well," Laramie was philosophical, "you know the old man."

"Yeah," agreed Earl. "I know him."

Their horses moved off and after a moment Chet got up and threw off his blanket and began to put on his still damp clothes.

Laramie and Earl Keelin were not the only ones to discuss Chet Minor that Sunday afternoon. Barney Loveless and Joe French, Joe with a pipe and Barney smoking a cigar, sat in the living room of the Screwplate headquarters and talked things over.

"He's tryin' to work," Barney admitted. "I'll say that for him. He's tryin' to earn his money."

"But what are you goin' to do with him when that vega's cut?" Joe asked.

Barney waved a hand. "Fix fence, feed hay, somethin'," he said. "Hell, Joe, you know there's always work around a ranch."

Joe nodded. "As long as he don't think we're makin' work for him," Joe agreed. "That might put him cocked again."

"It might," Barney agreed, and then, "You know, Joe, I've been thinkin'."

"Yeah?" said Joe French.

"Pete McGrath came by yesterday," Barney said. "Overman an' Mitchell are havin' a meetin' down at the Triangle. They want me to come."

"Meetin' about what?" Joe asked.

"Pete didn't say for sure but I think about the nesters," Loveless drawled, eyeing the end of his cigar. "Pete said, kind of in passin', that they're goin' to have to do somethin' about the nesters. He complained that the Triangle an' the Gunhammer both had lost some cattle. That's the way it will start, Joe."

"But . . ." Joe French said.

"It's an excuse," Barney continued. "The thing is that the nesters are takin' land that we've always used."

Joe French nodded. "So you'll go?" he asked.

Loveless nodded. "That don't mean that I'll join 'em though," he said. "We're pretty far from the railroad an' Rifle Rock up here."

"Yeah," Joe French agreed, not seeing where the conversation was leading.

"Yeah." Loveless's voice was placid. "I've always been forehanded, Joe."

"You have," Joe French agreed.

"An' the nesters are goin' to work into this country."

"In time," Joe French admitted cautiously. "They're comin' this way."

"They're comin' close. There's a man an' his daughter got a homestead on the creek now."

"But that's twenty miles away," Joe French said. "We don't run down that far an' never have. They ain't on us."

"I know," Loveless waved his cigar. "But we join on that country."

"You built that fence . . ." Joe began.

"A drift fence. We don't even own an acre of that land." Blue smoke came from Barney Loveless's lips. "We've got a camp at Rock Springs."

"Well?" prompted Joe.

"Well," Barney Loveless said succinctly, "if you own the water you control the range. I'm goin' to buy what patented land we run over, lease the state land if I can get it, an' put my men on the water we use an' get title to it. I'm goin' to do it now, before some crazy farmer from Kansas comes along an' grabs it up an' plows it. The Triangle an' the AC an' the Rockin' Chair an' them couldn't see it comin'. They're fightin' but they're too late. I don't aim to be late."

Joe French nodded at the wisdom of his boss. He could see the point. "Then you'll . . ." Joe began.

The door of the room banged open. Chet Minor, face very white, trousers shrunken by the washing they had undergone, shirt damp across his chest, and eyes flaming, walked into the room. Joe French started to his feet but Barney Loveless sat calmly and smoked his cigar.

"I'll go back to town," Chet said hoarsely. "I take no man's charity."

"Why, Chet . . ." Joe began.

"I know why you brought me out here," Chet flamed. "You thought that I was crippled an' that I was drinkin' too much an' you'd just be charitable. You thought . . ."

"Set down, Chet." Old Barney Loveless did not lift his voice but there was the ring and snap to it that had turned out trail crews on bitter nights for forty years, given orders that men obeyed. Chet Minor sat down on the edge of a chair.

"Yo're feelin' sorry for yorese'f again," Barney accused. "Yo're touchy. You think, because you got one short leg an' had yore insides mixed up some, that you ain't a whole man. You think we think that!"

"You do," Chet began hotly. "You been makin' work for me to do. You aimed to let that vega go an' use it for pasture this winter. You . . ."

"Boy," Barney Loveless drawled, "you earned yore week's wages. You cut hay, didn't you?"

"Yes, but . . ."

"Shut up! When a man's got friends he uses 'em. That's what a friend is, a fellow that will side you, somebody that when you take him along you don't have to look back an' see if he's comin', no matter what kind of goin' there is. Did you ever try to use yore friends?"

Chet made no answer but Barney needed none, he answered the question himself. "No, you didn't," Barney Loveless said. "Yo're high-headed. Yo're proud as hell. You say to yorese'f, 'Here I am, crippled an' broke. All the folks I know pity me, so I won't take nothin' off of 'em. I'll show 'em!' So you make a damned fool out of yorese'f an' go out an' get drunk. An' that's a hell of a way to show people that you amount to somethin'."

"But I couldn't get a job," Chet expostulated. "I . . . I'd been rooked out of a job I was supposed to get. Powell Overman . . ."

"Sure," Barney waved a hand. "Powell Overman. He got the job on the Triangle an' he married Maida Scotia. He'd be tickled as hell if you stayed drunk an' if you made an ass out of yorese'f. You sure were accommodatin' to Overman, son."

"But what can I do?" Chet demanded. "I can't stay here, doin' work that you make for me out of charity. I can't . . ."

Barney Loveless squinted his eyes. "You got somethin' I want, son," he said. "Somethin' that I'll buy. There's somethin' that you can do for me an' it won't be charity, neither."

"What is it?" Chet demanded eagerly. "What have I got?"

"Yore homestead right," Loveless snapped. "I want you to go down to my Rock Springs camp an' homestead it. I'll stake you. When you get it proved up I'll buy yore homestead, takin' out the money I've put in to keep you goin'. There's somethin' you can sell. There's somethin' you can do that don't depend on charity. Want to do it?"

Chet Minor sat very quiet for a long minute, his eyes fixed firmly on the old man. "Yes," he said suddenly, out of that quiet, "I want to do it."

48

Barney Loveless let smoke go out from his thin lips. "We'll take you down as soon as you can get an outfit," he said. "Joe, you an' Chet will go to town tomorrow an' buy what he needs at Wolfbarger's. Git the things he can't take from here."

"Sure," agreed Joe French. "Sure, Barney."

Barney Loveless turned to Chet and suddenly his face was stern. "An' let's not hear any more about this damned charity an' feelin' sorry for yorese'f!" he snapped. "Yo're a man, ain't you? Then act like one!"

Chet Minor made no reply. The old man was right and Chet knew it.

When Barney Loveless gave an order at the Screwplate that order was obeyed. Monday, just after dinner, Chet Minor and Joe French went to Rifle Rock. They reached town shortly after sundown, put the light wagon that they were using in the wagon yard and stabled the team. It was too late to do any buying and Joe French, looking at Chet, asked a question. "What do you want to do, Chet?"

"I'll hang around," Chet said. "I don't . . . Well, I don't reckon I want to bum around town much, Joe."

"Stay in the wagon yard, huh?" Joe French grunted. "All right, Chet. But we'll eat some supper first."

To that Chet agreed and they went from the livery barn on down the street to Murphy's restaurant. While they ate Joe made a sudden announcement. "In the mornin'," he said, "I'll draw some money from the bank. Barney give me a check. You take it an' do yore buyin' an we'll pull out. You know what you want, don't you?"

Chet nodded. Relief flooded him. He had been afraid that Joe French would go into Wolfbarger's with him like a parent buying a kid a new suit of clothes. "I know what I want," he agreed.

Joe said nothing more and when they had finished their meal they left the restaurant, Chet signifying his intention of going back to the wagon yard. "We got a bed roll," Chet said, "an' I can throw down in the feed room at the barn. You go on, Joe. I'll just go to bed."

Again French grunted agreement and leaving Chet, went on down the street toward the Staghorn.

Chet, left alone, walked slowly back toward the livery barn. He wanted to stay out of sight. He didn't want anyone to see him. There was a raw spot on Chet, a place that he had rubbed himself, and meeting anyone he knew in Rifle Rock would simply be rubbing salt in the wound. Chet hoped that he could go to the barn, turn in, and in the morning get his buying done and get out of town.

He did not get his wish. Before he reached the barn, some distance along Utah Street, a woman coming hurriedly around the corner, bumped squarely into him and would have fallen save that Chet caught her. Regaining her balance as Chet freed her from his arms the woman stepped back and in the light from a street lamp on the corner Chet could see that she was Maida Overman.

The lamp burned yellow in its square glass box, the dim glow spreading around the post, and Chet stepped aside to give Maida room to pass. She paused on the boardwalk.

"Why . . . why, it's Chet," Maida said, making no movement to go on. "I didn't know you were in town, Chet."

Chet Minor looked at the girl. She was handsome, with the high, imperious features of Mark Scotia, and with coal black hair that glinted in the lamp light. Chet did not know what to say and so, "Hello, Maida," he said inanely.

The girl smiled. She had gone to dances with Chet Minor. She had ridden with him across the grama grass of the Rifle Rock. She had, in the dim recess of Mark Scotia's front porch, kissed Chet Minor when his awkward lips sought hers. Chet had thought that kiss a confirmation of their love. To Maida Scotia it had been one of numerous experiences, albeit a pleasant one. Smiling, she put out her hand and gripped Chet's lax arm.

"I'm glad to see you, Chet," she said. "Awfully glad."

Chet flushed red. He was recalling the last time he had seen Maida sitting on a bench in the K. P. Hall. "Well . . ." he said awkwardly, "well, Maida, I got to go on. I was just . . ."

"But you haven't been to see me since you came back," Maida protested. She was enjoying herself, all the more so because she knew that Chet Minor was suffering. "It isn't nice of you to avoid your old friends."

Chet braced himself. He could not handle the situation; it was in the girl's hands and she knew it. Still there was no escape for Chet. It seemed to him that he just could not step around the woman and go on down the street. He did not know what to do.

"I been busy," he said uncomfortably. "I've been out at the Screwplate. I . . ."

"I'm staying in town now," Maida said swiftly. "Daddy isn't feeling well and I'm staying with him. You could come to see me, Chet."

Getting a grip on himself Chet made answer. "You're married now," he said hoarsely. "Powell an' I . . ."

Maida pouted prettily. "Powell is at the ranch," she said, "and I'm all alone, except for daddy. I . . . I haven't been very happy, Chet." She sighed.

"I wrote to you," Chet said hoarsely. "I wrote from the hospital. I never got an answer."

Maida disregarded that. "You used to like me, Chet," she said softly. "If you would come in to see me . . . Powell needn't know, and I'm so lonely."

A distaste welled up in Chet Minor, a dislike that amounted suddenly almost to loathing. He took a step back. "You're in a hurry," he said. "I won't keep you."

The half-smile left Maida's face. Her eyes darkened with anger. "Oh," she said, her voice cold, "so you think . . ."

"I think you're a married woman," Chet said. "I think I'd better go on." He moved again, forward now, skirting around Maida Overman. The anger in her eyes had suddenly become fury. She opened her lips to speak, withheld the words and half turned. Chet was limping on down the street, his shoulders square and broad. He did not look back. Maida Overman watched

52

him go and then, turning again, walked on, her heels striking hard against the board sidewalk.

Chet Minor went along toward the livery barn, shaken, disturbed by the meeting. Maida Scotia had been on a pedestal in Chet's mind. He had loved her and now . . . now she had shown him just what she was. Chet's face was very white when he walked into the wagon yard and dragged his bed from the back of the buckboard.

In the morning, with a thin sheaf of bills procured by Joe French from the bank, Chet made his purchases. Clothing he bought, a scant amount. Supplies, the necessities that would see him through for a month at the Rock Springs. Joe French stood silently by, looking on.

"That's the size of it," Chet said to Wolfbarger's clerk.

Joe French stepped forward. "Better put a couple of boxes of thirty-thirties with that," he commented.

Chet looked his surprise.

"I put my rifle in the wagon for you," Joe French said. "You can keep it at camp. You'll want a gun around."

From Wolfbarger's Chet and Joe went to the U.S. Commissioner's office. There, with the Commissioner looking on, Chet Minor filed on one hundred and sixty acres of land and paid his sixteen dollars. The Commissioner, an old cowman who knew every foot of the country, blinked when Chet filled the description of the Rock Springs on his application. The Commissioner knew that Barney Loveless used the Rock Springs as a camp. He knew too, must have known, that there was some sort of deal between Loveless and Chet — the very presence of Joe French told that — but the Commissioner was not asking questions. His sympathies were with the cowmen. He had, almost every day, men appearing before him filing desert claims that would never be irrigated, timber claims on which no trees would be planted, stone claims where no stone would be moved. The influx of settlers into the Rifle Rock was causing the cowmen to fight back desperately and they were using every legal means and some that were extra-legal, to preserve their grazing. Chet walked out of the Commissioner's office, his filing made, the potential possessor of one hundred and sixty acres of land. In six months, if he chose to pay $1.25 an acre, he would own it. Otherwise he could stick on the land and prove up. He was committed to make improvements: a house, a barn, a source of water. These were already in place at the Rock Springs. Chet and the Commissioner both knew that, and said nothing about it.

"Well," said Joe French when they left the Commissioner's office, "that's that. Let's go home, Chet."

From Rifle Rock Chet Minor and Joe French went straight to the Rock Springs, not returning to the Screwplate. The wagon was loaded with the clothing and supplies that Chet had bought, with a bed roll and an old saddle and riding gear from the ranch, with

54

rope, with wire and staples, with a shovel and an ax and a saw and a hammer, with all the necessities that Chet Minor would need to live for a month or more. Joe French and Chet Minor reached the Rock Springs just at dusk.

The camp lay beneath a little mesa. From the side of that mesa the spring welled out, a never-failing water supply. Below the spring and to the south of it was the cabin, tight-built and sturdy. Further down were the shed and a corral. There was a forty-acre horse pasture at the Rock Springs and coming in, Chet could see horses against the fence.

"Barney had 'em sent over," Joe explained, speaking of the horses. "Laramie brought 'em." He looked narrowly at Chet. "There's a couple of young horses in the bunch," he added.

Chet made no answer. He was looking at the camp, at the cabin, the shed, the corral, the hay stacked close by the shed. This was his. Temporarily it was his. There was a little tingling all along Chet's spine. He could understand the nesters now, could understand their wants, their desires, the deep necessity of having their feet planted firmly on land that was their own.

"You'll stay the night, Joe?" Chet Minor asked, Chet Minor who owned land.

CHAPTER
FIVE

Joe French stayed the night at the Rock Springs. He cut wood while Chet unloaded the wagon and he stood by, as a guest should, while Chet cooked supper. Bedding was scant at the Rock Springs camp but Chet gave Joe the most of the soogans, a host making his guest comfortable, and shivered through the night under a quilt and a saddle blanket while Joe snored peacefully. In the morning Joe French left for headquarters.

"Barney said to leave the team an' the wagon for you to use," French said, in parting. "There'll be some things you'll want 'em for an' we've got another wagon an' plenty of horses at the ranch. So long, Chet. Take care of yourself." With that Joe mounted and rode away toward the north, and Chet Minor, left alone, surveyed his domain.

There was not a great deal of it. One hundred and sixty acres, a quarter section, is not a whole lot in a land where men count their pastures by townships, and where, in a winter storm, cattle may drift fifty miles. Chet climbed up on the mesa behind the camp and looked out over the land.

He had lived in the country all his life. He knew it as intimately as he knew the palm of his hand, but standing there above the claim it seemed as though he had never seen it before. North of him the sharp beak of Tramparas Mesa cut into the valley. The Screwplate lay against the base of that mesa on Tramparas Creek. To the south, Tramparas joined Willow Creek, and south lay the great Triangle range, cut now along the creek by the homesteads of the nesters. Due east was Alec Crow's AC, and away down south, below Rifle Rock, was the Rocking Chair. Chet, riding with the round-up wagon, had covered all that country.

A little southeast from where he stood was the landmark that gave the valley, the town, the whole country, its name: the Rifle Rock. Black against the morning sky it stood, jutting up out of the valley. There on the north was the sharp climb of cliff that formed the butt of the rifle, sloping south to make the grip, climbing again to make the breech. The rock stood there, for all the world like a great rifle, only its top outlined against the sky, the lower portion buried in the earth. The old-timers, heading west, passing down the valley, had named the rock. They had camped below it, where the Rock Creek and Willow came together, staring up at the black basalt that made the bluff, their own rifles across their arms and their eyes alert and keen. "Rifle Rock". It had seen the country grow and change. It would see it change again.

Chet came slowly down from the mesa side. He was walking across his own land. Momentarily he forgot his bargain with Barney Loveless. He had bet the Government sixteen dollars against one hundred and sixty acres that he could live on the land for five years.

That was the way the cowmen spoke of the nesters and their claims. Well, he, Chet Minor, was a nester, and if he was going to win his bet there were things to be done.

And for a while Chet Minor did those things. The work in the hayfield at the Screwplate had hardened him somewhat. Still, he was not as yet capable of any great exertion. He tired easily and so, temporarily, he stayed close to the cabin.

The Screwplate had kept up the cabin, using it occasionally for a camp, keeping a man there to ride the lower drift fence that kept Screwplate cattle from going down the valley when the storms blew in from the north, using the hay that was cut from the vega below the spring, to feed weak cattle. The cabin was in good shape; but not good enough to please Chet Minor who knew the ferocity of the storms that blew into the valley.

He worked around the cabin. He banked more dirt against its sides and he patched the broken pane in the single window. He rebuilt the chimney of the fireplace, bringing down rock from the mesa slope and mixing a mortar of thick adobe to lay the rock. He worked slowly and, as he worked, he forgot that this was not his own. Cutting posts to repair the corral he saw other growth from which posts might be made. He had some wire. He could build a fence.

Barney Loveless, riding over a week after Chet had come to the Rock Springs, saw the fresh dirt banked against the cabin's walls, and the new posts in the corral and heard the ring of an ax away up the slope of the mesa. Barney grinned a leathery, wrinkled grin, and did not stay but rode back the way he had come. Leave a man alone, Barney Loveless thought, and he will work out his own salvation. Chet, coming in with the wagonload of posts, did not suspect that he had been spied upon.

Gradually Chet Minor hardened. Gradually the muscles toughened. Gradually his mind, tight and tense, eased. Leave a man alone. Leave him alone and he will be a man if it is in him.

At night, sitting in the cabin, the fireplace making light because the supply of kerosene was scanty, Chet considered ways and means. He was holding this place for Loveless. Loveless would pay him for it, taking Chet's expenses out of that payment. Chet's eyes narrowed as he looked at the fire. There was a chance of making a stake. The less he spent, the more he would have. Well then, he must cut down expenses. There were posts on the mesa. Perhaps he could sell some posts. He had seen tracks around the spring and down the creek. Muskrats had made houses. There was a tiny dam made by beaver; coyotes and skunks, and coon used along the creek. Pelts were worth something.

Joe French, riding in with a sack on his saddle, was met by Chet Minor at the cabin door.

"We butchered," Joe said. "Barney sent you over a fore quarter." Joe dismounted and unloaded the sack, carrying it in and planking it down on the table.

"Thanks," said Chet Minor. "I can use some beef."

Joe French looked around that tight, tidy cabin. Here was no sloppiness, no shiftlessness. Joe had seen Chet's washing on the clothes line as he came in. The cabin was swept, the bed made. There was amusement and content in Joe French's eyes. "We're goin' to shove some cattle down this way," French commented. "Some old cows that Barney bought this fall."

Chet nodded. "You'll want the hay," he said quietly.

"Barney said that you could feed what you needed to the horses," French said innocently. "We're pretty heavy stocked this year. Might have to put a man down here to feed the cows."

"I'll feed 'em," Chet offered eagerly. He wanted no interloper on his domain.

"We'll pay you for it then," Joe drawled. "You know, Chet, Barney has got a bunch of young horses this year. First time I ever knew him to buy any. We're havin' a poor time gettin' them started. Got six head." He watched Chet closely. Chet said nothing. He was not thinking about young horses.

"Joe," Chet said suddenly. "I want some traps. When is the next time you're goin' to town?"

"Pretty soon," French answered.

"You get me some traps," Chet said, and detailed his desires.

"I'll get 'em," French promised.

Joe French ate dinner with Chet that day, drawling along as he ate, retailing the happenings in the Rifle Rock. Chet listened with only half his attention. Joe French spoke of the nesters and of the cattle shipments and of the men and women in the valley. He was talking about Powell Overman when, right in the middle of the tale, Chet interrupted.

60

"You know, Joe," Chet said, "if I had some cement I'd build a big tank down below the spring. I could haul the rocks for it this winter."

Amusement glinted in Joe's eyes. "I'll mention it to the boss," he said.

Joe French had a report to make when he got back to the Screwplate. "It's his place," Joe said to Barney Loveless. "He's fixed it up. He's talkin' now about buildin' a big tank down below the spring. Barney . . ."

"What?" growled Barney Loveless.

"Well, hell," said Joe French. "It's his place, Barney."

Within a week Laramie brought over the traps Chet had requested. Chet was not in when Laramie dumped the traps beside the door. Chet had put a saddle on an old and gentle horse and was experimenting. He had not ridden for a long time. He wanted to get the feel of the saddle again. There were two young horses in the five that were in the horse pasture, and the Screwplate had six more and no one to break them. Surely Barney Loveless would pay five dollars for breaking a young horse, and a man could live a long time on forty dollars. If he could just ride . . . Chet saddled the gentle horse and took a ride. He had to shorten the leather of the right stirrup, and the saddle galled him, but . . . well, there was the forty dollars to consider.

With the traps that Laramie had brought, Chet set a line down the creek. Mornings, early, he rode that trapline. He had a neighbor down the creek. Joe French had mentioned someone that was called Doc Laird. Chet had never seen the doctor, but at the end of his trapline he encountered a fence. He did not go below it. His days were filled now. He hauled rocks for the proposed tanks, believing that surely Loveless would furnish the cement when spring came. He cut posts and piled them, good cedar posts. He rode his trapline. He cooked, he ate, he slept and he stake-broke the young horses. Maybe he couldn't ride them but at least he could begin their education. Chet Minor was busy and, being busy, was content and proud. October wore away. November came and was finished. December drifted in with a little snow. Supplies came over from the Screwplate, Joe French or Laramie or Amador bringing them. On Monday in the first week of December, Chet Minor rode his trapline.

The thin snow was crisp under the hoofs of the gentle horse when Chet rode out that morning. The old horse had a little hump in his back and bucked a few jumps and Chet took the bucking. It did not even hurt his hip where the bone had been broken. The old horse was pretty rough, too, being big and stout for all his age. Chet felt good.

He had a floursack tied under his chin to keep his ears warm and the sheepskin he had bought in Wolfbarger's was fleece-lined and comfortable. His hands were cold without gloves and there was a hole in the sole of one boot, but that was all right. He was going to halfsole the boots himself as soon as he got around to it, and in the meantime the hole was not very big.

Chet made straight for the end of the trapline. He would pick up what pelts he found on the return journey. Just seven o'clock when Chet rode out and the sun was low against the southeast and the little wind was brittle.

Reaching the fence at the end of the trapline, Chet stopped. There was a rider coming up along the creek, someone who was not familiar with a horse and who rode an outsized mount. Chet stopped and waited. It would be kind of good to talk to someone.

The rider came on, reached the fence and stopped. Chet Minor's nester neighbor. The rider was a girl with tawny red hair and the wind had whipped her cheeks until they were red beneath her brown eyes. The eyes were anxious, as was the girl's voice when she spoke.

"Marybelle's having a baby," the girl announced without preamble.

Chet was astonished, so startled that he could not say a word.

"Can you come and help me?" the girl asked.

"Marybelle . . . ?" Chet gasped.

"It's her first," said the girl. "She's having trouble. Won't you come?"

"But . . ." Chet began. "A baby?"

"A calf. I went out to the barn . . ."

Chet began to laugh, his relief was so great. "Marybelle's a cow?" he asked.

"A Jersey." The girl had straightened and there was a trace of anger in her brown eyes. "She's a very fine Jersey cow and she's having trouble. I don't know what to do for her. Dad's gone to the Olsons'. He's been there all night. I knew that you lived up the creek and I came . . ."

"Cows do have calves," Chet drawled. "Mostly you just let 'em alone an' they have 'em."

"But Marybelle's different," the girl announced. "If you won't come I'll have to get someone else. I suppose I could get Mr. Olson . . ."

"I'll come," Chet said. "Sure, I'll go with you." He got down from the old horse and, limping to the fence, began to kick down the wire. The girl watched him.

"You're Mr. Minor, aren't you?" she asked when Chet had the wire down and had led the horse across.

"Chet Minor," Chet agreed, mounting.

"I'm Sally Laird." The girl turned the big horse she bestrode and rode up beside Chet. "Let's hurry."

The plow horse broke into a lumbering trot, the girl clinging to the saddle horn with both hands. Chet's old mount took up a running walk.

"I'm . . . afraid . . . about . . . Marybelle . . ." The words jolted out of Sally Laird.

"We'll look after her," Chet assured. "If you kind of ease forward an' put some weight on the stirrups that horse won't jolt so much."

Sally Laird eased forward and straightened her legs. The plow horse kept the trot.

Not far below the fence, where the creek formed a cove, the roofs of a house and barn appeared. Smoke was coming from the chimney of the house. The two riders swung into the cove and made straight for the barn. There they dismounted and went in. A Jersey cow was lying on the hay spread upon the dirt floor. She looked up with big brown bovine eyes as Chet and the

64

girl entered. Chet, a veteran of range obstetrics, took in the situation at a glance. Marybelle *was* having trouble.

"You go on to the house," Chet directed, peeling off the sheepskin coat. "I'll handle this." Not waiting to see if his order was obeyed, he advanced upon Marybelle and knelt beside her.

For the next thirty minutes Chet was busy. At the end of that time a tawny, fawn-colored calf lay beside Marybelle. Chet looked at his red hands, looked at the cow and the calf, and grunted. It had been more difficult than even he had anticipated.

"There you are," he said. "I'll come back after a while an' tail you up, an' the calf can suck."

Marybelle, nosing the calf, made no objection to the program. Chet walked out of the barn and went toward the house. Sally Laird met him at the door with a washbasin, soap, and a teakettle full of hot water.

"Marybelle's got a calf," Chet announced. "A heifer." He took the washpan from the girl's hands and put it on the bench beside the door. The girl poured hot water.

Now that the excitement concerning Marybelle was past, there was a diffidence between the two. Chet washed and dried his hands and pulled on his sheepskin. "Well," he said awkwardly, "I reckon I'll go back to Marybelle for a minute an' then go. She's all right but I want to let the calf suck an' . . ."

"I've got some gingerbread and some coffee," Sally Laird offered. "Won't you come in? I haven't thanked you and . . . Here comes Dad!"

A horse, drawing a buggy, was coming through the gate. Leaving the steps, Sally Laird ran toward the vehicle.

"Marybelle's had her baby," she called, as the buggy stopped.

A plump, round-faced man, glasses on his nose, the smile on his face overshadowing the weariness, climbed down. "And Mrs. Olson has a nine-pound boy," the man said. He put his arm about the girl and looked inquiringly at Chet. The bay horse in the buggy shafts looked around questioningly.

"This is Mr. Minor, Dad," Sally Laird explained. "He helped Marybelle. You didn't come and Marybelle was having trouble so I went to get help, and found him and he came." The words came out all in a rush.

"Calf had a front leg doubled under it," Chet explained.

"Well . . . well . . . Lots of trouble bringing these youngsters into the world," Dr. Laird said. "Mrs. Olson had some difficulty, too. Come in, Mr. Minor. Come in. Don't I smell coffee, Sally?"

The girl, breaking away from her father, ran to the house and disappeared. Dr. Laird smiled. Somehow he seemed to include Chet in that smile, as though there was some secret between them. "Come in, Mr. Minor," Laird said again. Chet found himself preceding the doctor into the house.

There was coffee and gingerbread in the kitchen. There were curtains on the kitchen windows and the room shone. The coffee was ambrosia and the gingerbread manna in the wilderness. Sally Laird fussed around, making her father and their guest comfortable. Presently Chet found himself talking, talking naturally about cattle and about horses and the country and things that he had not talked about before. After a time the doctor and Sally and Chet went out to see Marybelle. Marybelle was on her feet and the calf, wobbly legs spread, had her head beneath Marybelle's flank. Marybelle's great brown eyes were proud.

"Did it all yourself, didn't you?" Chet said, running a hand along Marybelle's sleek neck. "You won't want to use the milk for the first two, three days, doctor. After that you can build the calf a pen an' break it to drink out of a bucket if you want. Generally though, we let the calf suck one side an' milk the other."

Dr. Laird nodded. "I'm afraid that I can't milk," he said doubtfully. "I know that Sally can't."

"Well," Chet offered, "I could come down an' show you. It isn't far."

"We'll be eternally grateful if you will," the doctor said. "Won't we, Sally?"

Sally nodded her bright head.

"I got to go now," Chet announced awkwardly. "I've got a trapline to run an' the pelts to skin out an' stretch."

"You can't stay for lunch?" asked the doctor.

"I better not," Chet said. "I better go on. Thanks."

Despite the doctor's expostulations he was obdurate. Mounting the old brown horse he rode off, following along the creek, leaving the doctor and his daughter at the door of the barn. At the bend of the creek Chet looked back. Dr. Laird and Sally Laird were still beside the barn, watching his departure. Chet waved a hand. Now why in the devil had he offered to come down and teach the doctor to milk? Why had he done that? Blame' nester coming into the country and didn't even know how to milk!

The brown horse, knowing that his rider was engrossed in other matters, walked sleepily along and stubbed a toe over a stone, stumbling. Chet jerked him awake.

"Jug, you damn' sleep-walker!" Chet snapped. "Wake up or I'll . . ."

Why in thunder had he made that offer anyhow?

CHAPTER
SIX

With winter finally shutting down upon the country, the town of Rifle Rock basked in a kind of lethargy, stirred only for the moment by the Christmas preparations. Maida Overman stayed in town where she could play the great lady, preferring her father's home to life at the ranch. Maida's father, Mark Scotia, was slipping rapidly. The Triangle was not entirely owned by Scotia, the ranch in reality being a company, but Scotia was principal holder of the stock and had devoted his life to the building up of the Triangle. Now, as winter became more and more evident, and as the *Conejos Examiner*, the newspaper from the county seat, carried more and more telegraph reports on its front page of the terrible conditions in the East, Mark Scotia became more and more preoccupied. The mail brought him letters which he took to his study and pondered over for hours. There came a morning when Mark Scotia did not get up when he was called and Maida, going to his room, found him in his bed with blood on the coverlet. Dr. Frawley, hastily summoned, made an examination and looked grave. Mark Scotia had suffered a slight stroke. The breaking of a blood vessel in his nose had relieved the pressure. He must have rest and quiet. Powell Overman, called from the Triangle, listened to the doctor's report, his face sober but inwardly elated. Now, for the first time since his incumbency in the manager's position, he would have free rein.

With her father ill, Maida added another maid to the staff of servants in the house, and regardless of her concern for her father, went ahead with her plans for a Christmas celebration: a party to be given at the house in town.

It was in the midst of these preparations, a scant week before Christmas, that a stranger arrived in Rifle Rock. The stranger came on the evening train, a well-dressed, quick-moving man with sharp black eyes and gray touching the temples of his black hair. He took a room at the hotel, registering as Norville Kirkpatrick, with a home address of Kansas City, and having seen his grips bestowed in the Parker House, inquired the way to Mark Scotia's residence. The curious clerk gave him instructions and Kirkpatrick left the hotel.

Maida was tying Christmas packages when Rosa Revilla, the new maid, called for Mark Scotia. Leaving the dining room, Maida met Kirkpatrick in the hall. The work of tying packages had caused Maida to be charmingly disheveled, and Kirkpatrick returned her welcoming smile.

"Father is ill," she told the caller. "He has had a slight stroke and Doctor Frawley says that he is not to be disturbed."

Kirkpatrick shook his head in sympathy. "I'm sorry to hear that," he said. "I've come from Kansas City purposely to see him. Of course . . ."

"He simply can't talk business now," Maida interrupted. "My husband, Mr. Overman, will be in from the ranch tonight. He is the manager. Perhaps he . . ."

"I'll see him," Kirkpatrick decided. "When will he be in, Mrs. Overman?"

Maida gave an approximate time for Powell's arrival and Kirkpatrick took his departure, assured that Maida would inform her husband of his being in town.

Powell Overman called on Kirkpatrick at the hotel that evening and when he returned home his face was grave. Maida, coming into the hall as her husband entered, saw the expression and hurried to him.

"Is anything wrong, Powell?" she asked.

Powell Overman made no direct reply. "Kirkpatrick will be here for a day or two," he said abruptly. "I'm going to take him out to the ranch tomorrow and I want you to have him here for dinner tomorrow night."

"But the party!" Maida protested. "I'm so busy getting ready for it, I won't have to . . ."

"I've already invited him," Powell stated. "And you be nice to him, Maida. You be mighty nice to him, you hear?"

The urgency in her husband's voice frightened Maida. He was gruff and abrupt and turned her questions aside, and finally shut himself in Mark Scotia's office, locking the door against intruders. It was late when he came to bed and although Maida had

71

lain awake to question him, Powell undressed and went to bed without satisfying her curiosity.

The next day Powell Overman and Kirkpatrick went to the Triangle, coming in late in the evening to the meal that Maida had ordered prepared with especial pains. At the table Kirkpatrick was urbane and smiling . . . and uncommunicative. It was not until after the meal when Powell had gone into Scotia's study for cigars, that Maida had opportunity to air her charms. She did so beautifully, sitting beside Kirkpatrick on a divan in the parlor, smiling at the man and talking to him. Kirkpatrick was appreciative. Filled with a good meal, having drunk good wine, in the company of a pretty woman he expanded. It was there that Maida learned a little of Kirkpatrick's business. Kirkpatrick was a vice-president of a Kansas City bank.

Maida Overman was not a typical Western product. She had been born in the East and while she had spent most of her life in Rifle Rock, her education had been in Eastern schools. She extended herself to be charming to the visitor. Powell Overman, coming back with the cigars, heard part of the conversation that came from the parlor.

"I should think," Kirkpatrick's deep voice was saying, "that you would find it very narrow here, Mrs. Overman. A woman of your talents and education must find this country trying."

"Oh no!" Maida's voice carried a plaintive note as though, in refuting Kirkpatrick's statement she was in reality agreeing with it. "I love this country. I was raised

72

here. And there is so much good that I can do, and my husband is so kind to me . . ."

Powell Overman slipped back along the hall, an appreciative grin on his face. Maida was softening Kirkpatrick. Better leave her alone awhile. At the end of the hall Powell encountered Rosa Revilla. He stopped the girl, placing one hand on her shoulder.

"Bring the decanter and glasses into the parlor directly," he ordered.

Rosa smiled up at the big man. There was something provocative in the smile, something a little bold in the black eyes that flashed a glance from beneath lowered lashes.

"Si, Señor," Rosa said demurely, and hurried away.

Powell watched her go. The girl's hips swayed under the closely fitting black dress. At the sideboard she picked up the tray containing the decanter and the glasses, turning her head to look at Powell as she did so. Again she smiled. Powell Overman grunted. Rosa's shoulder had been soft and silken under his touch, and the black dress was low at the throat, the ivory satin skin temptingly in contrast with the white ruffles at the dress's neckline. Again Powell Overman grunted and swung back along the hall.

"You had better stay here for Christmas, Mr. Kirkpatrick," he said when he entered the parlor. "We're goin' to have a big celebration. Maida is havin' a party an' . . ."

Kirkpatrick did not take his eyes from Maida's face. "I'm only sorry that I can't," he said. "Mrs. Overman has been pressing me to stay but this is a business trip and I must get back." He smiled at Maida.

"However," he continued, "business will bring me back this way again after the first of the year. If Mrs. Overman will be so kind . . ."

Maida flushed faintly. "You must come and stay with us of course," she said. "Whenever you are in Rifle Rock you must make this your home."

Gallantly Kirkpatrick picked up Maida's hand and raised it to his lips. "Who could refuse so charming a hostess?" he asked.

Rifle Rock was not alone in preparing for Christmas nor was Maida Overman the only one to plan a celebration. All along Willow Creek the nesters were getting ready for the Yuletide and, in Dr. Laird's house, Sally was busy.

The preparations of the settlers were scanty enough. There is not much that a man and his wife can do for Christmas when they are on a shoestring. A little piñon tree, cut from a mesa slope, some red berries, a few pine boughs, perhaps a pair of shoes for a youngster, maybe a few yards of calico to make a dress, some hard candy from the store . . . Christmas can be mighty gaunt in a nester country.

In Dr. Laird's tight new house Sally baked a cake and made pies, Dr. Laird watching his daughter with amused eyes. "Christmas, Sally?" he asked. "What do you want for Christmas?"

"You, Dad," Sally answered, hugging her father and leaving the marks of her floury hands on his coat.

"And what else?" Laird insisted.

Sally released her father and a faraway look came into her eyes. "I don't know," she confessed. "At home, with grandmother, we always had turkey and dressing and all the relatives came and . . . it *felt* so good, Dad!"

Laird nodded soberly. "There isn't much Christmas Spirit here, I'm afraid," he said slowly. "Olson was telling me that his fence had been cut and torn down all along the east side. I'm afraid, Sally. We aren't welcome in this country. The cowmen don't want us here. All my life I've read about the West. I've treasured the idea that someday I would own land in the West. Now we're here and the people . . ."

"Not all the people," Sally interrupted swiftly. "There's that old man, Barney Loveless. He looks like an old gnome out of a book, and that big, black-bearded man that was with him. They were friendly, Dad. And then there's Chet . . ."

The girl flushed. Dr. Laird smiled slowly. "You like Chet, don't you, Sally?" he asked, stroking his daughter's hair.

"He's been good to us," Sally answered. "He's . . . Dad!" her voice was scandalized, "I've got flour all over your coat!"

Chet Minor had been good to Dr. Laird. He had, as he promised, gone down and taught the doctor to milk. He had helped the doctor build a pen for the calf and, with some trepidation, because he did not like the job, had taught the calf to drink milk from a bucket. Chet's advice and help had been invaluable to the Lairds. Chet

Minor knew instinctively how to get along in the country. Why shouldn't he know? He had been raised in it. Some of that knowledge he had imparted to the doctor and to Sally. They were dang' nesters, Chet told himself, and unworthy of a cowman's notice, but he butchered a calf for the doctor, and he hauled wood for the doctor, and he had showed the doctor how to set a corner post for a fence, and he had suggested that the new house would be warmer if banked with dirt and lined with paper. Shucks, the Lairds lived right down the creek, at the end of the trapline, and it wasn't any trouble to ride a little further along and drop in and see how they were coming.

Right at the moment Chet was being good to the Lairds again. With Joe French's thirty-thirty he was prowling the top of the mesa behind the Rock Springs camp. There was a bunch of turkeys up there and Chet was looking for the roost.

He found the roost and waited while the day grew cold with coming night. The turkeys came in and with the thirty-thirty's spiteful crack a big gobbler, proud in his glossy feathers, came down to flop on the snow, his head shot off. That night, burning precious kerosene, Chet plucked and drew the gobbler and in the morning he carried the bird in a gunnysack when he rode down the creek.

Chet rode a young horse that morning. He had worked up his nerve to try one of the broncs and had made the grade. The bronc had bucked but Chet had ridden him, taking the punishment that the horse dealt out. Now old Jug rested and Chet rode the broncs. He had even carried a wolf hide on one of the green horses, no inconsiderable feat. A far different Chet Minor from the crippled, mentally troubled boy who had come to the Rock Springs rode down Rock Creek that morning with a turkey tied to his saddle horn.

There was a gap in the Laird fence that Chet had made and he rode through it. Dr. Laird hailed him from the barn when he reached the house and Sally opened the door and smiled at him. Chet, climbing down, untied the turkey. "Christmas dinner," he said, holding it out.

Sally's mouth made a little round O of surprise and admiration and Dr. Laird, coming up behind Chet, put his hand on the rider's shoulder.

"And you'll come to Christmas dinner with us," Laird announced.

"You've got to," Sally echoed.

So it was that later in the week, Joe French, coming over to the Rock Springs camp bearing an invitation for Chet to eat Christmas dinner at the Screwplate, met with an unreceptive answer.

"I can't, Joe," Chet said. "I'm goin' to eat dinner with them nesters down the creek. I couldn't get out of it."

Joe French looked grave and expressed sympathy and sorrow. "Likely you'll have beans an' corn bread an' rabbit gravy," Joe said. "You better call it off, Chet, an' come to the ranch."

"I can't, Joe," Chet answered.

Joe French kept a straight face but he grinned all the way home. Joe French and Barney Loveless had stopped and visited with Dr. Laird and his daughter.

And so Chet Minor ate Christmas dinner with Dr. Laird and Sally. Clean and scrubbed until he shone, he came in carrying a burlap sack, which he placed beside the door. He had done a washing two days before Christmas and on Christmas Eve he had dragged an old half-barrel into the cabin and filled it with hot water and scoured himself with yellow soap. He could still smell that dang' yellow soap as he rode down the creek and even while he stabled old Jug in the Laird barn. But when he came into the house and was welcomed by Dr. Laird, the aroma of turkey and stuffing and of coffee and spices drove the odor of soap away.

Laird welcomed Chet at the door and Sally thrust her tousled head into the kitchen from her bedroom door and smiled at him. "I'll be out in a minute," Sally called, and Chet, somehow bashful, somehow feeling like a small boy, took the chair that Laird offered.

Sally came in, neat and clean, her cheeks rosy. The turkey came from the oven. The dressing and the mashed potatoes and the gravy and the canned corn went on the table. Chairs were drawn up and Dr. Laird asked a blessing and then fell to sharpening the carving knife.

"See what's in your package, Chet," Sally said.

There was a tissue-wrapped parcel beside Chet's plate. He opened it. There, inside the tissue, was a pair of gloves, warm gloves, strong leather gloves, and with the gloves a note. "To our friend, Chet Minor. Merry Christmas."

Chet pulled on the gloves, the color staining his cheeks beneath the tan. "Say . . ." said Chet Minor. "Say . . ."

"They fit!" Sally beamed.

Chet pushed back his chair and got up. Going to the gunny sack he had brought in, he reached into the burlap and from it produced a wolf hide, beautifully stretched, fleshed and tanned. Chet had taken a great deal of trouble with the wolf hide.

"Here, Doc," said Chet, "you can use it for a rug, mebbe." Dr. Laird took the wolf hide and made no attempt to conceal his pleased smile.

Again Chet reached into the gunny sack. The pelts he brought out now were the pride of his winter trapping. There had been a few beaver at the little dam. Chet had taken them. Now he extended the glossy beaver pelts to Sally Laird. All the beaver he had taken, the most valuable portion of his catch. The best he had.

"It ain't much," Chet Minor said. "It ain't a lot but . . . Merry Christmas, Sally. Mebbe you can use 'em for somethin'."

For a moment Sally Laird stood stock still. She did not say a word. The light went out of Chet's eyes and the smile left his lips. He lowered the pelts. "It ain't . . ." Chet Minor said again, and stopped. Sally Laird cried one word, "Chet!" came up out of her chair and, throwing her arms around Chet's neck, kissed him full on the mouth while Dr. Laird stood by beaming.

"A whole coat!" Sally exclaimed, freeing Chet from her arms. "They'll make a whole beaver coat. Or a big muff and stole. Oh, Chet . . ."

The light was back in Chet's eyes now and his cheeks were red. "Well," he said defiantly, "they ain't much . . ."

"Chet Minor!" Sally flared, "if you say that again I won't . . . I won't feed you any turkey!"

Filled with turkey, stuffed to repletion after the meal, Chet leaned back to enjoy the cigar that Doctor Laird had given him. Sally would not hear to the men's helping with the dishes and their smoke was accompanied by a pleasant rattle of plates being washed and the girl's brisk footsteps as she crossed the kitchen.

"You've been a help to us, Chet," Laird said, eyeing his cigar. "You've helped Sally and me more than I can tell you."

"Shucks," Chet answered uncomfortably, "I haven't done much. I've been in this country quite a while an' I know the ropes. That's all."

Laird nodded. "You know the ropes," he echoed. "I wonder . . . Chet, why you don't help the other settlers?"

Chet flushed. "I'm a cowman," he said. "I don't have much truck with the nesters."

"Sally and I are nesters."

"You're different," Chet answered quickly.

"When I came out here," Laird said, "I planned not to practice medicine any more. Since I've come I have done more work and driven further than I ever did in Ohio."

"An' been paid less," Chet surmised shrewdly.

Laird had the grace to flush. "What of it?" he demanded. "They come to me, and what can I do? Turn them down?"

"No," Chet agreed, "you can't turn 'em down."

"Neither can you."

"But they don't come to me," Chet said triumphantly.

"I'm coming to you." Laird held his cigar in his fingers and leaned forward. "You were right in one thing, Chet: Sally and I aren't in the same shape as the average nester. I've money enough to see me through, at least until I can raise a crop. The others haven't. That is, most of them haven't."

"You won't never raise a crop," Chet said. "This is a range country. It'll be plowed up an' mebbe some wheat raised, but it won't produce every year."

"I realize that." Laird waved the cigar. "That means that we'll have to depend on cattle or sheep for a living. Now, Chet, I'm asking you a question. We haven't any hay. I've bought some but the men that haven't the money to buy hay are in a bad spot. Some of them have cattle and they're going to lose what they have if they can't find feed. What would you do, Chet, if you had a little bunch of cattle and no feed for them?"

Chet considered the question. "I haven't any cattle," he said.

Sally had come to stand in the door and look in on her father and their guest.

"But suppose you had," Laird insisted.

Chet's eyes narrowed. "Well then," he said reluctantly, "I'd take a boy an' a horse an' I'd hold what cattle I had on the chamisa. That is, if there was chamisa. Cows'll eat that an' get along."

"Suppose you had no chamisa, then what would you do?"

Chet grunted. "There's cactus all over the country," he said. "One time we had it dry here an' we cut a lot of prickly pear an' burned off the stickers. The cows ate that an' it carried them through."

Laird's hand came down on his leg with a loud slap. "I'm going to send Olson up to see you," he announced. "I want you to talk with him. He needs help . . ."

"I won't help a nester," Chet interrupted stubbornly.

Laird laughed. "You just have," he said. "Anyhow . . . can you turn them away, Chet? Can you?"

"Mrs. Olson has the sweetest baby boy," Sally interposed, apropos of nothing. "A little tow-headed fellow. There are seven children in the family. The baby's sweet."

"Olson is a good, honest Swede," Dr. Laird said. "He's slow but he will work, and he's honest. The other settlers seem to look up to Olson. He has fifteen cows. I'd hate to see them starve to death."

Chet's face was fiery red. "It ain't the cows' fault that the man that owns 'em is a nester," he growled reluctantly. "All right, I'll see Olson then."

"And help him?"

"I'll show him how to burn the thorns off a cactus," Chet agreed — ungraciously. "Even a dumb Swede could learn that."

From the door Sally laughed gleefully and Dr. Laird smiled and put his cigar back into his mouth.

"Well," Chet said, "you shoved me into it. It isn't my fault an' it don't mean that I like a nester."

There was something tender in Sally's eyes and her laugh had a little tremulous ring. "You don't like them, Chet," she said. "You . . . well, you and Dad are a pair."

CHAPTER
SEVEN

On the second day of January Powell Overman sat in Mark Scotia's study, a frown wrinkling his forehead and his eyes narrow as he considered the papers spread on the desk before him. He had been in town for New Year's Eve and New Year's Day and was postponing his return to the ranch. There were several things to keep Powell in Rifle Rock but most important of these was a meeting to be held among the cowmen of the valley. Powell Overman and Royce Mitchell had called that meeting and ranchers were coming in from as far north as Stevens' on the upper Tramparas, and as far south as Bob Jumper's JK below the town.

At the moment Powell Overman was considering his own situation. Upstairs Mark Scotia lay in his bed, a weakened, tired Mark Scotia whose long body made a narrow line under the bed clothes. Mark Scotia was all through with being the big man of the Rifle Rock. It was just a question of time before Mark Scotia would be a mound in Rifle Rock's cemetery.

Looking forward to that time Powell Overman was worried. Spread upon the desk were letters from the Easterners who held the majority of the foreign-owned shares in the Triangle. They were short letters, terse and pointed, and they told a tale. The Triangle, save for only a part of Mark Scotia's interest, was now security for loans. There was a panic in the East, a panic whose fringes spread across the country, and the men who owned the Triangle had placed their shares in the ranch with banks to make security for their loans. And the banks were beginning to act as if they were afraid.

Powell Overman did not worry about the Eastern men; he worried about himself. In the hands of the banks there was enough of the Triangle shares to control the ranch. Mark Scotia was slowly dying. When he was dead there would be an accounting. At that accounting Powell Overman must appear in a favorable light. He was manager of the Triangle and to retain that position he must produce. In the Rifle Rock there were forces at work that would hinder and hamper that production. Grass and water and cattle made the Triangle. Now, encroaching upon the grass and water, the settlers had come. Sections of land owned by the railroad had been sold to settlers. Other land, unowned, was now claimed by homesteaders. The holdings were small individually but large in the aggregate, and coupled with the loss of land was another factor: the ranches of the Rifle Rock were losing cattle.

There had always been a certain amount of rustling in the Rifle Rock. There had always been a few cattle short on the fall count. Any country has in it men who will take from other men, and the Rifle Rock was no exception. This fall there were more cattle missing than usual. Powell Overman and the other ranchers, alarmed by the encroachment on their range, chose to place the shortage at the hands of the newcomers. They disregarded the fact that the nesters were far apart and unorganized; they chose to ignore the sudden prosperity of men who had lived in the country for a considerable length of time, men like Ben Revilla and Julio Tidd who owned no land, but had a brand and cattle that ran free on the open range. One sore spot can make a man forget other lesser aches and pains, and the nesters were the sore spot in Rifle Rock.

Hearing a knock, Powell Overman got up and went to the door.

Royce Mitchell was first to arrive at Mark Scotia's house, closely followed by Tom Neil. Overman took them to the study and they sat smoking, their talk desultory, while they waited for the others. Alec Crow came in, and Stevens who had stopped the night with Crow, breaking his long journey from the upper Tramparas. Old Bob Jumper arrived, and presently Barney Loveless. The big cowmen of the Rifle Rock were all present. Powell Overman, seated behind Scotia's desk, broke the subject of the meeting.

"We've been losin' cattle," he said without preamble. "Royce an' me talked it over an' we thought we'd better get together."

Solemn nods went around the semi-circle, only old Barney Loveless, his yellow eyes flashing from one man to another, keeping out of it.

"What's your idea, Powell?" Tom Neil asked. "Form an anti-rustler association and put up a reward for information an' convictions?"

Powell Overman and Mitchell exchanged glances. They had already talked this thing over.

Barney Loveless spoke quickly. "That ain't a bad idea," he said. "It gives us a sort of organization an' we can put up a little money for rewards an' such." Barney hoped that he would be able to control this meeting and keep it sane.

Royce Mitchell shook his head. "That won't work," he said quickly. "Suppose we do have an organization, an' suppose we do catch somebody rustlin' cattle an' bring him in to trial? Who's goin' to be on the jury? Nesters!"

The word was out. There, in that single word the purpose of the meeting was stated. There was not a man present, save only Loveless, who had not lost land and water. Not a man was present, with that one exception, who did not feel that he was being encroached upon, who did not think hotly of some particularly desirable location where formerly his cattle had grazed and that was now fenced.

"The juries would turn 'em loose as fast as we caught 'em," stated Alec Crow.

"They've got the votes," Royce Mitchell added. "They'll be able to control the county offices next election."

Young Tom Neil blurted it out. "They're takin' our range an' water!"

Barney Loveless looked slowly around the half-circle of faces. "There's lots of room in this country," he stated casually. "I remember when some of us were startin'. Alec, you used to work for the Diamond Dot.

You got a place of your own now. Remember how you got it? Tom, yore daddy come to this country with three head of horses an' a saddle rope. That was all the start he needed. It'll take a little time but we got the country with us. Ten years from now, after we've had a drought an' a hard winter or two, we'll be runnin' our cattle where they've always run. The nesters will be gone."

Again he looked at the faces about him, hard, stern faces with no relenting in them. Old Barney Loveless got up slowly. "I reckon," he said whimsically, "I'm out of place here. I'll leave before you begin to talk about your plans. Good day."

It seemed as though the old man's bones creaked as he walked to the door. Then men in the office could hear him out in the hall, struggling into his coat. Then the front door slammed and someone in Mark Scotia's office let go a pent-up breath.

"What's your idea, Powell?" Clyde Stevens asked quietly.

"My idea," said Powell Overman, "an' I've talked it over with Royce here, is to get somebody into this country to look after things for us. Somebody who knows how to handle a rifle."

Silence followed that statement and then, beside the desk, Alec Crow nodded his head. "That way," said Alec Crow, "we get results."

"Powell an' me," Royce Mitchell's deep voice boomed, "have kind of looked over the field. We think we've got a man in mind. Over at Globe one of the copper companies had some trouble with independents cuttin' in on their holdin's, an' they got a man. He got results. Now . . ." Royce lowered his voice and the others bent their heads to listen.

There were other meetings besides that in Scotia's house, held on January second. In the back room of Juan Salas' cantina, over in Rifle Rock's Chihuahua, Ben Revilla and Julio Tidd, together with Frank Oakes and a sharp-featured man named Runkle who occasionally bought cattle, were gathered round a table. Tidd ran cattle in the Rifle Rock although he had no ranch of his own, nothing but a house in town. Ben Revilla was a rider and Oakes was a tinhorn gambler. There was a whisky bottle in the center of the table and small glasses stood about the edge.

"They'll blame it on the nesters anyhow," Tidd said. "There ain't a cowman in the Rifle Rock that don't hate a nester. How many cattle can you handle, Runkle?"

Runkle tapped the edge of the table with his fingers. "Plenty," he said. "You get 'em to me with the brands changed, an' I'll market 'em."

Oakes' poker face did not change expression and Tidd shifted nervously. "We've got no place to work on 'em," he said. "We've got to get a place. It'll be all right for Carl an' me to be out lookin' around. We both got a few head of cows an' if anybody asks we can say we're lookin' after them. But how about you, Ben?"

"Me?" Ben Revilla grinned his flashing smile. "I think I'm goin' to be a nester. I take up a little claim over in the Amarilla Mesa country. There is a house there."

"An' we can shove 'em right through the canyon an' over into that rough country west of it," said Tidd. "That's a good idea, Ben."

"But not too many at a time," Oakes added his word. "An' we won't want to work 'em over on Ben's place. Somebody would get wise if we did."

"You fellows settle it among yourselves," Runkle said casually. "I'll buy 'em. It looks like we'd ought to make some money. I'll buy a drink."

Tidd lifted his voice. "Juan!" he called. "Juan!" And then, as Juan Salas' swarthy face appeared at the door, "Bring another bottle!"

And a third meeting was held on that second day of January. On the flats down below Rock Creek there were perhaps ten men assembled. Dr. Laird was there, and Chet Minor and Olson, big and slow and blue-eyed, and Ray Quick, who had a homestead clear down by the railroad and who had spent the night with Olson. Ten men and three wagons and a fire burning briskly and a youngster holding a little bunch of cattle, Olson's fifteen cows.

"You don't want to cook 'em," Chet Minor said, shoving a hayfork into a pile of cactus that had been unloaded from a wagon. "All you want to do is burn off the spines." He held the loaded fork over the fire and cactus spines crackled as they burned and the sap hissed on the hot wood. Chet revolved the fork and the snapping of the burning spines came again.

"See?" said Chet.

Olson took a fork and loading it with prickly pear, held the cactus over the flame. Chet tossed his forkful to the ground.

"This is one way of handlin' the stuff," Chet said. "If you just got a cow or two an' are keepin' them penned you can cut cactus with a scythe like we done today, an' pile it up an' burn it off when you need it or when you pile it. That way you can kind of treat it like it was hay an' have some on hand."

Around Chet, men nodded solemn heads. Quick had taken Chet's fork and was burning spines from cactus. The pile was growing.

"I've seen it," Chet said, "where the cactus wasn't cut at all. If you've got a bunch of cattle to feed you can make a kind of torch an' take a line of men an' work along a pear flat, burnin' off the stickers. The cattle will follow you right along." He glanced at Dr. Laird and the doctor nodded his head in approbation.

"An' that's about all I can tell you," Chet said. "Turn your cows loose, Olson, an' they'll eat this stuff."

Olson called to his boy and that youngster, riding his rawboned horse around the cattle, brought them slowly toward the fire. The first cow, gaunt from lack of feed, came to the little pile of cactus, nosed it with lowered head, and then tentatively tried a mouthful. She chewed, swallowed and took another bite.

"Damned if they won't eat it," Quick marveled. "I guess this kind of fixes us up, don't it, boys? There's a lot of cactus around my place."

"They won't get fat on it, but they won't starve to death," Chet said shortly. "I'll go along now. I reckon there's nothin' else you want, is there?" He turned and started toward his horse tied to the wheel of a wagon.

"Hold on a minute, Chet," Laird requested.

Chet stopped.

Olson and Quick, standing together, exchanged glances. "How much do we owe you, Mr. Minor?" Quick asked.

Chet's eyes were wide with astonishment. "For showin' you how to burn cactus?" he asked incredulously. "Say, the cactus is free, ain't it?"

Olson nodded. "But we took your time," he said.

"You don't owe me a thing!" There was anger in Chet's voice. "Not a damned thing!"

A smile spread over Olson's square face and Quick stood grinning. Every nester in the bunch was smiling. "We're much obliged to you," Quick said. "Maybe sometime we can help you out."

Chet made no answer to that but went on toward his horse, his back expressing his indignation. Laird, with a nod to the others, hurried after Chet.

"I'll ride back with you," the doctor offered, catching up. "I'm ready to go."

"Yore buggy's too slow," Chet answered rudely. "I'm goin' straight across." And then, his anger breaking bounds, "That's the trouble with a damned nester. Always wantin' to pay for somethin'."

Laird grinned. "They didn't know you, Chet," he apologized. "You go along. And say, Sally's planning on your dropping in for supper tomorrow night. Think you can be there?"

"Mebbe," Chet's voice was less gruff. "I'll try to make it, Doctor."

He had untied his horse now and had his left toe in the stirrup. The bronc circled away. Chet hopped on his short leg, swung up, got the leg across the saddle and found the off-stirrup. He circled the bronc back toward the fire where now Olson's lean cows were eating prickly pear.

"You better get a bunch of that stuff burnt in the next week," Chet warned. "We're about due for a storm."

All the way back to the Rock Springs, Chet was angry with himself. He had been imposed upon, he felt. Dr. Laird had taken advantage of their friendship. Just because the doctor looked after half the nesters when they were sick and charged them nothing was no reason that he should rope Chet Minor into the same sort of deal. Still, those nesters had been grateful and the cows were eating the cactus. Chet remembered how those men had looked, how solemn their eyes had been, how those eyes had lighted up when the cattle began to eat. He was of two minds, halfway between anger and gratification, when he rode into the Rock Springs and saw Barney Loveless's buckboard standing beside the fence.

Barney was in the house when Chet came in. The old man had built a fire and the house was warm. Chet put his horse in the corral and Barney met him halfway between the corral and the cabin.

Their exchange of greetings was short. Barney went on down toward the corral and Chet went back with him. The old man looked at the green horse and then at Chet.

"Breakin' broncs?" he asked.

Chet was uneasy. "There were two green horses here," he explained. "I've got a trapline down the creek an' I didn't think it would do to ride Jug all the time. I took a whirl at the green horses."

Barney said, "Hmmmm," deep in his throat. "Give you any trouble?" he asked.

"I carried a wolf hide on him about a month ago," Chet said with pride.

The two went back from the corral to the house, Barney stopping to inspect the stack yard in the journey. In the house, while Chet rustled around putting more wood on the fire and making things straight, Barney wandered about. He told Chet that he intended to stay the night, and Chet, putting on his coat again, went out to do the chores and get a bucket of water. Chet unsaddled, unhitched Loveless's team, fed the horses, throwing down hay into the rack, carried in wood, and brought two buckets of water from the spring. When finally he was done and was taking off his coat in the house, Barney Loveless spoke up.

"We'll throw two-hundred head of cows down here next week," he announced. "I want to use that hay."

Chet nodded. "Feed 'em an' I'll pay you thirty a month an' furnish chuck," Barney growled. "I'm goin' to bring the rest of my green horses down for you to start. You won't get to 'em until spring so I'll send a couple of gentle horses along. There'll be a wagon come down when the cattle come. It'll have some grain for yore horses."

Two months ago Chet would have received a thrill from the simple statements. Then he would have considered them as coming from the boss to a rider. Now, while he agreed with Loveless, the thrill was lacking. After all, Chet thought, this is my place. He might . . .

Loveless seemed to sense Chet's thoughts. "That will be all right with you, won't it?" he asked. "It'll accommodate me a lot."

Now the thrill came. Barney Loveless had recognized Chet as a free agent, not just a Screwplate hand. "That will be fine, Mr. Loveless," Chet said, and turned toward the sheet-iron stove. Barney Loveless suppressed a grin.

The old man was silent while Chet set about preparing supper. When the meal was on the table and Chet invited him to come, Loveless took a seat and fell to eating.

"I could send a couple of calves down with the cattle," he said. "You could use some beef."

Chet thought that over. "I'm tryin' to get by as cheap as I can," he answered finally. "I figured to have a stake out of this, Mr. Loveless."

"That why you been trappin'?" Barney asked.

Chet nodded.

"That why you ain't sent to the ranch for supplies?"

Again a nod.

"I see," Loveless said slowly. "Well . . . looks like you might have a stake, all right."

Nothing more was said during the course of the meal. With supper finished and the dishes done, Chet set about making a bed for the older man. He gave Loveless the bunk and the soogans and spread down his own bed beside the stove, borrowing from his pile of skins for covering. A wolf hide, some coyote pelts, and a blanket made the bed. Loveless watched Chet work.

"Trap them coyotes?" he asked.

"I shot some of them," Chet answered. "I'm about out of shells."

Loveless made no comment to that but changed the subject. "You were out when I came in," he commented.

Chet flushed. "I went down on the flats," he said. "Dr. Laird down the creek, wanted me to show some nesters how to burn the stickers off cactus so that cattle could eat it."

"You show 'em?"

"Yeah."

The old man sat quietly, seeming to study over an idea. Presently: "I thought you were a cowman," he said.

"I am," Chet agreed instantly.

"But yo're helpin' the nesters?"

Again the hot color came to Chet's cheeks. "They're human, ain't they?" he snapped. "Anyhow, it ain't right to let cattle starve when it's not their fault. Those folks don't have any hay."

For a long time Loveless made no comment. When he spoke, his voice was troubled. "Trouble comin' in this country, Chet," he said. "The cowmen had a meetin' in Rifle Rock today."

Instantly Chet was alert. "Yes?" he questioned.

"I pulled out. Didn't stay," Loveless said. "Time'll take care of the nesters. Them that has got what it takes will come through all right. They'll be little cowmen. The country will be fenced all over an' there'll be room enough for all of us. Them that can't get along will pull out. I tried to tell Overman an' Mitchell that."

"An' they wouldn't listen to you," Chet surmised.

"They didn't seem to want to." Loveless grinned ruefully. "I left."

"What are they goin' to do?"

"I didn't stop to find out."

Chet was silent, lost in his thoughts. He knew what cowmen generally did when they were pushed. They took things into their own hands. Dr. Laird and Sally lived down the creek. Olson, big and slow and honest, was five miles below the Lairds. There was that little, swift-moving man, Quick, and there were others.

"Damn it," Chet said suddenly, "why the hell can't things work out peaceful?"

Old Barney Loveless shook his head. "I don't know," he acknowledged. "I just don't know, Chet." Again he was silent and then, lifting his head to look Chet fully in the eyes, he spoke once more. "Yo're kind of a nester yorese'f, Chet," he remarked, "an' you been throwin' in with them."

"What of it?" Chet demanded.

Barney Loveless's words were slow. "Yo're workin' for me in a way," he drawled, "an' that will help you some. Nobody will buck the Screwplate very hard, I don't think. But . . ."

"But what?"

"If I was you I'd go to town pretty soon," Barney Loveless concluded. "You want to sell yore pelts anyhow, an' you need some supplies, an' when you go to town, Chet, don't forget to get some shells for yore Winchester."

CHAPTER
EIGHT

The cows came down as Barney Loveless had promised, Joe French and Laramie with them, Amador driving the wagon that accompanied the cattle. French and Laramie helped Chet put a rack on the running gear of his wagon so that he would have something to feed from. They unloaded the sacked grain that Loveless had sent, and helped Chet stack it in the shed, and they stayed the night with him. In the morning the Screwplate crew pulled out and Chet was alone once more.

Acting upon Loveless's advice he had made a trip to town, taking a full two days to go and come with the wagon, and as a result of that trip he had a little money in Claypool's bank from the sale of his peltry. He had, too, made purchases in Rifle Rock, buying necessities such as a barrel of flour, and not forgetting shells for Joe French's thirty-thirty. In Rifle Rock he had been treated just as always. Chet Minor was not missed from Rifle Rock. The town had other things to think about.

Now, with cattle to feed, with his trapline to tend and shift, with wood to bring in, with salt to take out and place, with all the one hundred and one things that go to make up the work of a winter camp, Chet was busy.

He got up and dressed by lantern light. He went to bed with kerosene furnishing the light by which he undressed. And he was no longer solitary. A week after the cactus-burning lesson Olson had come up to the Rock Springs with a problem for Chet Minor. Olson was having trouble with his water supply. Chet took time off to show Olson how to locate a well where the water would not be alkali.

That was the beginning. Olson, Laird, even Quick from away south, brought their difficulties to Chet Minor, seeking his advice. Chet did the best he could for them. It was a nuisance, he told himself, a damned imposition, but he had let himself in for it, and while he fumed externally to Dr. Laird, inwardly he was pleased. It is nice to be the big man in a country, the man that others came to for advice and assistance.

Of all the newcomers, Chet saw the most of Sally Laird and the doctor. That pleased him. He liked Laird; and Sally . . . well, Chet had had an experience that made him gun-shy of women, but Sally Laird was just a little something special.

Among the callers that came to the Rock Springs camp was Ben Revilla. Revilla rode in and stayed the night with Chet, sure of his welcome. Chet was astonished to see Revilla and more astonished when Ben told him that he was homesteading a place in the Amarilla Mesa canyon and that he had brought out one of his sisters to keep house for him. It was so little typical of Ben Revilla to be homesteading that at first Chet could hardly believe it but thought that Ben was stringing him. Revilla left the following morning, riding on to the north and mentioning his intention of visiting the Screwplate. Chet watched Ben go, still wondering about what he had been told, still trying to figure out a reason for Ben's sudden desire to own land.

January ended with a storm, a heavy fall of snow. In the first week of February a chinook blew and then the weather turned bad in earnest and winter shut down on the Rifle Rock country like a man might close his hand upon a silk neckerchief. The only travel was by horseback and men went out only on business.

For a week Chet saw no one, not even the Lairds. He could, when he rode southeast, see the smoke from the Lairds' house at times and he knew that they were all right. But he was busy now, hardly finishing his feeding before the quick dusk came. Naturally he was surprised when he received a visitor.

It was nester Olson who came to see Chet, riding in on a big, rawboned horse. Chet was on a stack loading his rack to go out to feed when Olson came in, and he continued to work while Olson came close to the stack.

"Mr. Minor," Olson said.

Chet arrested his work with the fork and, leaning on it, looked down at the man on horseback.

"I . . . you've helped us out before," Olson said, his voice troubled. "I wonder if you'll give me some advice."

"What is it?" Chet asked, mentally preparing himself to say "no" to anything that Olson asked. He couldn't, he just couldn't leave the camp now. Not with cattle to be fed.

"Ray Quick was killed day before yesterday," Olson said.

"Quick killed?" Chet's surprise sounded in his voice. He could not believe that that little, swift-moving man was dead.

"He was shot in his yard," Olson continued somberly. "His family had gone back to his wife's folks for the winter and Ray was alone. His neighbor, Morton Burgess, found him."

Chet remembered Mort Burgess, a lanky man with a big hooked nose. "Who shot Ray?" he asked, unconsciously using Quick's first name.

Olson shook his head. "We don't know," he answered. "Mort got the deputy to come out from town and they looked around and couldn't find anything. We had to bury Ray. There wasn't enough money to send him back to his wife's folks."

Chet nodded, quick sympathy showing on his face. "Did the sheriff come over?" he asked.

Olson nodded soberly. "He came yesterday," the nester answered. "He didn't do anything either."

"Jim Clarke is a good man," Chet announced. "He's made a good sheriff."

Olson's voice took on a stony tone. "Maybe," he said. "He didn't look very hard for the man that killed Ray. I was there. I saw what he did."

Chet made no answer to that. Jim Clarke was a cowman; he would not place too much importance upon the killing of a nester.

"Now," Olson said, "I have come to you. Yesterday when I got my mail, I had a letter. Burgess had a letter too, and I do not know who else." The big man pulled off a worn glove, reached under his coat and took a letter from his pocket. He handed it up to Chet.

Examining the envelope Chet saw that the address was printed and that the letter had been mailed in Rifle Rock. He slipped the folded sheet from the envelope and, opening it, read the printed message. The words were direct enough and to the point.

NESTER, YOU HAVE BEEN STEALING CATTLE. YOU ARE WARNED THAT YOU ARE NOT WANTED. LEAVE THE COUNTRY.

REGULATORS.

"Huh!" Chet grunted, passing back the note. "Short an' sweet."

"I have not stolen any cattle and I will not go." There was utter finality in Olson's voice. "I am honest and I work. I have not complained too much about my fence being cut and about the things that have been done to me. I know that we are not wanted here but this is free country. I will not go."

"That settles it then," Chet said. "You won't go. What did you want me to do, Olson?"

"You have helped us," the big man said ponderously. "We talked and we thought that if you went to Mr. Clarke, the sheriff, and to the judge and to the prosecuting attorney, you could talk to them. You could tell them that we are going to stay and that we will fight back."

Chet leaned on his fork. Here it was. He had helped the nesters and now, when the trouble broke, they came to him. "Will you go?" Olson asked.

Chet shook his head. "I'm a cowman," he answered. "You know that. I . . ."

Olson did not wait for Chet to finish. He turned his big horse and with the letter still held in his ungloved hand, rode away from the stack. Chet wanted to call him back, but could not. He wanted to yell at the big man, telling him to come back, that they would talk it over; wanted to offer his help. Somehow he could not call. Olson rode away, a gradually diminishing dot against the gray sky and the snow, and Chet, suddenly feeling the chill, fell to work again.

Chet finished work early that evening and without cooking his supper, saddled a horse and rode down the frozen creek. When he reached the Lairds' he found the doctor doing his chores, and stopped at the barn to talk with the older man.

Laird had fed his stock and was finishing with the milking, his head pressed against Marybelle's flank. He looked around as Chet came to the barn door, spoke a greeting and resumed stripping Marybelle's udder.

"I thought I'd come down an' see how you were makin' out," Chet said awkwardly. "Haven't seen you all in a long time."

"No," Laird answered, "we've been pretty busy. I suppose you have too."

"Some," Chet agreed. "I'm feedin' a bunch of cattle for Loveless."

The last spurt of milk rang against the side of the bucket and Laird got up. "You couldn't quite come over to us, could you, Chet?" he asked sorrowfully.

"What do you mean?" Chet asked.

"Olson stopped here on his way home," Laird said. "He told us that he had been to see you."

"See here, Doctor," Chet's voice was quick, "I've been a puncher all my life. I was born an' raised in this country. You wouldn't expect me to go against every friend I had, would you?"

"Not even when the friends are backing murder?" Laird asked.

"But you don't know that it was murder," Chet said eagerly. "Maybe Quick had some enemy we didn't know about. Maybe it was an accident. Maybe . . ."

"You can't believe that in the face of the letter that Olson got," Laird said. "No, Chet, it won't do."

Chet made no answer and Laird, placing the milk stool in a corner, spoke again. "You've helped us, Chet," he said. "You've been good to us. We don't think that you are mixed up in this."

Chet's eyes widened. "Why, Doc . . ." he began.

"Olson is calling a meeting," Laird said. "We're going to fight this thing. If we can't get the county officers behind us perhaps we can do something else. It's murder, Chet, and you know who is behind it!"

Suddenly Chet Minor was frightened. What chance would these greenhorns, these tenderfeet, have against the Rifle Rock? The Rifle Rock was hard, how hard Chet Minor knew. "Stay out of it, Doc," he pleaded.

"Don't you have a hand in it. You're a doctor; they'll leave you alone."

Laird picked up the milkpail. "I'm a nester," he said. "You know I can't stay out, Chet. Are you coming to the house to see Sally?"

Chet shook his head. "I'll ride back," he answered. "I guess there's no use of talking to you, Doc."

Laird made no reply but walked toward the house, carrying the milk bucket. Chet mounted his horse and turned back the way he had come.

Tired as he was Chet Minor did not sleep that night but lay awake pondering the questions Olson's visit had evoked. The next day, occupied with his work, his mind was busy. By nightfall Chet had made up his mind. That night he slept, calmly, without tossing or turning.

In the morning he was out betimes, loading his rack. He worked rapidly, scattering the hay in bunches across the feed ground. He grained the horses and threw down an extra supply of hay for them, and then he saddled the biggest of his mounts and, leaving the cabin, rode toward the north, bound for the Screwplate.

He was ten miles from the cabin when a black dot against the snow spoke of a man traveling toward him. Chet pushed on and as the paths converged saw that the man coming toward him was Joe French. The two met in the middle of a snowswept flat and reined in their horses.

"Just comin' down to see how you were makin' it," French said. "Anything wrong, Chet?"

"Not at camp," Chet answered. "I wanted to go to the ranch to get a man to spell me for a while. I need to go to town."

"I'll ride back with you," French offered. "I could stay down at camp for a while. Why go to town, Chet?"

"Business," Chet answered briefly. "Come on, Joe."

French made no further inquiry and Chet turned his horse. Together Chet and French rode back to the Rock Springs.

At the camp, having attended their horses, they went into the cabin and Chet stirred up the fire. Joe French pulled off his coat and put a bundle on the table: a few newspapers, a saddle catalog, a letter. Mail brought from town to the ranch and then on to Chet.

"What's the business in town, Chet?" French asked suddenly. "You out of grub?"

Chet shook his head. "A man named Ray Quick was shot four days ago," he said. "A nester down by the railroad."

Joe French waited.

"Vance Murray didn't do a thing to find the killer," Chet said. "Neither did Clarke when he came over. I'm goin' in an' talk to Vance. Clarke, too, if he's there."

"What good will that do?" French asked.

"I don't know," Chet answered. "All I know is that they can't scare these nesters out. Maybe they can kill 'em, but they won't scare."

"You know that the Triangle an' the lower ranches have been losin' cattle?" French asked. "There's been some big wads run off. I heard that the Triangle lost fifty head in one jolt."

"I don't give a damn," Chet's voice was calm. "Killin' nesters won't stop the cattle stealin' an' you know it. Most of these nesters wouldn't know how to go about stealin' a cow anyhow. They'd get caught."

Joe French shook his head. His eyes were troubled. He started to speak, stopped, and began again hesitatingly. "But Chet . . ."

Chet had gone to the table. He pushed the papers aside and picking up the letter, opened it. He glanced at the sheet of paper and then threw it out, face up, on the table for Joe French to read. Printed there in pencil, was the same message, word for word, that Olson had shown Chet Minor.

"I'll be obliged if you'll look after the feedin', Joe," Chet Minor said. "I'll go to town in the mornin'."

Joe French shook his head. "Barney was afraid it would break," he said. "He was afraid."

"Suppose, Joe," Chet Minor drawled, "that you cook supper, and I'll do the chores. I want to get to bed early an' take an early start."

Slowly Joe French laid down the letter and turned toward the stove. "Damned if I blame you," he said. "Damned if I blame you a bit."

There was starlight and the morning was clear and cold when at three o'clock Chet saddled a horse and put a lead rope on another. He would go to Rifle Rock in about eight hours, the going being slow because of the snow. He would return on a fresh horse, if he did return, in about the same length of time. Joe French had risen when Chet did and there was a light in the cabin as Chet led his horses to the door. Joe had hot coffee and warmed biscuits and salt pork and gravy on the table. He ate with Chet, neither of the men speaking. When Chet had finished he put on his coat, tied his neckerchief around his head to protect his ears, pulled on his hat and donned his gloves. He picked up the thirty-thirty from beside the door.

"So long, Joe," Chet said.

"So long, Chet," Joe French replied soberly.

Chet closed the door behind him and walking to his horse, slid the rifle into the scabbard under the fender. Then, mounting, he rode away from the Rock Springs camp, the feet of the horses crisply crunching the snow.

It was almost noon when Chet Minor rode into Rifle Rock. He stopped his horses at the bank, went in and drew some money from the account there. That treasured bank account was pitifully thin when Chet came out of the bank.

Mounting again, Chet rode on to the livery barn. There he left his horses, giving terse orders that they be fed, and paid spot cash. From the barn he walked back up the street. Vance Murray was usually to be found at the saddle shop. Entering the shop Chet did not find Murray. Wayt Higlow, the grizzled little saddlemaker, came to attend his wants and Chet made them known.

"I sold you a belt an' holster an' a 32-20 awhile back, Wayt," Chet said. "Have you still got them?"

Wayt nodded and reaching into a bin under the counter brought out a belt and a holstered gun. Chet put money on the counter. "How much?" he asked.

"You can have them for what I gave you," Wayt answered.

Chet's eyes flashed a gleam of appreciation to the saddlemaker. "You're a white man, Wayt," he said.

Higlow made no answer. He counted part of the bills that Chet had put down, and pushed the rest back to Chet. Chet took the money, pocketed it and, unbuttoning his sheepskin, belted the gun around his waist.

"You're makin' it now?" Higlow asked.

"I'm makin' it," Chet answered. "Thanks, Wayt. Know where Murray is?"

"I think at the hotel," Higlow said. "Clarke is down there an' they'll likely eat together. It's almost dinner time."

Chet again said, "Thanks," and went out of the shop, Wayt Higlow's eyes following him reflectively.

At the Parker House Chet did not hesitate but went directly into the lobby. It was small and crowded and in a corner Jim Clarke and Vance Murray stood talking with Powell Overman and Royce Mitchell. Chet pushed his way to them, passing several townsmen who regularly ate their dinner in the Parker House dining-room, and a little group of traveling men. As he came up and stopped, Vance Murray greeted him.

"Hello, Chet."

Clarke turned and also spoke a greeting. Royce Mitchell held out his hand, but Powell Overman maintained an aloof silence.

"Long ways to town from the Rock Springs, ain't it, Chet?" Murray asked cheerfully. "Must be somethin' important that brings you in."

110

"It is," Chet agreed. "Jim, what do you an' Vance aim to do about that man that was killed?"

For a moment neither Murray nor Clarke could answer. The door of the lobby opened and a cold draft struck the men. Chet did not look around but Clarke's eyes widened as he saw the four men who came in.

"I'd kind of like to know," Chet said impatiently.

"Why," Jim Clarke brought his eyes back to Chet's face, "we're tryin' to find out who done it, Chet. Have you got any information?"

"No," Chet shook his head. "I don't know who did it. I know who's behind it." He turned abruptly so that his eyes met those of Royce Mitchell, and flashed on to Powell Overman's face. "I got your letter," Chet said.

Overman said nothing, made no movement.

Mitchell blustered. "I didn't write you."

"No," Chet agreed, "maybe you didn't. But you were there when the letter was written. You can have it." He dipped his hand into his pocket, pulled out the letter and thrust it forward. Mitchell, not realizing what he did, took the letter, held it a moment, and then let it fall. Chet turned back to Clarke.

"Listen, Jim," he said soberly, "I know that you're on a spot. I've known you a long time an' you've been a good officer. I want to tell you somethin'. You can either take it or leave it. There's trouble in the country. You know who's behind it an' so do I. A man has been killed. You can stop that trouble now or you can let it go till it's too big to stop. I tell you, Jim, it'll be bad."

Clarke's eyes were harried. They flashed from Chet Minor's face to Powell Overman and on to Royce

Mitchell, returning to Chet again. "What do you mean, Chet?" Clarke asked.

"I mean I'm askin' you to stop the trouble before it starts, Jim," Chet answered, his voice almost gentle.

"You damned nester!" Mitchell spat the words.

Chet wheeled to face him. "I'm a cowman an' you know it," he snapped.

"You come in here tryin' to tell an officer his duty!" Mitchell snarled. "Who do you think you are, Minor?"

Chet turned wearily away from Royce Mitchell, back to Jim Clarke. "I can't talk to him, Jim," Chet said. "You can. Tell him what's happening. Can't you see, Jim? For every nester that's killed, some cowman, some puncher that isn't mixed up in it at all, will be downed. Tell him, Jim."

Jim Clarke cleared his throat. He had made up his mind but his voice was uncertain. "I'm doin' what I can to apprehend the murderer," he said. "I'm the sheriff of the county. I don't need you to tell me what to do."

Chet read his defeat in Clarke's eyes. Jim Clarke had been elected by the cowmen. He would stay with them.

"All right, Jim," Chet said wearily, "you know what you want to do." He turned then, limping away from Clarke and Overman, Murray and Mitchell, his eyes on the floor, not looking where he walked. A hand grasped his arm and Chet stopped. When he looked up he saw that Olson was holding his arm and that behind Olson was Dr. Laird and Burgess and a nester from north of town named Hill.

112

"Minor," Olson said, "I thought . . ."

Chet jerked his arm from Olson's grasp and without a word walked through the door.

CHAPTER
NINE

Chet Minor left Rock Springs a little after one o'clock but the Rock Springs camp was dark when he rode in, Joe French having long before gone to bed. For the last part of his return trip Chet had a weak moon, heavily ringed with haze. That meant a storm. Chet was glad to see the black bulk of the cabin under the mesa, glad to hear the horses neigh a greeting, glad to see the pinpoint of light spring to life in the cabin as French got up and lit the lamp. Chet unsaddled, turned his horses loose and went wearily up the path to the cabin. It was eleven o'clock. He had been in the saddle about seventeen hours, had ridden down two horses and had been going for twenty hours, at least. Recognizing Chet's weariness when the man came in, Joe asked no questions and Chet undressed and went to bed, not realizing that Joe had made a bed down beside the stove and left the bunk for Chet.

In the morning French would have let his friend sleep late but Chet, hearing Joe moving, sat up, stretched, yawned and got up. The two went silently about the chores there were to do. Until he has eaten breakfast a man's temper is uncertain and a cow camp is, before breakfast, a silent place.

French asked a few questions concerning the trip to town, after breakfast had been disposed of. Chet answered them. He told Joe what he had done, the amazement growing in Joe's eyes as he listened.

"They've brought a killer into the country," Chet said bitterly. "Hired somebody to do their dirty work. You sabe that, Joe?"

French nodded. "But I don't know why you side with the nesters," he said.

Chet shrugged. "I don't either," he confided, "but I'd made up my mind to go to town before you brought me that letter. I didn't do a damned bit of good. Might have known that Clarke wouldn't listen to a cripple."

The bitterness and some of that old self-pity was creeping into Chet's voice. Joe heard it and was worried. "They'd listen to you if they would to anybody," he said. "Say, Chet, when I get back to the ranch I'll talk to Barney. Maybe he can do somethin'. He's not in with the rest of the cowmen, you know. He . . ."

"Nobody's got on him yet," Chet interrupted. "Maybe Loveless will change his mind when he has some cattle stolen an' some land grabbed out from under him."

"Not Barney," French refuted. "I know him."

Chet grunted disparagingly.

French helped Chet with the feeding, and as a result, the work was done before noon. There were signs and portents in the air that corroborated the mist around the moon. A storm was brewing.

"Makin' bag," Joe said, looking at the sky. "I'd better get back home, Chet."

Chet agreed and Joe French, saddling his horse, bade the young rider good-bye and rode away toward the north. He was worried, was French, and he wanted to talk with Barney Loveless. Chet had been right. Barney had not been stepped upon as yet by the encroaching settlers. Joe wondered if Barney would be as equable when some Screwplate cattle were missing. He thought that Barney would.

Still the storm held off. Still, at night, the moon was ringed with haze and during the day the clouds hung lowering over the northern mesas. Chet, gloomily satisfied to be alone once more, went about his business. He rode, he fed, he did the chores, but he did not go down to Laird's and he had no company.

Two days after Joe French left, Chet finished feeding and drove the team and rack to the shed. He unhooked the team, stripped off the harness and put the horses up. He was keeping the work team in the shed and feeding them, a little grain and plenty of hay. One horse was always in the corral and the other horses came in regularly from the pasture to be fed. Chet, done for the time being with the outside work, went to the house and saw that the water bucket was empty. The spring, being living water, did not freeze solid and so Chet had only thin ice to break. He picked up the buckets, went out of the door and started around the corner of the cabin. He had taken two steps beyond the corner when something smacked into the logs just beside his head, and up on the mesa a rifle cracked viciously in the timber. Chet dropped both buckets and sprang back. His short leg played him false and, at the cabin corner, tripped him. He fell, and perhaps that fall saved his life for the rifle cracked again up on the mesa slope. Chet rolled around the corner of the cabin, scrambled up and ran for the door. Inside the door he dropped the bar in place and stood, panting.

Chet Minor was no gunman. He had never, in all his life, shot at a man. Like most riders of that day and time he was familiar with firearms. He owned a 32-20 Frontier Model Colt and with it he had shot numerous prairie dogs, tin cans and bottles. He could shoot a rifle as well as most. He had killed a few deer, an antelope or two, some coyotes and wolves. He was not a marksman, not a gunhand, but Chet had something in him that beat being a gunslinger: Chet was a fighting man. He was not panic-stricken, standing there inside the cabin door. He was not frightened particularly nor was he raging. Instead Chet's mind had sharpened to a razor-like keenness and his muscles were not tense but rather relaxed and ready for instant action. It was not with any deliberate thought that Chet caught up the rifle from beside the door and went swiftly across the cabin's single room, nor did he plan and decide on a position of defense. Simply he had the rifle and was kneeling beside the window, his eyes searching through the grimy glass along the slope of the mesa.

There was movement on the mesa slope. A piñon stirred, a cedar bent and sprang straight again. Chet Minor fired three times, as rapidly as he could finger trigger and work the lever of the Winchester, once to

117

the right, once to the left, and once squarely into the center of the cedar. The bullets crashed through the glass and powder smoke was acrid in the cabin. Chet dropped down from the window, leaning against the wall. The heavy logs of the cabin would stop any bullet. Only the window and the door offered vulnerable spots.

Silence hung, heavy as death, over the Rock Springs camp.

Presently Chet moved. He peered cautiously out of the broken window, watching the mesa slope. Nothing moved or stirred. He crawled beneath the window to the northern wall, pried out chinking with his knife and looked through the loophole he had made. The shed and the corrals were unchanged. And still Chet Minor waited.

He smoked a cigarette as he alternated his vigil between the window, the loophole on the north, another that he made in the southern wall, and the hole in the door where the latch string came through. He saw the horse in the corral. He saw the piñons and the cedars on the mesa slope, he saw the cleared ground, marked by tracks and cattle droppings where he fed the dry cows; he saw the long slope to the south, and nothing more.

The day grew dim. As night came so, at length, came the impounded snow, great flakes that fell silently with no wind to blow them. Chet watched the coming of night and as it fell, busied himself within the cabin. The window he barricaded. He stuffed rags into the loopholes, keeping out the cold. He pulled the table over until it was close to the door so that it could be used for a barricade. These things he did and then, with night fully come, he put on his sheepskin and his hat and slipped out to the shed.

There was water in the half-barrel in the shed. Chet broke the ice in the barrel and let the team drink. At the corral he opened the pasture gate so that the horse within the fence could go out to the others and get to water. He scooped the buckets full of snow and took them to the cabin, careful lest they clink or rattle and so expose his position. There was wood enough in the cabin but Chet brought the ax from the woodpile and then he went in and unstrapped the Colt from around the sheepskin and pulled off his coat and hat.

The fire had died in the stove. Chet rekindled it, knowing that there was as much danger from the cold as from anything. He drank hot coffee after the fire had grown strong, and he ate cold biscuits and a piece of steak that he had fried at breakfast time. At intervals he listened, and heard nothing.

Chet did not light the lamp. He stayed in utter darkness and as the night grew older he heard the wind begin to rise and moan around the cabin. He dozed during the night, not sleeping but resting, as a cocked weapon rests, reposing in a holster, ready, instantly, to leap out and into action. With the gray light of morning he was fully awake. The storm was raging now and with the storm came safety. Chet pulled the table away from the door, opened the door and looked out. Snow was drifted three feet high across the opening and all outdoors was a blurry white mass of wind and flying snow. Chet Minor shrugged his shoulders, closed the door and methodically set about preparing a meal as though nothing had happened.

When he had eaten he bethought himself of the work there was to do. He could not ride but the horses would be in the corral and must be attended, and the team was in the shed. Chet put on his coat and hat, pulled on his gloves and sallied out.

The mesa behind the Rock Springs camp formed a lee in the storm. The wind eddied and while the snow was thick Chet could see the shed dimly, and walked toward it.

The horses were in the corral. Chet let them into the shelter of the shed. From shed to stack, from stack to shed he worked, feeding, carrying hay. He went to the spring with his pails and carried water, breaking the ice free in the half-barrel in the shed, dumping out the round cake of ice that had formed and filling the barrel, once, twice, three times as the horses drank thirstily. He carried wood into the cabin, glad that he had cut so much when the weather was fine. And with those things done Chet went back to the cabin. Later, when the storm lessened, he would look after the cattle. Now to venture a hundred yards from camp was to invite death.

The fire roared up from a cedar log in the sheet-iron stove and the cabin was warm and tight, only the cupboard across the window and the air that seeped in through the rags that stuffed the broken pane, speaking of what had happened the night before.

By ten o'clock a change had come in the wind, its whine becoming more urgent. When Chet looked out the door he saw that the snow was finer and it stung against his face like tiny needle pricks. Once more Chet donned his outer clothing and went out into the storm. This was bad. This was as bad as he had ever seen. This was the sort of blizzard that the old-timers talked about.

A brief survey showed that the horses were in the shed, sheltered from the wind, their breaths steaming. They must do without water now, for Chet dared not venture to the spring, close as it was.

As Chet started back toward the cabin an eddy in the wind caused a momentary visibility in the storm. Chet could see, perhaps two hundred yards away, a slight movement, something black against the snow, low and close to the ground.

It might be a cow but was not large enough. It might be a wolf but the wolves and the coyotes would be bedded down in this blizzard, safe in shelter. Through the lull, Chet started toward the black object, plowing through the drifts, his limping-run a slow, plunging fight. The storm shut down again. Chet could not see five yards. He stopped and then went on, the wind buffeting him, the snow biting into his cheeks. And then, suddenly, he stumbled over something soft, and throwing out his hands as he fell, struck against a man's body.

The man was down, flat on his belly, but a slight movement showed that there was life in him. Chet got up. He caught, with numbing fingers, at snow-filled clothing, turned, and dragging the man he had found, started back toward the cabin. For a long distance he struggled with his load and then, suddenly, fright possessed him. He should have reached the cabin by now. He had missed it.

Here, for a bare moment, was panic. Chet tried to pierce through the storm, and could not. He could see perhaps eight feet. He was panting with his exertions and his breath froze upon the lifted collar of his sheepskin. His nose dripped with the cold and the drops of moisture froze on the coat collar. His hands were numb and the cold was striking into his feet and legs. Once more Chet caught the man's coat, and tugging, resumed his painful way.

The stackyard fence stopped him. He had been going directly away from the cabin. There were fences on either side of the cabin, perhaps two hundred yards of fenced territory, and between those fences Chet Minor was lost. But the stackyard fence gave him a point of departure. He turned his back to it and resumed his labor and then, suddenly, the cabin wall was in his sight and relief flooded his mind.

It was the work of moments now to reach the door, shove it open and pull his inert burden into the warmth of the room. Chet let the man lie on the floor while he forced the door shut. Then, leaning against the door he panted, catching his breath, relaxing from his struggle.

Somewhat recovered from his exertion Chet bent to the man on the floor. He half-carried, half-dragged the man to the bunk, and there fell to stripping away the snow-packed clothing. The rescued stranger was not a big man, hardly as large as Chet himself, and Chet was no giant. There were compact, hard muscles under the clothing and a marble white skin that was cold to

122

touch. The man's hands were so tanned that he appeared to wear gloves, and his face and neck were as brown as the hands. These marked the outdoorsman, the rider. Chet rubbed the white body with a blanket, the rough wool rasping against the flesh. He laid the blanket over the naked man, put fresh wood in the stove and set the teakettle forward so that it would boil. There was no whisky in the Rock Creek cabin. Chet had not dared trust himself with whisky, but perhaps hot coffee would serve equally well. Chet returned to the rubbing. Presently the man on the bed breathed deeply and opened his eyes. He stared around the cabin and then the eyes, gray and wide, came to rest on Chet.

"Horse went down," the man on the bunk said hoarsely. "I tried to make it to shelter. Got lost."

"I'll have some hot coffee into you in a minute," Chet promised. "How d'you feel?"

A little smile came to the gray-eyed man's lips. "Like hell," he muttered.

Chet, going to the stove to make the coffee, knew that the man on the bed spoke truth. He did feel like hell. The blood returning to his cold muscles must burn like fire. Chet had been cold himself and knew just how it felt. He carried a steaming cup of coffee to the bed and stood by while the gray-eyed man drank it.

"What time did your horse play out?" Chet asked.

"Last night." The stranger's voice was stronger now.

"An' you been comin' ever since," Chet marveled. "You were clear down when I picked you up."

"More coffee," the stranger said.

Chet filled the cup. When the coffee had been swallowed, the gray-eyed man, grimacing with the aches that were in him, sat up under the blanket. "Just whereabouts did I get to?" he asked.

"This is the Rock Springs. I'm Chet Minor," Chet answered.

"My name's Ames." The gray-eyed man held out his hand. "I'm obliged to you. Guess I wouldn't have made it if you hadn't picked me up."

"It's a ripsnorter outside," Chet said, embarrassed. "Regular blizzard."

Ames nodded. "I found that out," he said ruefully. "You know, gettin' cold doesn't hurt except at first. It's the thawin' out that's hell."

"Well," Chet said, "you'll thaw after a while. I'm goin' to cook some dinner." He left the bunk, picking up the clothing he had pulled off as he moved, and carrying it toward the stove. A belt and holstered gun lay on the floor where Chet had dropped them as he undressed Ames. Ames's eyes sought and found the gunbelt, scrutinized it, and they went on to where Chet was hanging clothing on a chairback and on the short length of line behind the stove. The wind moaned around the corner of the cabin. Under the blanket Ames shivered.

Methodically Chet set about cooking. He moved from cupboard to table to stove and back again. Ames stirred beneath the blanket.

"I'm thawin' out," he announced.

Chet stopped the preparation of the meal. He brought a suit of his own underwear, a clean pair of levis and a shirt, and laid them on the bed. "Can't do much about boots," Chet said apologetically. "I got just the one pair."

Ames sat up and began to dress. Chet went back to the stove. Ames was dressed before the meal was ready. He went to the cupboard that stood in front of the window and peered around it. "Sure blowin'," he commented.

"Dinner's about ready," Chet answered.

By three o'clock Ames's clothing was dry, his boots only faintly moist. He sat on the bed, sucking on a thin cigarette, watching Chet. There had been little talk either while the two ate dinner or after the meal. Ames had helped with the dishes.

"You got a nice place here," he said suddenly.

"Old line camp," Chet said. "I'm homesteadin' it."

"Goin' to keep it?" The question was direct and blunt. It was out of place. Chet made no answer. "It used to belong to the Screwplate," Chet said by way of answer.

"You ride for the Screwplate?"

"I rode for the Triangle before I got hurt."

Ames got up and put the cigarette in the stove. "Looks like I'll be with you a while," he announced.

"You'll have to stay until the storm blows out," Chet agreed. "I don't mind. It's lonesome here."

"I reckon," Ames agreed.

"I think I can make it to the barn," Chet stated. "I want to look after the horses. If you want to you can fill the buckets with snow an' put 'em on the stove to melt." He took his coat from a nail beside the door as he spoke, pulling it on. Ames walked to the bench and lifting one bucket, poured the water it held into the other container.

"Don't take chances," he warned. "The storm's bad."

Chet pulled on his hat and opened the door. "I'll be right back," he announced.

When he came back in Chet saw that Ames was melting snow in a bucket on the stove. Chet stamped snow from his boots and shook the flakes from his coat. "Seems to be lettin' up a little," he announced.

Ames had pulled on his still-damp boots to get the snow.

Now he moved a box toward the stove, sat down, and extended his feet toward the heat. "They'll dry better on," he observed, speaking of the boots. "Funny, I never had a pair of boots till I was about twelve years old. Always wore moccasins." The man's voice was smooth, pleasant, drawling.

"I don't remember when I didn't wear boots," Chet said. "My dad got me a pair about the time I learned to walk, I reckon."

"I didn't have a dad to get 'em," Ames drawled. "Closest thing I ever had to a father was old Two Elk down on the Jicarilla reservation."

"Indian?" Chet asked.

"Apache," Ames corrected. "He brought me up. It don't get cold down there like it does here. We don't have the snow."

The man seemed in a reminiscent mood. His face was impassive but pleasant, his eyes keen. "Looks like you were forted up," he observed, gesturing toward the cupboard in front of the window. "You got your window blocked an' I see you got some loopholes stuffed with rags."

"Had a shot taken at me last night," Chet answered, watching Ames narrowly. "Man just missed me."

"So?" Ames said.

Chet nodded. "Until the storm hit I thought he might come back," he commented.

"It would take a hard case to be out in this storm," Ames said. "I wouldn't worry if I was you."

Chet's eyes were still on Ames. "I don't worry," he returned.

"That's right." Ames nodded.

"The Jicarilla is in Arizona, isn't it?" Chet asked.

Again the gray-eyed man nodded. "South," he agreed. "I was born down in that country. They tell me my father was a missionary that come out to save the Indians. In place of that the Apaches killed him."

"An' you lived with the Apaches?" There was some disbelief in Chet's voice.

"Until I was about twelve," Ames agreed. "Two Elk adopted me. He'd lost his own kid. When I was twelve I tied up with a freightin' outfit. Of course I've been back an' forth on the reservation a lot since then. I've got a lot of friends there."

"Friends? An' they killed your father?"

"My mother too," Ames said. He was fashioning a cigarette as he answered. Looking up from the paper and tobacco he smiled faintly at Chet. "I didn't hold it against the Apaches," he announced. "That's just their

127

way of gettin' along. It's kind of their trade, you might say."

Chet shook his head. "I don't quite sabe," he admitted.

"Well," Ames wet the flap and finished the cigarette, "it's this way: an Apache lives by raidin', killin' people. You can't hold it against 'em. They're fair about it. They didn't hold it against me when I guided for Crook. That was the way I earned my livin'. Of course they tried to kill me an' I did for some of them, but when they were back on the reservation we were friends again. It was all right."

Chet sat down on the bed. He was beginning to get an insight into this gray-eyed man who calmly smoked Chet's tobacco. "So when you fight that's just business," he mused, "an' when you don't fight you get along all right."

"That's right," Ames nodded.

"Didn't they have it in for you for killin' some of them?" Chet's curiosity was aroused.

"Mebbe some of the relations did," Ames drawled. "I don't know. I'd done it in the line of business, you see. An Apache don't think there's any harm in killin' a man."

"Well," Chet said, "maybe there ain't. I wouldn't feel good about it though."

"Why not?" Ames's eyes were mildly curious. "What's wrong in killin' a man if he needs killin'?"

"Well . . ." Chet searched for words, "I don't exactly know. I reckon it's just that . . ."

"You ain't never killed a man," Ames surmised.

"No," Chet said, "I haven't."

"That's why you think like that." Ames shrugged.

"Damned if you ain't a cold-blooded proposition!" Chet exclaimed. "You sit there an' talk about killin' a man like it was butcherin' a calf."

"Speakin' of cold," Ames got up, "it's gettin' cold in here now. That window leaks some air. Where's that woodpile? I'll bring in some wood."

"I'll help you," Chet offered. "You couldn't find the woodpile in this snow."

They went out together to return, snow-plastered and laden with fuel. When again they removed their coats, Ames reached into a pocket and produced a deck of cards. "Ever play rummy?" he asked.

Chet said that he had. Ames placed the deck on the table and moved a box around until he faced the door. "Come on," he invited. "I'll play you a game."

"There's nothing we can do outside," Chet said. "All right, I'll play you."

The two played rummy until it was time for supper. After the meal they went to bed.

By the following morning the snowfall had stopped but the wind was still blowing and it was bitter cold. Snow, lifted from the earth by gusts of wind, whipped against Chet and Ames when they went out to attend the horses. They played rummy for the remainder of the morning but by noon the wind had dropped away somewhat and Chet knew that he must do some riding. There were two hundred head of cows to look after and where they had been scattered by the storm, only the Lord knew. Of course the drift fence, south of Rock

Springs, would have caught some of them, but the rest would be in whatever shelter they had found and some might be hopelessly lost or even killed by the blizzard.

"I've got to make a little ride," Chet told Ames. "Can't go far this afternoon, but I've got to look around."

Ames nodded. "If you had a saddle I'd go with you," he offered.

"I've just got the one saddle," Chet said. "You'd better stay here. There'll be somebody down from the Screwplate as soon as they can get through, an' get their own work done."

"Well," Ames said, "I'll look after things around the house anyhow."

Chet agreed to that. He dressed, belted the Colt around his sheepskin and took the Winchester out to his horse after he had saddled. Ames watched these preparations, saying nothing. Chet rode off, looking back to see Ames down at the corral, forking hay into the feed rack for the horses.

All through that bitter afternoon Chet rode, finding some cattle, bunching them and throwing them back toward the camp. He worked automatically for his mind was filled with other business than cattle. There was a shrewd and strong suspicion in Chet Minor concerning Ed Ames. The way the man talked, the casual way he spoke of killing, his arrival at the camp, his horse's being missing, all of these were facts that made Chet suspect the man. And yet the dry-gulcher who had shot at Chet from the mesa side must have pulled out before the storm struck, must have made for shelter. That intended murderer would have been long gone from the Rock Creek vicinity when the snow struck down. Chet pondered the thing over and finally shrugged his shoulders. At any event Ames could not do him much damage. Chet had taken occasion, when Ames was out of the house, to unload the Colt that Ames carried, and to strip the cartridge belt of shells. They were in the pocket of Chet's sheepskin at the moment. No matter what Ames was, he was harmless right now and Chet, coming along slowly behind the little bunch of cattle he had collected, ceased worrying about Ed Ames and looked eagerly into the growing dusk for the pinpoint of light that would mark the Rock Springs cabin.

When Chet came in Ed Ames had supper on the table.

For three days, following the tailing-off of the storm, Chet worked from the time he could see until the time he couldn't. During those three days he was thankful for the two young horses he had broken. They were stout and they could stand the gaff. The old horses played out. Good as they were they couldn't buck the snow. Chet rode the old horses, all three of them, one day, and the two young horses the next. It was tough going. There were cattle along Barney Loveless's drift fence. Chet picked them up and brought them in. Some were cows that he had been feeding, others were drifted down from above. The second day, coming in late, he nursed a bunch along as far as he could, dropped them and went back the next morning and brought them in. During those three hectic days Ed Ames took Chet's place in the stackyard, feeding hay.

Chet had almost two hundred head when, about noon the fourth day after the storm, Joe French and Laramie came down from the ranch. Joe and Laramie had been en route since six o'clock and they had horses with them.

The snow had hit as hard at the Screwplate as at the Rock Springs. It was all over the country, French reported. There would be a lot of cattle killed, perhaps more than cattle. Laramie and Joe threw down their beds and turned their horses into the corral while Chet rustled grub. Laramie looked oddly at Chet after he had been introduced to Ed Ames. Ames said that Chet had pulled him out of the snow. He didn't make a whole lot of it but Chet could tell that Ames meant the praise he spoke. They ate and then the three riders left to see what they could do about bringing in more drifted cattle.

When they came in that night, Ed Ames was gone. There was a note for Chet on the table and Ames had done the chores. The feed rack was filled and so were the water buckets.

"I borrowed a horse and bridle," Ames's note read. "Will leave him in Rifle Rock. So long and thanks."

The note was not signed. Laramie looked at Chet again, an intent expression on his face. "Know who you pulled out of the snow?" he asked.

Chet shook his head.

"Just the toughest man that's hit these parts, that's all," Laramie announced. "I knew about him in Wyoming before I come down here. He was a mine guard when they had a strike at Hanna. Run the guards for the company."

"Well," Chet said, "tough or not, I couldn't let him lie out an' freeze, could I?"

"It might have been a good thing," Laramie commented.

CHAPTER
TEN

The three riders cleaned up after the storm. A lot of cattle had drifted down on Chet in the storm and when they were brought in he had more cattle to feed than before the storm. They dug a few out of snowbanks and brought them in, and they found some cattle winter-killed. It was tough. Joe French, with Laramie assisting, wormed information from Chet. They found out about the attack upon him. There was evidence around the cabin that they could not overlook, the loopholes and the shattered glass of the window.

"You think it was Ames that taken that shot at you?" French asked bluntly.

Chet shook his head. "I don't know," he answered. "I don't see how he could have. He came in the day after that happened. He'd have had to lay out all night if he was the one."

"He could do that," Laramie stated. "He's about half Injun. Injun-raised, anyhow. I think I'll . . ." Laramie did not complete what he started to say. Laramie, Chet and Joe both knew, was dangerous. He had seen plenty of the seamy side.

French wanted to leave Laramie with Chet when he went back to the Screwplate. Chet dissuaded him, knowing that Laramie was needed at headquarters; and anyhow he felt that he could take care of himself. Unwillingly Joe took Laramie along when he left.

During the riding, in the course of the work, Chet managed two things: he saw the Lairds and he took up his trapline. There was too much work now for him to tend his traps properly and Chet did not propose to leave them out. The Lairds were glad to see him but his visit was brief. Chet simply wanted to reassure himself that the Lairds were not in need of help, and when he had done that he left.

After Joe and Laramie had returned to headquarters, it was easy for Chet to settle down once more into the old routine, feeding cattle, doing the chores, and always keeping a wary eye out for his own safety. It became second nature for him to keep under the ridges and off the skyline, to come into the cabin by devious and varying routes.

February wore out and was done. March came, and with it thawing weather and winds that blew constantly, whining about the cabin, tugging at Chet as he rode, jerking the hay from his fork as he tossed it from the wagon when he fed. But March softened winter and the end of March broke winter's back.

By the end of March calves were commencing to drop; under the brown grass the tender green was sprouting, and in the Rifle Rock the nesters were plowing.

The Rifle Rock was quiet with the temporary silence of a teakettle set on a hot stove. The kettle was not boiling; not yet.

As the weather softened and Chet had more daylight to work by, he started on the horses that Loveless had sent down. There were four green broncs and Chet, stake-breaking them, began the wearisome process of their education into cow horses. By Earl Keelin, who brought down the horses, Chet sent a letter to the ranch, asking that it be given the bootmaker in town. Chet needed a pair of boots, needed them badly, and the bootmaker in Rifle Rock had his measurements.

Early in April, returning to camp atop a green horse that he was educating, Chet saw a buggy tied to the fence in front of the Rock Springs camp. When he reached the corral and was stripping the saddle from his horse, Carl Olson and Dr. Laird came out of the house where they had been waiting, and approached the corral.

"Hello," Chet said, pulling the hackamore off the horse. "Been here long?"

"Not very long," Laird answered. "We came over to visit you, Chet, and made ourselves at home."

"That's right," Chet commended, letting the horse go. "What's on your mind, Doc?"

"Let's go to the house," Laird suggested.

The three walked back to the cabin together. Chet put wood on the fire that had been built by his visitors, and slid the coffee pot forward on the stove so that it would heat. Olson had seated himself stiffly on a box and Laird took the one chair. Chet peeled off his coat and sat down on the bunk. There was a purpose to this visit and he wondered what it might be.

"Chet," Laird said suddenly, "Olson and I had visitors yesterday."

"Yes?" Chet said.

The doctor nodded. "Mr. Overman and Mr. Neil, with a man named Ames, and several others, called on us," he continued.

Chet's eyes were sharp as he fixed them on the doctor. "So?" he commented.

Laird smiled ruefully. "It seems that there have been some cattle stolen from Mr. Overman's ranch and Mr. Neil has missed some. I understand that they are visiting all the settlers in this region. They seem to think that we have been stealing cattle from them."

"Ames was along, huh?" Chet asked.

"In an official capacity," Laird said. "I understand that he is a stock detective."

Chet made no comment on that explanation and Olson, shifting nervously on his box, spoke out. "We come to see you," he said bluntly. "We got a plan."

Chet rolled a thin cigarette. "Overman an' them didn't get up here," he commented. "I didn't see 'em."

"Carl and I have been talking things over." Laird's eyes were bright. "We have an idea, Chet."

"Yeah?" Chet said, and lit his cigarette.

"We want you to run for sheriff next election."

Chet was startled. His eyes flashed from the doctor to Olson and back again. Suddenly he laughed. "That's rich," he said. "I couldn't be elected dog-catcher in Rifle Rock."

The doctor's smile was amused. "I don't think you quite realize that this country has changed, Chet," he reminded. "You have a good many friends that you didn't have a few months ago."

"No," Olson's voice was guttural, "we don't forget who helps us."

There was something about that big, stolid man that made Chet suddenly become serious. "Election comes next fall," he said. "That's six months away. You . . ."

"It's not too early to begin talking," Laird interrupted. "Now, Chet, don't say anything yet. Let me talk. Olson and I have thought this out."

Chet nodded and Laird went on. "You know that Ray Quick was killed," he said. "You know that a good many of the men who have come into the country were ordered out of it. Some of them have gone. There has been a good deal of trouble. Now the newcomers are being accused of stealing cattle. We want protection, Chet."

"Anybody does," Chet agreed.

"We think," Laird said, not noting the interruption, "that you are the man that can give it to us. We think that if you are in the sheriff's office we will have a man who will treat everyone alike. We're not asking favors, but just fair treatment. And we believe that if you will consent to run, we can elect you. There are quite a lot of us nesters, Chet!" The doctor was smiling as he spoke the last words.

Chet's face was somber. "I can't do it," he said. "I . . . well, I made a fool of myself when I came back to this country. The cowmen blackballed me. I've got this claim. Loveless wouldn't stand . . ." He broke off.

There was no need of telling about the arrangement with Barney Loveless. "Anyhow," Chet concluded lamely, "if there's goin' to be trouble you'll need your protection right away. It won't do to wait till fall an' election time."

Again Laird and Olson exchanged glances. Olson cleared his throat. "We think that we can wait," he said. "If the sheriff knows that there will be a fight in the election, he will be careful. He will not let anything happen that would hurt his chances of being reelected."

"There's somethin' to that," Chet admitted. "You can do better than me, though. Why don't you run, Olson?"

"I would not make a good sheriff," Olson said stolidly. "I don't know enough an' I do not know the country."

Olson was right. Chet was forced to admit it. Conejos County was a hundred miles long and more than sixty miles across. The Rifle Rock took up more than half the county. What chance would a nester, a plowman, have in a range country? How could he enforce the law?

"Don't say what you'll do yet," Laird urged. "Talk to Loveless before you make up your mind. Talk to French. They're friends of yours."

Again the doctor's eyes slid across to Olson's face. Laird smiled faintly. He and Carl Olson had not come directly from their claims to the Rock Springs. Since early morning they had been in the doctor's buggy and among other places they had visited the Screwplate.

"Well," Chet agreed reluctantly, "I'll talk to Loveless, but I tell you right now I won't run. You'll have to get somebody else."

Laird got up. "We won't take that as final," he said. "We'll talk about this again. Carl and I have to go now if we're to get home before dark."

Olson too had risen and Chet got up from the bed and followed his guests to the door. "Doc," he said, as Olson and Laird went out, "you get the damnedest ideas. Just think of it. Me, runnin' for sheriff! It's funny!"

"Not nearly so funny as you think," Laird replied. "Good-bye, Chet. You think it over and come down and see us."

"I'll come down and see you but I won't think it over," Chet grinned. "So long, Doc. So long, Olson."

But when Laird's buggy had rattled away Chet went back to the bed and sat down. Presently he shook his head. He had been right. There was no chance. Laird's idea had simply been humorous.

It was not so humorous when, during the week, Barney Loveless came down to the Rock Springs. Barney went out with Chet and they looked over the cattle. They rode most of the country, talking about the calf crop, the grass, the water, the weather. Back at the cabin Barney estimated the amount of hay that was left and suggested that Chet need not feed any more. Chet said that he was only feeding a little bunch of weak cattle now. They talked over what had been done and what there was to be done, then Barney exploded a bombshell.

140

"Yo're goin' to run for sheriff next fall," he announced suddenly.

Chet grunted, as though he had been hit, and stared at the wrinkled little man.

"I mean it," Barney said.

"I couldn't be elected lamp-lighter in Rifle Rock," Chet announced. "You know . . ."

"You won't be runnin' for lamp-lighter," Loveless snapped. "I said sheriff!"

"But Mr. Loveless," Chet expostulated, "there's no use of even thinking about it. Why, Overman an' them blackballed me. They . . ."

Loveless sniffed. "Powell Overman ain't Gawdawl-mighty!" he snapped. "See here, Chet, the nesters are already talkin' about runnin' you. There's quite a bunch of nesters, too."

"But the cowmen . . ." Chet began.

"The cowmen are a tail tryin' to wag a dog," Loveless announced. "Anyhow, I'll back you an' I'm a cowman, ain't I?"

"Yes," Chet agreed, "but . . ."

"An' if I do there'll be more," Loveless announced.

"But what about the claim?" Chet asked. "I've got to live on it. I can't go galavantin' off an' . . ."

"Election's next fall," Loveless interrupted. "You'll have been on the claim six months. I'll advance the money an' you'll pre-empt it. Then I'll buy it from you."

Chet looked toward the cabin from the corral by which they stood. Loveless, watching with knowing eyes, saw that look and played a card. "The sheriff's

141

office pays nice money," he said shrewdly. "I'm spread out a lot, Chet. It might be that you could buy this place with what you'd make."

Chet shook his head. "I couldn't be elected," he said slowly.

"We'll find out about that in the fall," Loveless answered. "I ain't said anything yet, but I want you to go with the wagon this year, Chet."

Chet looked at Loveless and raised his eyebrows inquiringly.

"Stevens an' me are goin' to run a wagon together," Loveless amplified. "Goin' to try it for a year."

Chet wondered as to the reason for the change. Heretofore the Screwplate had always thrown in with the Triangle wagon in the round-ups and Stevens had run a pack outfit to brand his calves.

"Most of the Bar O7 stuff an' mine don't get below the drift fence," Loveless said. "We think we can put reps with the Triangle wagon an' do a better job of cleanin' up our own country by ourselves. Joe's goin' to run the wagon, but I'll pay you top wages."

"I guess I can go all right," Chet answered. "I've got to go into town. I got a pair of boots ordered. I'm pretty near barefooted."

"When will you go in?" Loveless asked.

"Next week."

"Better make it the middle of the week," Loveless said. "About Wednesday, say."

That was an order. Chet wondered why it had been given but said nothing. Barney Loveless always had a reason for his commands but he did not always state that reason.

"We're goin' to start the wagon the fifteenth," Loveless said. "That's two weeks off. You come up to the ranch the fourteenth an' be ready to go. Bring your truck up in the wagon. I don't want to leave it here."

"All right," Chet agreed.

There was some further talk concerning the green horses and the round-up arrangements, and Barney Loveless left for the Screwplate.

On Wednesday, as Loveless had requested, Chet went to town. He had the remainder of his peltry with him on a pack horse, for he wanted to dispose of the hides and not leave them at the cabin. He stopped at the Lairds' on the way in to town but found the house was closed. Their buggy tracks were in the soft dirt of the road Chet followed and, halfway between the claim and town, Chet passed the buggy, waving to his neighbors as he passed.

Wolfbarger's store was the first place he stopped when he reached Rifle Rock and the first man he met in Wolfbarger's was Barney Loveless. Laramie was with Loveless and he grinned at Chet when he came in.

Barney came over while Chet disposed of his furs to the merchant and received payment. "What you goin' to do with that money?" he asked Chet.

"Take it to the bank," Chet said.

Loveless nodded. "I'll be around town," he announced. "See you before you pull out."

Chet, with the payment from his furs, left Wolfbarger's and went to the bank. There he met with an unusual reception. Stevens Claypool, ordinarily an austere individual, greeted Chet cordially, accepted Chet's deposit himself and invited Chet into his little glassed-in office. There he gave Chet a cigar and gestured toward a chair. Chet sat down wonderingly.

"I hear you're going to run for sheriff in the fall," Claypool announced, lighting a match and holding it out to Chet. "That's fine, Chet."

So surprised was Chet that he almost forgot to puff on the cigar. "Why . . ." he began. "Why . . ."

"I've already written to Jones in the bank at Conejos," the banker interrupted. "He has just answered my letter. I told Jones that we would support their candidates for assessor and clerk if they would support you for sheriff. Jones was agreeable."

"But . . ." Chet expostulated.

"I know it is early," the banker continued, "but I believe in getting a candidate's name before the public. We'll nominate you this fall and elect you sure. There's a good deal of sentiment against Clarke. He's done nothing about that man Quick's being murdered."

Chet shook his head. Things were coming a little fast for him.

"Now don't do much talking," Claypool advised. "Leave that to your friends, Chet. Come in and see me whenever you're in town and I'll keep you posted on how things are going."

Chet got up from his chair. Claypool rose and put his hand on Chet's shoulder, ushering the dazed young

144

man out of the office. "Don't worry a bit," Claypool said. "We'll look after your interests here in Rifle Rock."

Chet left the bank in a daze. He did not know whether he was afoot or riding as he walked up the street. Across the street Barney Loveless and Joe French, with Laramie loitering behind them, watched Chet's progress.

"Claypool kind of jolted him," Loveless chuckled. "Look at the way he walks." French laughed, and Loveless's chuckle became frankly a giggle. Barney Loveless owned a quarter of the stock in Stevens' bank and was its biggest depositor. Barney had done a little missionary work with Stevens Claypool.

Chet went to the bootmaker's. His boots were ready and while he tried them on, the bootmaker, a little gnome of a man, stood by to see how his handiwork stood the test. The boots fitted and Chet paid for them. As the bootmaker made change, he asked a question.

"Is that right about yore comin' out for sheriff next fall?"

"Where'd you hear that?" Chet demanded.

"Everybody's talkin' about it," the bootmaker said. "It's about time somebody from Rifle Rock was elected. Clarke's had it long enough. He ain't done nothin' about that murder an' he ain't been able to stop the rustlin'. The Triangle an' the Rockin' Chair an' the Gunhammer, all three of 'em, have been losin' cattle."

"Well . . ." said Chet, surprise in his voice.

"I'm for you if you want to run," the bootmaker announced. "There'll be a lot more for you, too."

145

Chet left the bootmaker's shop more dazed than before. He had received almost as great a jolt as at the bank. Going down the street he encountered the nester, Burgess. Burgess, too, stopped him and questioned him concerning his running for the sheriff's office. Carl Olson, Burgess said, had talked to him and to a lot of the nesters. They were all for Chet. Chet felt the need for reinforcement. Here, fully fledged, was a political boom and he was the object of it. He crossed the street and stopped. Loveless had called to him and as Chet waited, Loveless and Joe French, still with Laramie following along behind, came toward him.

As he stood waiting for his friends, a buggy passed by. Maida Overman held the reins and beside her was a man that Chet had never seen before, a well-dressed stranger, his clothing bespeaking the East. Chet followed the buggy with his eyes. He was examining his own mind. For the moment he had forgotten Stevens Claypool and the bootmaker and Burgess. He had seen Maida Overman and, oddly enough, had experienced no feeling whatever. It was just as though he had seen her as a total stranger.

"Where you headed, Chet?" Loveless asked as he came up.

"I was goin' to the Staghorn," Chet answered honestly. "I felt like I needed a drink."

Loveless's eyes were sharp. "I'll buy you a beer," he offered.

"That's just what I was goin' to get," Chet answered.

They went on to the Staghorn, Loveless and Chet in front, Joe French and Laramie bringing up the rear.

146

The four arrayed themselves in front of the bar and nodded to Vance Murray and Jim Clarke who were talking with Alec Crow and young Tom Neil further down the bar.

Otto Hahn served the ordered beer. "How are you, Chet?" he asked, pushing out the glasses.

"Good," Chet answered, sipping beer.

"I hear talk that you're goin' to run for sheriff?" Otto said, glancing from the corners of his eyes toward Clarke and the others with him. "That right?"

"I . . ." Chet began.

"You bet he is," Barney Loveless said swiftly. "We're goin' to win with him, too."

Chet gulped at his beer.

"It's time," Loveless grinned wickedly, "that we had some law enforcement around here."

Clarke pushed his way from the bar and came toward Chet. Barney stepped back so that no one was between Clarke and Chet. Behind Clarke, Murray and Neil and Crow stood, their faces revealing their resentment.

"So you think you'd make a better officer than I do?" Clarke demanded, scowling at Chet.

Suddenly Chet was cool. He met Clarke's eyes and did not turn away. "Have I said so?" he asked.

Clarke, for the moment, was taken aback. "I've been sheriff of this county a long time," he blustered. "If you think . . ."

"I'm beginning to think you've been sheriff too long a time," Chet said quietly. "I haven't said I'd run, Clarke."

"But yo're goin' to!" Clarke snapped.

"Now that you're askin', I am!" It seemed suddenly to Chet as though things clicked into place. He was calm, all the internal dissension gone.

"If you think yo're so damned good I'll give you a chance," Clarke rasped. "I'll make you a deputy an' . . . ."

"Just what Chet wants," Barney said cheerfully. "Get out the badge an' the commission, Clarke."

"Jim!" Alec Crow's voice was hard. "Don't be a damned fool!"

"You wouldn't call Jim a fool for makin' a good man deputy, would you now, Alec?" Loveless asked innocently. "We need another deputy up here. The job's too big for Vance to handle."

"Jim!" Alec Crow said again, paying no attention to Loveless.

Clarke turned. Crow was shaking his head, frowning.

"Well," Loveless said cheerfully, "you was goin' to make Chet a deputy, Jim."

"I won't do it!" Clarke said suddenly. "Think I'm a damned fool?"

"I know yo're a fool," Loveless said complacently. "Come on, boys. We'll go if you finished yore beer."

Silently the four Screwplate men filed out of the Staghorn, Laramie lingering until the last, his eyes on Clarke and Neil and Crow. Out on the street Barney Loveless began to laugh. "Won't that make talk?" he chuckled. "Ain't that somethin' for the campaign? So yo're goin' to run after all, Chet?"

"You crowded me into it," Chet said angrily.

Barney continued to laugh. Reluctantly Chet began to smile. "Wasn't Jim Clarke hot?" he said.

"We'll make him a lot hotter," Loveless prophesied. "Let's get out of town. Are you through, Chet?"

Chet said that he was finished and, leaving the others, crossed the street to where he had left his horses. Laramie, Loveless and Joe French went on to the livery barn for their horses. It was apparent that they had stayed in town all night. Chet wondered why, then he grinned. It was just like Barney Loveless to do this! The little cuss had come to town with just this idea in mind.

Laird's buggy was in front of Wolfbarger's, the doctor and Sally just alighting. Laird spoke to Chet and went on into the store but Sally lingered a moment on the sidewalk.

"Took you a long time to get to town," Chet said, as he came up to Sally. "You must have stopped."

"We went to the Triangle," Sally said. "Dad wanted to see Mr. Overman."

Chet's eyebrows shot up. Now what business could Dr. Laird have had with Powell Overman!

"Dad is worried," Sally amplified. "He has something on his mind. Did he say anything to you when he came up to see you, Chet?"

Chet shook his head.

"Maybe it's that woman over by Amarilla Mesa," Sally said thoughtfully. "Dad has been going over there to look after her. Are you going to run for sheriff this fall, Chet?"

"Fall is a long way off," Chet answered, "but it looks like I might."

Sally gave his arm a slight pressure with her hand. "I'm glad," she confided. "I've got to go in now. Dad's waiting."

CHAPTER
ELEVEN

All through the Rifle Rock men were busy that May. The nesters were planting, trying to get corn in before the middle of the month, the kids out in the fields with their fathers, the women sometimes coming to help. On the ranches there was also activity. Summer horses were brought in for the remuda, wagons were mended, tires shrunk on wheels, grease applied to the skeins, harness patched, riveted or sewed. Supplies were coming out from town. On the ranches smithies' forges flamed where some cow hand, impressed as a blacksmith, forged an iron. In the corrals, horses were thrown and shoes tacked on their hind feet so that there would be no cripples in the rocky country. All the Rifle Rock was at work and the Triangle was no exception.

Powell Overman was at the Triangle, an unhappy, dissatisfied, worried Powell Overman with only half his mind on his work. He had come to the ranch due to no desire of his own, but because he must; and Maida was not with him. Maida was entertaining Norville Kirkpatrick at the town house.

Just after the blizzard in February Mark Scotia had died, slipping quietly away in the night, and with Scotia's death all the weight of the Triangle had come to settle on Powell Overman's shoulders. That was no inconsiderable thing. While Scotia was alive Powell had not worried greatly, but now all the troubles were his own and there were many troubles.

First the Drovers' Bank in Kansas City had been forced to take over the Triangle shares it held as security for Eastern loans. Scotia's shares were still intact and in Maida's name, after her father's death, but the bank now held almost as much stock as Maida. Then, late in March, Kirkpatrick, as representative of the bank, had come to Rifle Rock to look after the bank's interest in the ranch. And Kirkpatrick had stayed an unreasonable length of time. The business was finished and still Kirkpatrick lingered, and that brought a scowl to Powell Overman's face.

Overman visited his wife in her bedroom the morning of the day he went to the ranch to stay throughout round-up. Powell had eaten his breakfast alone in the big dining-room. Maida did not come down to breakfast and Kirkpatrick had not yet risen. The big ranchman knocked at his wife's door and obeyed her summons to enter. Maida sat in the bed, propped by frilly pillows, her eyelids heavy and her face still flushed from sleep.

"I'm goin' to the ranch, Maida," Powell said awkwardly. "I can't stay in town any longer. Are you comin' out?"

Maida shook her head. "I don't want to go to the ranch," she pouted. "I hate it out there. It's so inconvenient."

"How long is Kirkpatrick goin' to stay?" Powell asked abruptly. "Did he tell you?"

Again Maida shook her head. "He's taking a vacation," she said.

"Well," Powell's voice expressed his feelings, "I wish he'd go home. We've been over everything an' there's nothin' more that he needs to do here. I wish he'd go."

"He's having a good time," Maida said.

"It was a mistake bringin' him here to the house," Powell announced. "It won't look right, me bein' at the ranch an' him here in town with you. People'll talk."

"Let them!" Maida snapped the words. "I don't care what people say. You've got to be nice to Norville, Powell. You must remember that he represents the bank and that they have a big interest in the ranch."

"That ain't any reason for him stayin'," Powell Overman persisted stubbornly. "If you wasn't so nice to him he'd pull out."

Maida scowled. There was no other word for the black look that came over her face. "I suppose you think I'm having an affair with him," she said sharply. "Well, let me tell you, Powell Overman, you're the last man on earth to talk. After I've had to let Rosa go because of the way you carried on with her, I suppose you think . . ."

"Please, Maida." Powell's face was flushed as he interrupted. "I thought we'd settled all that. I'm not sayin' anything about you an' Kirkpatrick. I . . ."

"Well, I hope not!" Maida flashed. "Mr. Kirkpatrick is a good friend and that is all. Now you'd better go,

Powell. Remember that I own most of the Triangle. You're the manager."

There was a threat there and Powell Overman heeded it. "I'll go then," he said, not able to keep the anger from his voice. "I suppose you an' your good friend will come out an' visit us while we're brandin'?"

"Norville will probably want to see the round-up," Maida admitted. "We may come out. Good-bye, Powell."

She turned her cheek toward her husband and, bending awkwardly, Powell Overman kissed it. At least the pretenses of affection were kept up in the Overman family.

"Good-bye, Maida," he said, and went out of the room. Maida Overman heard her husband's boots clumping on the stair. She smiled a small secret smile. Later, joining Kirkpatrick in the dining-room, Maida pulled her lacy negligée tightly about her and smiled provocatively up at the man.

"Powell had to go to the ranch," she pouted. "He's leaving me all alone."

"Not all alone, my dear," Norville Kirkpatrick said gallantly. "I'm still here, you know."

"But you'll have to go back to Kansas City," Maida said, "and then I *will* be alone. And . . ."

"I'll not leave while your husband is gone," Kirkpatrick interposed. "Certainly I'll not leave you."

Maida clapped her hands together softly. "We'll have such fun!" she exclaimed. "Norville, I think you're the nicest man I've ever known."

154

"Just nice, my dear?" Norville Kirkpatrick's eyes were calculating.

"Oh . . ." said Maida Overman, "you're . . . more than nice, Norville!"

Chet Minor went up to the Screwplate on the fourteenth of May, as Barney Loveless had desired. He found there, when he drove in in his wagon, that the three men that Clyde Stevens hired on the Bar O7 were already at the ranch. These three, with Chet, Joe French, Laramie and Earl Keelin, comprised the wagon crew. Jesse Lauder had been sent down to the Triangle to represent Loveless there. It was a small crew for the country and the work there was to handle. Amador was going along to cook and both Loveless and Clyde Stevens would visit the wagon, but they could not be constantly with it. Stevens and Loveless were too old to stand up under the grueling work, and then too they had other interests to occupy their time. Take a day jingler and a night hawk out of this bunch and this would be a mighty short-handed crew, Chet thought.

Later in the day the crew was augmented. Ben Revilla came in and closely following Ben, Sven Olson, Carl Olson's oldest boy. The kid was grinning all over, on his first step to being the thing he wanted to be: a cowpuncher. Barney Loveless had taken Sven on as day wrangler.

That day the final preparations were made and early on the morning of the fifteenth the wagon pulled out from the ranch, the riders helping Sven along with the remuda and Laramie driving the bed wagon. Laramie

155

was to act as night hawk and Chet wondered why Joe French had put so good a man on that job. They pulled the wagons down across country all that day and the next, going clear to the east side of the Rifle Rock and skirting around the point of Tramparas Mesa. The night of the second day Pete McGrath joined them, coming up from the Triangle, and Pearl Suplan rode in to represent the AC.

In the morning work started, Joe French taking his crew out on the first circle. Joe kept Chet with him while he dropped the others off and rode the circle with Chet. They brought in the drive they had gathered, throwing it into the herd on the bed ground and holding the growing herd. When the last of the gathers had come down, three men stayed to hold the herd and the rest went to the wagon to eat a hasty meal. Sven brought in the horses, throwing them into a rope corral formed by the wagons and saddle ropes, held by men who closed the gap after the horses were in. Joe French did the horse roping, pulling out the mounts that were called for and turning them over to the riders. Horses were pulled out for the men at the herd, and wagon-wheeled. Sven having eaten his dinner, riders went out to relieve the men holding the cattle and they came in, changed saddles and ate. Then, while Sven took the remuda out again, the crew went back to work.

Laramie, as night jingler, tended irons and the fires that he had kindled with wood that had been dragged in at the end of a rope. Chet was given the roping to do while Joe French ear-marked and castrated the calves and kept tally. Two men were put to hold the herd and

156

the rest made flanking and branding crews. Chet, riding a fresh horse into the herd, was a little nervous. He had not done any roping for a long time.

Selecting a calf with a Screwplate cow, Chet shook out his loop. His wise old horse maneuvered for position, the calf took a step, Chet's rope flipped out and he came out from the herd, standing off in his left stirrup, the horse dragging the calf and the anxious cow following her bawling offspring. McGrath caught the rope, Ben Revilla the calf's tail. A jerk, and the calf was down. Ben sat down, left leg under him, right braced against the calf's left foot, his hands holding the calf's right leg back almost against his belly. Pete McGrath put a knee on the calf's neck and held its head.

"Screwplate," Chet said.

Joe French bent down, straightened with a bloody knife in his hands and put a bit of ear cartilage in his pocket. Revilla had freed Chet's rope and, coiling it, Chet was on his way back to the herd. Earl Keelin applied a hot iron and the calf bawled while hair sizzled.

"Let him go," Keelin directed.

The calf struggled up. Ben Revilla, on his feet, waved his hat and the cow and the branded calf trotted off to the herd. Around the branding ground the cow-ponies stood in a tired semicircle, watching with blasé eyes this beginning of beefsteak.

When they finished with the herd, Suplan and McGrath rode through and then rejoined French, taking their tally from him and checking it against the bits of bloody hair, the ear marks, that he took from various pockets. Amador had come with a bucket to collect a mess of mountain oysters. Suplan and Chet, with the men who had done the holding, gave the cattle a shove back into the country that had been worked. Joe French and the rest were riding back toward the wagons where now the supper fire crackled. The remuda was coming in, young Sven Olson, straight as a ramrod in his dilapidated saddle, bringing up the rear. The sun was setting beyond the western mesas and on the branding grounds a fire died in a trickle of smoke and the last dust from the departing herd settled down. All over the range country that scene had been enacted that day. The West was at work, pursuing its business.

Chet Minor was tired. After supper, after the horses had gone out, gaunt Laramie with them, he got his bed out of the wagon and unrolling it, turned in. The fire was pleasant and the odor of cigarette smoke good, and the voices were a low murmur, interspersed with the rattle of the dishes as Amador cleared out the wrecking pan. At that moment Chet Minor would not have traded places with any man in the world, not excepting young Sven, filled with the elation that at last he was on the road to heart's desire.

The next day the crew worked another circle from the same bed-ground, branding in the afternoon. The morning after that they moved, working cattle as they rode and gathering on the Corbellus flats, still to the east of Tramparas Mesa. That night, coming in from the herd, they found a visitor at the fire. Ed Ames, smiling pleasantly, walked out to meet the riders as they came in.

It was a shock to Chet Minor to see the compact, smiling man. He had, for the time, forgotten all about Ed Ames and the trouble deep beneath the surface of the Rifle Rock.

Ames ate supper with the Screwplate crew. It was noticeable that he was the last man to go up the line to fill his plate and that he took a seat at the outside edge of the circle while they ate, no man behind him. Ames gave no explanation of his presence and none was asked. He rode away after supper, thanking French for the extended hospitality, saying a collective "so long" to the riders. Twice that night tall Laramie quit his horses and rode a circle around the camp, and again, when morning was gray, the tall man sought a vantage point and looked over the country. Chet did not know of that, nor did he take notice of the rifle that Joe French carried in a saddle scabbard when they went out on circle in the morning coolness. How was Chet to know the thing that Barney Loveless had told Joe French?

"He'll be safer with the wagon, Joe," old Barney had said. "You take care of him. They tried to get to him once an' now, with this talk about him runnin' for sheriff comin' up, they'll try their luck again."

Joe French had nodded, and Laramie, standing by, had reached inside his shirt and there touched the gun in his hidden shoulder holster, the weapon that was his constant companion.

Ed Ames, when he rode away from the wagons, went south. For two hours he rode and then, stopping, hobbled his horse and choosing a little depression in the prairie, placed his saddle blanket on the ground and covered it with his slicker. He lay upon the scanty bed and slept while his hobbled horse grazed near by. In the morning he saddled and went on toward the south, passing by the black bulk of the Rifle Rock until, from a rise, he saw the Triangle wagon below him. Ames rode into the wagon and, uncommunicative as always, took food from the harassed cook. Then: "Which way did Overman go?" Ames asked, and when the cook had told him, Ames rode away once more.

Two miles from the wagon he saw men and cattle and riding down to them, gestured to Powell Overman. Overman joined him and they rode on together until they were out of sight of the men. Then stopping, Ames dismounted and squatted on one booted heel, the bridle reins trailing from his hand. Powell Overman too dismounted and stood above Ed Ames.

"Well?" said Overman.

Ames looked up. "There's not a chance," he said. "They're keepin' him covered. That Laramie circles around the camp at night an' French is always with Minor, packin' a rifle on his saddle."

"I thought you were tough!" Overman snapped. "I thought you'd take a chance."

"I'll take a chance," Ed Ames drawled without rancor, "but I'm no damned fool. Minor will have to wait a while."

Overman scuffed the toe of his boot across the ground. "That damned doctor," he said, "is all over the country, talkin' Minor up for sheriff. He's stirrin' up the nesters an' so is that big fellow Olson. You wouldn't have any trouble settlin' Laird."

Ames shook his head. "I'll kill no doctors," he stated definitely. "Doctors an' preachers are out of my line."

"Why?" Overman asked curiously.

"Because," said Ed Ames, "when one of them is killed the whole damn' country gets up an' goes to war. That's why."

"Well, then," said Powell Overman, "what are you hired for?"

"You hired me," Ames answered slowly. "You ought to know. I'll look over that Olson for you."

"Do that!" Overman ordered. "I'll have to talk to Mitchell an' Crow. Hell, I thought you could do the job."

"If you've got doubts," said Ed Ames, "you can always let me go."

"I'll talk to Crow an' Mitchell," Overman decided. "We're goin' to Rifle Rock from here. You can find me there when you've got somethin' to tell me."

"All right," Ames answered. "An' remember, Overman, I come to this country because I was asked an' the agreement was I was to work my own way. You've had some nesters pull out, an' any time you ain't satisfied I can roll my bed."

Powell Overman shook his head. "I'm just upset, I guess," he said. "All this stir-up about Minor, an' with Laird talkin' . . . Damn him!"

The utter ferocity in the last two words made Ed Ames stare at the speaker. Ames blinked his gray eyes, but said nothing. He arose from his boot-heel, put a rein over his horse's neck and, catching a stirrup, mounted.

The round-up wagons moved on across the Rifle Rock valley, following the old trails, dim, indistinct roads in the grass, trails that buffalo had made, or copper-skinned riders that followed the buffalo. Behind the wagons were branded calves, reaching around to lick at scabs on ribs or rump. May gave out finally and June began. The heel flies along the vegas buzzed viciously, tanned men became the color of old saddles.

Joe French, standing at the tail gate of the hoodlum wagon, spoke to Barney Loveless who was visiting the round-up. "We'll be through next Christmas, the way we're goin'," he said. "Barney, we got a lot of cattle winter-killed and there's some few just plain missin'."

"You'll be through by the end of June," Barney Loveless refuted. "Sure, there's some cattle missin'. You didn't think they'd overlook us, did you? Where do you go from here?"

"Over toward the Rock Springs. Ben Revilla's quit, Barney. He wants his time."

"I've brought all the checks down," said Barney Loveless. "Give Ben his time if he wants it. I'll pick up a man in Rifle Rock to take his place."

"We could use about four more," Joe French said.

Barney snorted and walked over to the buckboard to get the checks.

And so the round-up moved west across the valley, sweeping the country, cleaning it up as they went. That night after Barney left they were camped above Rock

Creek, perhaps ten miles from Laird's. Sven Olson asked Joe French if he could ride down home. He wanted to get some clothes, and he wanted — although he did not say this — to exhibit himself before the awed eyes of his younger brothers and sisters.

"Sure," agreed Joe French, "you can go tomorrow, Sven. You've made a pretty good hand an' I'll let you off a day."

Sven left in the morning and the wagon crew, a man short, rode their circles and threw a herd together. They were fortunate, for they had a wire corral to brand in that day, a corral built at a spot called "the mule pens" and so the absence of Sven did not noticeably slow them down.

Along in the afternoon, when the branding was well under way, Barney Loveless came back to the wagon on his return trip from Rifle Rock. Barney came out to the corral and Joe French laid off his job to talk to the boss, turning his work over to another man.

"Came past the Triangle wagon," Barney said, talking across the wire fence to Joe. "They've made pretty good time. Overman wasn't there but I talked to his straw boss an' they've lost a lot of cattle, winter-killed an' missin'."

Joe grunted. "We've lost some ourselves," he reminded. "Not so many though when you come to think about it."

"Did Ben pull out?" Barney asked.

"Goin' tomorrow," Joe said.

"The best I could do for a man to take his place was a fellow named Hall that's homesteaded down below

163

here," Barney announced. "He says he's punched a few cows."

Joe snorted. "You goin' on to the ranch or are you goin' to stop with us tonight?" he asked.

"I guess I'll stop," Loveless decided.

"Then we can talk after supper," said the foreman. "I'll go back to work."

Loveless, climbing back into his buckboard, drove back to camp.

Down below the mule pens a man lay on the rim of the creek bank, hidden by the willows. He had a rifle pushed out before him and his eyes were steady on the board shack below him in the creek bottom. Ed Ames had been there on the creek bank most of the day, patient, with an Indian's ability to wait, watching with all an Indian's concentration. Ames had seen the youngster, Sven, come riding in to the claim. He had seen the family greet the arrival of their brother. He had seen Mrs. Olson come out of the house and pass back and forth, and he had watched the children as they went upon unknown errands. But Ames had not seen Carl Olson. Carl Olson was confined to his bed with an infected foot. Ames surmised that something was wrong with Olson, for Dr. Laird's buggy had come down the creek and the doctor had gone into the house, carrying his medicine bag. The doctor came out after a time and under the eyes of the silent watcher in the willows, had driven away toward the southwest, toward Amarilla Mesa. Still Ed Ames waited. There was

164

just the chance that Carl Olson would come out of his house.

But as sundown approached the watcher on the bank lifted his rifle and slid back more deeply into the willows. Rising there, he progressed afoot to where a thicket spread toward the higher ground. From that thicket he took his horse and rode away, back toward the east and the Rifle Rock, keeping down below the ridges as he rode, watching the country narrowly.

And now another rider appeared from the west, silhouetted black against the sun, a man who pushed his horse along, urgency written in pace and posture. Ed Ames reined in.

"Overman," he said, half aloud. "Wonder what he's doin' over here? I wonder now."

CHAPTER
TWELVE

When the Screwplate finished branding they turned the cattle out of the mule pens corral and hazed them back toward the east, then, with the fire growing brighter as the dusk came down, they returned to the wagon. Revilla had acted as horse wrangler that day instead of the absent Sven, and he brought in the horses, putting them in the recently vacated corral. They left the horses there while they ate and after supper, now with dark almost fully come, Laramie stood talking to Joe French and Loveless before he went out with his charges. Chet, stretched out on his bed with a cigarette, was talking to Pete McGrath when, in the darkness, the sound of a running horse came faint but distinct from the south.

Conversation about the fire ceased abruptly. Amador suspended activity at the dishpan. The horse came on, urgency in the pound of hoofs against the sod.

"Now who . . . ?" said Pete McGrath.

"Comin' here," big Joe French announced.

As the rider closed on the camp, men stood up, waiting to see what and who this was. The kid, Sven Olson, came into the firelight, sliding his horse to a stop, coming out of the saddle, his foot hanging in the stirrup for a moment before he kicked it free.

"Doctor Laird!" Sven gasped. "He's killed!"

For a moment there was no other word, no sound except the crackling of the fire and then the questions broke about the boy, deluging him. Barney Loveless's high-pitched voice stilled the others.

"Shut up, everybody!" Loveless ordered. "Now, what is this, Sven?"

The boy was almost speechless with fright and excitement. Loveless's hand on the lad's shoulders steadied him and he gasped out his story. He had been on his way back to the camp and stood at Laird's to talk with Sally. His next smaller brother had ridden that far with him and while they were at the doctor's house, Laird's buggy had come in, the lines loose across the horse's back. Dr. Laird was in the buggy, bent forward over the dashboard, and when Sally had lifted him up she found the doctor dead, shot twice through chest and abdomen. Sven had ridden for the camp and his brother had headed back home.

Loveless looked around the circle of faces, ruddy now with firelight. "Some of us had better go down there," he said. "Chet . . ."

Chet Minor had already moved away to get his saddle. Loveless's eyes searched the faces about him. "I guess some of you won't want to go," he commented, his voice harsh. "We can't all leave the camp. I'll take Chet an' Joe an' Laramie. Earl, you run things till we get back. I'll borrow your saddle, Amador. You got it with you, haven't you?"

Amador Fernandez, the cook, ran to the chuck wagon and delving into it pulled out his battered saddle

167

that he had brought along just on the chance it would be useful. Chet had stopped beside his bed, and was pulling out the Colt and its belt and sheath from his clothes sack. Joe French had already started toward the corral, carrying his saddle; and Laramie, whose horse naturally was ready, for he was night jingler, came running from the hoodlum wagon carrying a rifle that he slid down into the saddle scabbard.

"Come on!" Barney Loveless snapped.

There was some dust and confusion in the corral as French roped horses, taking the first that his loop settled on, then the hasty preparations were simplified by Amador's appearance with a lantern. As the men mounted Loveless called directions to Earl Keelin, left in charge.

"Don't know when we'll get back, Earl," he called. "You use yore judgment about what to do in the mornin'. We'll get word back to you. Hurry with that horse, boy!" This last was to Sven, who, under French's direction, was changing saddles.

Sven finished with his latigo and mounted, crawling up on the horse in his eagerness. Loveless wheeled his mount around and they set out, pushing steadily, the horses at a long lope.

Cow horses can travel over rough country at night, can make it at a run or a lope or trot or walk. Sometimes one falls and a rider is thrown, but Loveless and his men suffered no such mishap. They came to the drift fence where Sven had left the gate down, went through the opening and on toward the south. Then ahead of them they saw a pinpoint of light that moved, and another light, fixed and steady, and suddenly they were coming down the bank into the creek bottom and were reining in before Laird's fence.

The horsemen dismounted. There was already a wagon in the yard, standing beside the buggy. Olson was at the wagon, his bandaged foot off the ground, a home-made crutch supporting him. Olson held a lantern shoulder high.

"Where's Doc?" Chet demanded of the big man.

"In the house," Olson answered, his voice a harsh rasp. "My wife's with Sally. I sent the boy on to get Hall."

As though to confirm that statement, a boy and a man came riding in from the creek, the nester Hall and young Jens Olson. The man and the boy dismounted and came forward. Hall's voice was gruff.

"I sent one of my kids to town," he said. "Got to get the sheriff out here, I guess."

"What do you know about this, Olson?" Loveless demanded.

"I talked to Sally," Olson said. "Her father came down to see me this afternoon. He was goin' on over to Amarilla Mesa. He was lookin' after one of the Revilla girls over there. Sally says that the buggy came in . . . you saw it, Sven. You tell them."

Sven Olson, pushed forward by his father's hand, repeated what he had told at the wagon. He could add no details. When he had finished, Loveless took the lantern and, with Chet at his elbow and Joe French and Laramie behind him made a careful examination of the

169

buggy. They found blood on the floor and seat and dribbled down the dashboard. That was all.

"I'd like to see Sally," Chet said.

"My wife's with her in the house," Olson answered.

Chet went to the door, the others hanging back. Sally Laird was in the kitchen, stony-faced, beside the table. Mrs. Olson, wide and ample and with her youngest in her arms, sat across the table from the girl.

The girl looked at him, no recognition in her eyes. Chet moved toward her. Mrs. Olson caught his glance and shook her head. Chet stopped and the woman gestured toward the bedroom. Passing by Sally Chet went to the door. There was a lamp burning dimly in the bedroom and Dr. Laird lay upon the bed, the wolf skin Chet had given the doctor, spread beside the bed. Except that he was fully clothed, the doctor might have been asleep. Chet turned slowly and came back to the kitchen. He knelt beside the girl, resting on one spurred heel.

"Sally," he began again, his voice gentle, "it's Chet."

The girl looked at him, seeing him for the first time.

"I'll do whatever you want, Sally," Chet said.

The girl's voice was low. "I'm thinking, Chet," she said. "I'm trying to believe that he's dead. I can't, Chet."

Chet reached up and put his arm about the girl's shoulders. It lay there, strong, comforting, reassuring, and suddenly, Sally Laird turned her head, hiding her face on Chet's shoulder and began to cry, great noiseless sobs shaking her body. Chet's free hand came up to stroke the girl's bright hair and his eyes sought

170

Mrs. Olson's face. The woman got up and, carrying her child, went out the door. In the yard the men were clustered around the lantern. Olson was in the wagon, sitting on the seat, his foot stretched out so that it was rested on the end gate. In the yard the men turned questioning eyes toward the woman on the stoop.

"She's crying," Mrs. Olson said, and came on to stand beside her husband.

Time wore on. In the yard there was no talk. Then, suddenly, Chet came out of the kitchen door and paused beside the step.

"She wants Mrs. Olson," Chet said, and came on down into the yard.

Carl Olson's wife went to the house and Chet, joining the others, stood silent.

"How is she, Chet?" Barney Loveless asked.

Chet did not answer the question. "By God!" he exclaimed fiercely. "He never harmed a soul. Not a soul!"

Loveless's hand shot out and caught Chet's arm. Chet was trembling. "Take it easy, boy!" rasped Barney.

Under the old man's hand the trembling ceased. Chet Minor took a long breath and let it go. There was a fiber in his voice, a timbre that Barney Loveless or any man about had not heard before. "It'll be mornin' pretty soon," said Chet Minor.

That was not a statement, not a detail of time, but rather a promise, and about Chet Minor the men accepted it as such.

"Mornin'," Laramie granted.

In that little group, men nodded their heads. It would be morning pretty soon.

When the first gray light came over the eastern mesas, Chet Minor spoke to Loveless. "I'll go along now," he said, almost casually.

"Where, Chet?" Loveless asked.

"Along the buggy tracks," Chet answered. "I'll get to them before they're messed up."

Loveless nodded his understanding. "You goin' to talk to the girl first?" he asked.

Chet shook his head. "Barney," he said, and he was giving directions now, not requesting a favor but demanding obedience, "you stay here. There'll be a bunch out from town pretty soon. I'd take it kindly if you'd look after things here. Keep 'em off Sally."

"Sure, Chet," Loveless replied.

"You can tell Clarke an' them I've gone out," Chet's voice was calm. "There'll be some dew and it might help the trailin'. I know who I'm lookin' for but I want to be certain."

Again Loveless nodded. "I'll tend to things here," he assured.

"Whatever she wants, Barney," Chet said, using the old man's first name.

Laramie had gone to the fence and now he came back leading his own horse and Chet's. "I'll go with you," Laramie drawled. "Comin', Joe?"

Joe French looked at Barney Loveless. Loveless tipped his head the barest fraction of an inch.

"I'll be along," Joe French said casually.

"You got the round-up, Joe," Chet said. "It will . . ."

"To hell with the round-up!" Loveless snapped. "Go on."

Mrs. Olson appeared at the kitchen door. "I've made some coffee," she said. "Sally wants to see you, Chet."

"Wait," Chet ordered, and limped toward the house.

Sally was standing in the kitchen and as Chet came in she moved toward him. Reading something that was in Chet's face, the girl asked a question. "Where are you going, Chet?"

"Out," Chet said shortly. "Don't try to stop me, Sally."

The girl saw the iron that was in the man. "You . . ." she began and then, "What are you going to do?"

"Find the man that killed your father," Chet answered levelly.

Sally Laird gasped. "Chet!" she exclaimed. "You must not!"

"I've got to, Sally."

Again the girl drew in her breath sharply. "Promise me," she demanded. "Promise me, Chet, you won't . . . you won't . . ."

"I can't promise a thing," Chet snapped, and wheeling, stalked out of the kitchen.

Laramie and Joe French were mounted. Chet stepped up on his own horse. He nodded to the men in the yard and with French and Laramie following him rode out the gate. Across the creek they went and then on toward the south, riding slowly, steadily, their heads bent as they studied the ground beneath them.

"I'd ought to have made them wait," Barney Loveless said to Carl Olson. "They'll maybe run into trouble. Maybe . . ."

"You couldn't have stopped Minor," Carl Olson said. "Help me down, Loveless."

Barney Loveless, cowman, stretched up his hand to the big nester.

Chet Minor and Joe French and Laramie rode on south. The buggy wheels had crushed the grass and the marks were plain. The horse had wandered but always toward home. The three men followed the tracks readily enough. The sun climbed up and up and the men held their steady pace and then:

"It happened here," Laramie announced. "The buggy stopped. The tracks ahead of here are straight like the horse was bein' drove. They kind of amble from here on back."

"We'll take a little circle," Chet said. "Maybe we'll find something."

The three rode out now from the buggy tracks, spreading apart, circling, cutting across the prairie. Not urban men, these, but riders, trained men, men who could follow a trail, read sign and interpret it. Chet headed toward a rise where a rocky rim jutted from the prairie, choosing that as the most likely spot. He rode toward the east but before he had gone fifty feet Joe French spoke.

"Here," he called sharply.

Chet and Laramie came back. Joe French had dismounted and was pointing to the ground. The other

174

two, alighting, examined the thing that Joe French indicated.

"Horse wore a number two shoe," Laramie said. "Just shod behind."

"He rode down," Chet said, "an' stopped the doctor. Likely talked to him. Then he shot him."

"Here's his tracks comin' in an' here's where he went out," Laramie said.

"Let's go then," Chet ordered.

Mounting again they rode toward the west, not so rapidly now, for the sign was not so plain. Occasionally the trail was lost completely. Then patient circling brought it to light again. The men were helped by the fact that there were practically no horses in the country that were shod. There were cattle tracks in plenty and once they lost the trail where cattle, going to water, had obliterated it. They followed patiently along the cowpath and, beyond the water hole, found the trail once more. Here a rock had been turned; here, in the dirt, was the mark of a shod hoof, here fresh droppings. On and on they went.

After a minute: "Lopin' his horse here," Chet announced.

Still the trail went on and now Chet stopped, puzzled.

"Here's where two horses went," he said. "Where'd this other trail come in?"

Laramie and French shook their heads. "Some place on that malpais where we had to stop and circle," Laramie surmised. "They go the same way. We'll follow."

175

"Both horses shod behind an' with the same size shoe," French commented. "Now what, Chet?"

"We know who's at the end of the tracks," Chet said grimly. "Let's go on to him."

The others nodded and the three rode on.

The country fell away in front of them, dropping off in a gentle slope. To the north was the Rifle Rock, black and grim. The sun had climbed high, the shadows of the riders almost beneath them. Over toward the west there was a trickle of smoke rising straight skyward.

"Camp," said Chet.

"The Triangle wagon," French corrected. "Are you goin' to ride in on 'em, Chet?"

"Why not?" Chet Minor grated.

They went on.

Now, presently, they could see the wagons, the chuck wagon with the canvas top rolled back and the bare bows of the hoodlum wagon. A man moved about the camp, one man only, and Joe French breathed a sigh of relief. He would have ridden in with Chet if the whole Triangle crew had been present, but he was glad, just the same, that they had not returned from their circles. Laramie, with the farsighted eyes of the man past forty, grunted deep in his belly.

"The cook," he said. "There'll be a night jingler too. Somebody's sleepin' under the wagon."

"An' there's a horse at the wagon wheel," Chet said. "Two horses."

As the distance closed, the details of the camp became more and more apparent. The cook, apprised of their arrival, looked toward them and a man came from a little sheepman's tepee pitched beside the wagons, and shading his eyes from the sun, peered at the approaching horsemen. Chet and Laramie and Joe, as they rode in, saw the cook turn and speak to the other man.

"The night hawk," grunted Chet.

As the three reached the camp the man from the tent walked toward them. The cook had returned to his duties at the chuck wagon and beneath the bed wagon a man slept.

Chet spoke tersely as he stopped and wheeled his horse. "Is Ames here, Gus?"

"Why . . ." the man who had come from the tepee hesitated.

Laramie had circled to the south until he was close to the bed wagon, his hand hidden inside his shirt. Joe French had swung his horse so that its right side was toward the camp, and was dismounting on the off-side, the horse between him and the wagons. French carried his rifle on the left side of his horse, the scabbard sloping forward. Now, on the ground, he moved, his motion hidden by his mount.

Chet knew the night wrangler, a man named Gus Ladd who had once worked for Chet. "I want Ames," Chet said, his voice flat. "He killed Dr. Laird yesterday evenin'."

"He's under the wagon, Chet," Laramie called, and now his hand appeared, filled with gun.

"Why . . ." Ladd said again, "Ames is here . . ."

Corroborating that statement, Ed Ames crawled out from beneath the wagon, rubbing sleep from his eyes.

Chet Minor, pushing his horse past Ladd, dismounted and walked slowly toward Ames.

"Hello, Minor," Ames said.

Chet made no reply to the greeting. "I've come to take you in," he said.

"Take me in?" Ames smiled sleepily and rubbed his eyes again. They darted to right and left as he lowered his hand, seeing grim Laramie, noting French's horse with just Joe French's head showing over the saddle.

"Yesterday," Chet said, "you killed Dr. Laird. Rode down on him an' stopped his buggy an' killed him. You shot him twice. I'll take you in, Ames, or you can take your chances with me."

Ed Ames smiled. "Yo're mighty sure," he said. "Yesterday I was here at the wagon. I . . ."

The cook, Fats Packard, had come up from the chuck wagon. Fats had cooked on the Triangle round-up for years and Chet knew him well. Chet saw the cook's eyes shift and spoke suddenly.

"Is that so, Fats? Tell me the truth!"

"I . . ." Fats' eyes darted nervously from Chet to Ed Ames and back again. "I . . ."

"The truth, Fats!" Chet commanded sternly.

"He wasn't here," Fats Packard blurted. "He come in late last night."

Ed Ames favored the cook with a long, slow look. "All right, I wasn't here. What are you goin' to do about it?"

"You've got your choice," Chet said.

Ames shrugged and looked toward Laramie. "Not much choice," he said. "I'll go with you. Wait till I get . . ."

"Stand still," Chet commanded, for Ames had turned toward his bed. "I'll get whatever you wanted to get. Watch him, Laramie."

Laramie, leading his horse, moved in closer. The muzzle of Laramie's gun had not deviated from Ed Ames, not even while Laramie dismounted. Chet, walking to the wagon, reached under it. From the bed he picked up a belt and holster and brought out a rifle.

"I'll take care of these," he announced. "Joe, you could get Ames's horse."

Joe French came in, leading his horse. He left his mount ground-tied and going to the horses that were tied to the wagon wheel, untied one of them. There was no hesitation in making the selection. Joe knew Gus Ladd's saddle and he had seen the horse that Ames had ridden on his visit to the Screwplate wagon. French brought the horse out.

"Get on," he said to Ames.

Ames mounted. French, going back to the bed wagon, got Ames's hat and carried it to the man. Ames put it on with an indulgent smile.

"An' now we'll go," Chet announced. "You can tell Overman what happened, when he comes in, Fats."

Fats Packard nodded solemnly. Chet stepped up on his horse, mounting with difficulty because of the rifle he held. The gun and belt he had looped over his saddle horn.

"Tell Overman," Chet directed, looking at the cook, "that his pet killer is in Rifle Rock, if he wants to come an' get him. Let's go, Joe."

Fats Packard and Gus Ladd watched them ride away, Ames in the lead, the other three behind him.

"By gosh!" said Gus Ladd when they were gone. "You see that look Ames gave you, Fats? What'd you want to give off head like that for? Why didn't you tell 'em he was here all day yesterday?"

"I wasn't lookin' at Ames." Fats Packard shuddered. "I was lookin' at Chet Minor. If he'd been watchin' you like he was me, you'd have told the truth too."

CHAPTER
THIRTEEN

Once on that long ride to town Ed Ames spoke to Chet Minor.

"How do you think you'll do this, Minor?" he asked. "Yo're not an officer."

"No," Chet agreed shortly, "but I'm takin' you in."

Ames, looking back over his shoulder, smiled dryly. "You won't get away with it," he predicted.

"Any citizen can make an arrest," Chet answered slowly. "We'll go in to Rifle Rock. When we're there I'll swear out a warrant an' turn you over to the peace officers."

Ames's smile was amused. "An' that will be fine," he agreed. "Just fine. Minor, yo're a damned fool. I'll be loose ten minutes after we hit town."

"I kind of hope you are," Chet drawled.

Ames said no more but rode along, the others following close behind.

When they reached Rifle Rock and came down Idaho Street they saw that the town was boiling. It was late in the day now, for they had come a distance and the morning trailing had been slow. There were wagons all along Idaho Street and at the very edge of town a youngster saw the little cavalcade and, shouting something in a shrill voice, ran, bare feet flying in the dust, ahead of them toward the town's center. Before they were two blocks from the depot which they passed on their way, a crowd was forming down on the bank corner, and as they neared the crowd Chet spoke quietly to his companions.

"Take either side of him," he ordered. "I'll come along behind."

Joe French and Laramie obeyed, closing in on either side of Ed Ames. Once again Ames looked back at Chet. Ames was smiling still, but now the smile was grim. "I reckon I'll just stay in jail, Minor," he said, "if I get there."

At the bank corner the crowd surged out into the street. There was no doubt concerning the mind of that crowd, no doubt of its sullen anger. The word of Dr. Laird's death had gone out over the country and men had quit their plows or their corn planters and come to town. This was a crowd of nesters, and dangerous.

As the men surged out from the sidewalk, Chet swung his horse to the left and pressed ahead. So he came between the forerunners of that would-be mob and the three men who held to the center of the street. Chet singled out a man he knew, from the many angry faces, and spoke to him.

"I'm takin' him to jail, Burgess," Chet said. "Don't try to stop me."

Burgess opened his mouth to shout something angrily and Chet pushed his horse forward, using the spurs. The cow pony, frightened, reared and came down pawing, kicked and bucked viciously in a circle. A man yelled as the horse kicked and the men in the street scattered, trying to avoid the lunges of the bucking horse. Chet let the horse go, riding easily. The pony was gentle enough and soon bucked out. He stopped and stood, head low. Chet looking down the street could see Ames and Laramie dismounting in front of the little building that contained the city offices and the jail. Joe French was riding back up the street toward him. The scattered crowd was re-forming slowly. Chet pulled his horse's head up and loped on toward Joe French.

When they met, French turned back and they went on to the jail together. The old man who acted as janitor and city jailor for Rifle Rock was arguing with Laramie. Ed Ames stood by, still with that rock-hard smile on his face. Chet ended the argument abruptly.

"Put him in your cell," he ordered, his voice carrying an impact like a blow.

The jailor quit his shrill tirade and shuffled into the building, fumbling with his keys. Chet watched the old man open the single cell.

"You better go in, Ames," he directed. "I'll stay outside a while."

Ames looked at Chet, swift appraisal in his eyes. "Thanks, Minor," he said briefly, and went into the cell. Chet closed the door, locked it, took the keys from the jailor despite his expostulations, and pocketed them.

"Now what?" Laramie demanded. "We'd have done better if we hadn't brought him to town, Chet."

"I didn't think the word would spread so fast," Chet admitted.

"We'd have saved a heap of trouble if we'd just shot him out at the wagons or on the way in," Laramie said wistfully. "A heap of trouble, Chet."

Chet did not answer. He gave his belt a hitch and limped toward the street door, opened it and went out, leaving the door open. Laramie looked at Joe French. French shifted the rifle that lay across his arm. His eyes were worried. Through the door they had a glimpse of Chet's back. Chet was sitting on the steps.

"By gosh!" French ejaculated.

A murmur of angry voices came through the open door. The murmur grew, becoming a roar. Laramie reached inside his shirt and brought out his revolver, holding it poised. "Had we better go out?" he asked.

French shook his head. "If it gets tight Chet will come back in," he said. "I'll take a window, Laramie. You look after the door."

Laramie nodded and stepped forward as French moved across to the window. Outside the crowd had stopped, confronting the man who sat calmly on the steps. One man came forward from that crowd. Burgess.

"We want that killer!" Burgess announced.

"What for?" Chet's voice was untroubled.

"To hang!" Burgess answered.

The voice of the crowd had quieted now. There were perhaps fifty men assembled before the jail building. Looking at them Chet saw that about twenty were nesters, men with legitimate grievances. The others were townsmen: riffraff such as a town like Rifle Rock can always produce; clerks from the stores, more curious than dangerous; others who had come to see and not to act.

Chet shook his head. "I brought him in," he said with finality in his tone. "I'll keep him."

"We'll hang him from the nearest sign," Burgess snapped.

"An' that," Chet drawled, "would be a pretty thing for Sally Laird to see when she brings her father's body into town."

The words gave pause to the mob. Burgess was a hard-headed man, a leader, the only one in the crowd. He spoke again.

"We'll take him out of town then. Don't try to stop us, Minor. They'll turn that murderer loose as sure as . . ."

Burgess stopped. Chet was shaking his head, moving it gently from side to side. "You could take him," Chet said, slowly. "You could kill me an' drag him out an' hang him, an' when you had it done there'd be hell loose in the valley. You'd better go home to your wife, Burgess. They won't turn Ames loose."

"Who'll stop 'em?"

"I will." Chet's voice was quiet but it carried a ring of utter conviction.

Burgess hesitated. "You . . ." he began.

"You've got too much to lose to lead a lynchin', Burgess," Chet said.

Still Burgess hesitated. Behind him, in the crowd, a man called out. "Don't let him bluff you. Go on, Burgess, we're behind you!"

Chet stood up. "The man that said that, step out!" he ordered, steel ringing in his voice.

No one moved. Chet slumped so that his weight was on his good left leg. "You see," he said to Burgess. "You'd better pull out. They want you to do it for 'em."

Sudden decision came to Burgess's face. "I'll take your word for it, Minor," he said. "There'll be no lynchin' now. But we won't go home. Not yet."

Chet sat down on the jail steps again. Methodically he pulled out tobacco and papers from his vest pocket. Methodically he began to roll a cigarette. "Suit yourself," he drawled. "Yo're a wise man, Burgess."

The big nester turned. He moved toward the crowd and it split before him. Chet, looking up from the cigarette forming in his hands, spoke once more. "You might as well go with your boss, boys," he drawled. "The excitement is over for right now."

At the edge of the crowd, split now as Burgess went through it, two men turned and began to move slowly away. That was the beginning. Others followed those leaders. The men that had for the moment been a mob, split now so that in place of one compact body, there were little groups of men all up and down Idaho Street. Chet lit his cigarette and thoughtfully broke the match in two and tossed it out into the street. In the office room of the building Joe French put down his rifle and wiped his sweating forehead with the back of his hand.

186

"He done it," Laramie stated, awe in his voice. "He done it, Joe, an' he never touched his gun."

"God!" Joe French said reverently, and then, "I couldn't have pulled it off, Laramie. Neither could you."

"I'd never have tried," Laramie answered. "Never!"

"Laramie," Chet called from out on the steps.

Laramie went out.

"I think we'd better eat," Chet announced. "You an' Joe go over an' bring somethin' back for Ames. When you get back I'll go."

"Sure, Chet," Laramie agreed.

It was sundown before the first of those returning from Laird's claim arrived in Rifle Rock. Jim Clarke and Vance Murray came in, faces black as thunder clouds. They rode straight to the jail and leaving their horses, walked into the building. Chet was at the desk, smoking a cigarette, and Laramie and Joe French were seated close beside the door. Disregarding Joe and Laramie, Clarke came stalking over to Chet, Murray right behind him.

"What in hell does this mean, Minor?" the sheriff demanded. "Yo're pretty high-handed, it seems to me. Who appointed you a deputy?"

"Nobody," Chet answered placidly. "I'm a citizen, though. There's your warrant on the desk an' there's your prisoner in his cell. What more do you want, Clarke?"

"You've got no business takin' a prisoner!" Clarke flared. "I'll turn him loose . . ."

"Look out the door before you do it," Chet warned ominously. "There's fifty nesters in town now, Clarke. Turn Ames loose an' see how long you all last."

"Nesters!" Clarke snorted. "They won't do nothin'!"

"Maybe they won't. But I will," Chet answered. "Listen, Clarke, Laramie an' Joe an' me followed trail this mornin'. We found where the doctor's buggy had been stopped an' the doc shot. We cut sign an' followed a horse trail right in to the Triangle wagon. Ames was sleepin' under the wagon an' Fats Packard said that he came in late. What more do you want? You try turnin' Ames loose and by God I'll lead a mob that will hang him an' you too if we have to! I've turned the prisoner over to you. You're sheriff. There's a warrant I've sworn out before the J. P. Now what are you goin' to do?"

Clarke's face had lost its livid anger while Chet talked. In place of anger a slow pallor had come and the sheriff's eyes were frightened. Chet got up from the chair. "You're responsible, Clarke," he stated. "You're the sheriff. Come on, Joe, you and Laramie."

Chet limped out of the office. Joe French followed him, but Laramie paused at the door. Everyone in Rifle Rock knew that Laramie was a tough old hellion and there was no mistaking the expression on his face or the tone of his voice when he spoke.

"Ames had better be here," Laramie growled, looking at Clarke, "because I'm comin' back to check up an' I'm goin' to be right close around."

With that, Laramie also left the building.

188

Jim Clarke and Vance Murray looked at each other. "We got to keep him in, Vance," Clarke said. "We got to."

"Mebbe when the cowmen get in," Murray began doubtfully, "we can . . ."

Clarke shook his head. Jim Clarke was, when all was said and done, an officer. He was angry with Chet Minor but now that he had calmed somewhat he was realizing just what he had on his hands. "Not us," he said. "If we turned Ames loose, cowmen or not, there'd be the damnedest fight in this town you ever saw. I ain't goin' to sit in on a game like that, not for any man. We'll hold Ames an' let the court turn him loose. I'm goin' back an' talk to him." Jim Clarke stumped off toward the jail's single cell.

It was odd that the Triangle, riders all, were not the next arrivals in Rifle Rock. The darkness came and still the cowmen did not come to town, but instead a wagon, escorted by a few mounted men and a buggy, came from the north. Clarke, leaving Murray at the jail, went out to the wagon and found Chet Minor standing beside it, talking to Carl Olson who drove. Dr. Laird's blanket-wrapped body was in the wagon box and Mrs. Olson was driving the buggy with Sally Laird beside her and the baby tucked between them on the seat.

"You bring the body inside while I round up the J. P. an' a jury," Clarke directed. "We'll hold the inquest right away."

Olson nodded and Chet and Joe French walked to the back of the wagon and took out the end gate.

The inquest was held in the jail office by the light of a smoking kerosene lamp and another that had a clean chimney. Clarke tried to get townsmen on the jury. Wolfbarger was the foreman and there were two clerks from Wolfbarger's and the Bon Ton, the blacksmith and Otto Hahn and the depot agent. Jerome Bloxom, a real estate man who was the Justice of the Peace, presided, and Dr. Frawley, the town's single physician, was present. It looked like a good jury to Jim Clarke. Every man on it was dependent upon the cattlemen of Rifle Rock for an existence. The jury heard the evidence.

Sally Laird came first and gave her testimony in a flat, stony-hard voice. When she had finished, Mrs. Olson took her to the hotel. Sven Olson, Chet Minor, Laramie, Joe French, all contributed, each testifying as to the trail they had followed, and adding the statement that Fats Packard had made at the Triangle camp. Wolfbarger took the jurymen over to his store to reach a verdict and Chet Minor went down to the hotel. Laramie and Joe French stayed near by the jail building. All up and down Idaho Street there were little knots of men talking, low-voiced. Jim Clarke stayed in the jail office talking with Vance Murray.

"It's funny that Overman don't come in," Clarke complained. "It's damned funny that there ain't any cowmen here in town." His voice was uneasy.

At the hotel Chet talked with Sally Laird. There was a grief-stricken expression in Sally's brown eyes but the girl maintained her composure. She was taking her father back to Ohio, she said, to place him beside her mother.

190

"Are you comin' back, Sally?" Chet asked.

The girl did not look at him. "I don't know," she answered dully. "I've asked the Olsons to look after things at the place. I don't know yet what I'll do, Chet."

Barney Loveless rose from his chair beside Chet and went out to find Stevens Claypool to make the necessary arrangements for Sally's funds. The nearest undertaker was at Conejos, further along the railroad to the east. The doctor would be shipped to Conejos and there prepared for the long journey east. Chet remained with Sally Laird, a strange Sally Laird, a girl who would not look at him and who did not speak.

"Didn't I do what you wanted, Sally?" Chet blurted finally. "Didn't I . . . ?"

"Let the girl alone!" Mrs. Olson ordered. "Let her alone. She doesn't want to talk to anybody."

Chet moved away then, going to the door of the hotel lobby. Just at the door Joe French met him and drew him outside.

"The jury's brought their verdict," French said.

"What was it?"

"They found that the doctor was shot by Ed Ames!" French could not keep the exultation from his voice. "An' Chet, Powell Overman has just come to town an' he's only got two men with him."

"What?" Chet demanded, amazement in his voice.

"Only two men," French repeated. "They won't try anythin' tonight, Chet."

Chet shook his head. "Maybe not," he answered, "but we'll kind of watch just the same."

French looked at his companion's drawn, weary face. Chet stood full in the light that came from the door of the Parker House and the lines on his face were those of an old man, deep and creased.

"One of us at a time will be enough," French said. "You an' me an' Laramie will split it up."

Chet nodded. Barney Loveless came out through the door and spoke to French. "Do you know where Doc Frawley is?" he asked. "Olson's got a fever an' there's pains runnin' up his leg from his foot. I've got him a room an' told him to go to bed, but I want Frawley to look after him."

"Doc was down at the jail," French answered.

Barney looked searchingly at Chet Minor and without further word went on down the street.

At the corner of the jail building Powell Overman stood talking with Clarke and Vance Murray. "I thought that there might be trouble," Overman said, "so I brought Shorty Thomas and Bill Honeyman in with me. They're good steady boys. You can appoint them deputies, Jim, and they'll help you out if you need help."

Clarke stared at Powell Overman, trying to see his face in the gloom of the street. "Ain't you . . . ?" he began.

Overman shrugged his shoulders. "I guess Ames is guilty, all right," he said. "He came into the wagon late yesterday, came in after I did. You say that French and Minor followed the trail he'd made?"

"Yeah," Clarke agreed.

Overman shrugged again. "I'm sorry that it was my wagon where they found him," he said. "Of course Ames wasn't workin' for me but it makes it look bad. You know how it is: you can't turn a man away from the wagon when he come in for a meal an' a bed."

"No," Clarke agreed, his voice hardening. "I know how it is."

"I'm goin' on to the house," Overman continued. "Haven't seen my wife for a week. I'll stay down there tonight, Jim."

Clarke nodded and Overman sauntered away. When he was gone the sheriff spoke to his deputy, Vance Murray. "By damn!" Clarke snapped, "if that's the way he feels about it you an' me aren't goin' to worry our heads, Vance. Hell! If I hired a man I'd stick by him!"

Murray made no answer and after a moment Clarke spoke again. "I'll make them two he brought in deputies, an' then I'm goin' down to the hotel an' get some sleep. Damn Powell Overman anyhow! You can look after things tonight, Vance."

Vance Murray grunted disgustedly. That was the way of it. The deputies always got the dirty end of the stick!

Powell Overman, crossing the porch of his house, pushed open the door and went in. There was a light in the living-room and Maida and Norville Kirkpatrick were seated beside the table. They both looked up as the ranchman entered.

"Hello, Powell," Maida greeted without moving. "Did you come to town because of the excitement?"

Overman nodded. Kirkpatrick had risen and was holding out his hand. Overman shook it briefly and let it fall.

"We went down town," Maida said. "We thought perhaps they would lynch Ames. We . . ."

"An' you didn't want to miss a good lynchin'!" Powell Overman said. "I'm tired. I'll go up to bed. Good night!" He stalked out of the room.

Maida watched him go. When the portières had swished shut behind him she turned to Kirkpatrick. There was a sardonic smile on Kirkpatrick's face. Maida was smiling too, in amusement. She spread her hands in a gesture as though to say: "You see . . ."

Upstairs a boot thumped down on the floor and then another followed it. Kirkpatrick reached across the table, cupped his hand behind the lamp chimney and blew. The lamp went out. In the immediate darkness the man reached out. His hands found a softly rounded body coming toward him. Kirkpatrick drew the woman close and bent his head.

"Why wait, Maida?" he asked. "Come with me."

Hands against Kirkpatrick's chest pushed him back. Maida's voice was mocking. "Not yet, Norville. Not yet. I want to see the end of the comedy."

"You devil!" the man whispered. "You cruel little devil! Come here."

CHAPTER
FOURTEEN

In the morning Chet Minor and Barney Loveless put Sally Laird on the East-bound train. The casket, brought from Wolfbarger's, that held Dr. Laird's body was loaded on the baggage car. Mrs. Olson, tears streaming down her face, kissed the girl good-bye. Sally Laird was calm with a forced calmness. She had refused all offers of companionship, had refused everything save only the financial help of Loveless and the old man's taking charge of arrangements in Rifle Rock. Barney had sent telegrams, had routed out Claypool and arranged for money, had done all the necessary things. The girl was deeply grateful.

Chet Minor watched the train go, feeling as though something had been taken out of him, as though he were empty. He turned to Loveless and Barney met his eyes.

"Now what?" Loveless asked.

"I don't know," Chet answered.

Barney considered the cinders of the station platform. "I think we'll stay in town today," he decided. "The boys can work short-handed. I think maybe you'd better stay in town quite a while, Chet. You're mixed up

195

in this. The district attorney is comin' in today an' he'll want to question you an' Joe an' Laramie."

Chet nodded.

"An' I'm worried about that big Swede," Loveless growled. "He's got a bad leg on him, Frawley says. Damn it anyhow! This had to happen just at round-up time!"

"Kind of tough," Chet said.

"Damned nuisance!" Loveless snapped. "I wonder what Overman an' them are goin' to do now. It would be just like Overman to make a break an' try to get him out."

Chet shook his head. "They'll hire a good lawyer an' get him loose," he said moodily. "There isn't much of a case against Ames. It's all circumstantial. Hell, Barney . . ."

"What'll you do if they do turn him loose?" Loveless asked, eyeing Chet curiously.

Chet shrugged. "Find him again," he answered. "Barney, why don't you an' Joe an' Laramie go back to camp? You've got cattle to brand."

"The calves will be just a little bigger if we wait," Loveless said. "Make the flankers earn their money. There's still lots of people in town, Chet."

"They're all right," Chet said casually. "They might have done somethin' yesterday but today they'll take it out in talk. Most of these grangers will pull out an' get back to work before the day's over."

Loveless nodded. There was amusement in his eyes. "An' if they don't you'll handle 'em," he suggested.

"They ain't bad people," Chet said. "Let's go get a cup of coffee. I'm dead for sleep an' I want to stay awake."

Leaving the depot, the two walked on down the street toward the center of town. At the jail Joe French was loitering, plainly in evidence. He nodded to the men as they passed. Beyond the jail Otto Hahn was sweeping the collected dirt from the door of the Staghorn and letting it drop down through the cracks in the board sidewalk. At Wolfbarger's Royce Mitchell was getting out of a buckboard. Tom Neil was with Mitchell and he turned and scowled at Chet and Loveless as they passed by.

"Friends of ours," Loveless commented dryly as he and Chet went into the restaurant. "That's what I was stayin' in town for, Chet. Wait till them two get ahold of Powell Overman, an' old Bob Jumper an' Alec Crow come up an' join 'em. Then we'll see what it's all about."

Chet nodded. "Coffee," he said to the waitress. "Are you goin' to talk to them, Barney?"

Loveless shook his head. "I'll let Claypool do the talkin'," he answered. "Crow and Neil get loans at the bank." The old man chuckled contentedly. He knew just about what Claypool would tell the cowmen: Trouble in the Rifle Rock and your loans will be called. That's what the banker would say. "Here's the coffee, Chet," Loveless completed.

Royce Mitchell and Tom Neil, leaving their team in front of Wolfbarger's, went into the store. They found Wolfbarger in his office in the rear and the merchant spent a stormy fifteen minutes with the cowmen. They could not understand why, as foreman of the coroner's jury, he had allowed that verdict to go through, and they said so plainly. When they started getting too rough Wolfbarger surprised them.

"I've carried both of you for years!" he announced. "From the time you sold your calves till you sold your steers and then till you sold your calves again. If you don't like my way of doing business you can trade someplace else, and see if they will carry you!"

Mitchell and Neil looked at the merchant with surprise. The cowmen had always been the kings in the Rifle Rock and it was almost as though a subject had rebelled against an overlord.

When they left the store the two cowmen took their buckboard and drove to Powell Overman's house. There, in Mark Scotia's old office, they found Powell Overman and gloomy Alec Crow. Jumper had not yet come in and Stevens had not been reached. The men sat down and scowled at each other. Mitchell, turning to Overman, broke the silence.

"Why'd you let Minor take Ames?" he snapped. "He took Ames right out of your camp."

"I wasn't there," Overman answered with asperity.

"Well," Neil snapped, "if you'd done somethin' last night you could have got Ames out. You could have brought your outfit to town . . ."

"Now see here," Powell Overman interrupted. "The time when you can do that sort of thing an' get away with it is gone by. There were fifty nesters in Rifle Rock last night and there'd have been a fight. If we'd tried anything like that the whole country would have been against us."

"Looks like they're against us now," Mitchell said moodily. "Tom an' me stopped to talk to Wolfbarger. He said if we didn't like the way he did business we could take our tradin' someplace else. The hell of it is I owe him about six hundred dollars an' I'm short of cash."

Neil nodded. Powell Overman spoke again. "There's no real case against Ames," he said. "I doubt if the grand jury will indict him. And if it does a smart lawyer will get him out."

"Well," Alec Crow agreed slowly, "that's so."

"And I don't think Ames has done a job for us anyhow," Overman proceeded. "There's been some nesters left the country and there's been these two killed. That's all he's done. He ain't worth the money we've paid him."

"That damned Minor," Neil flared. "He's throwed in with the nesters. They're goin' to run him for sheriff this fall. He goes out an' brings Ames in without firin' a shot. I tell you, Powell, we got to get rid of him!"

"I told Ames that," Overman agreed. "The Screwplate is watchin' Chet Minor like he was their baby. Ames went out an' looked it over an' said there was no chance of doin' anything about Chet Minor."

"I'm goin' to do somethin'," Neil vowed. "I whipped him once an' . . ."

"You try it now an' you'll find out it's different," Crow interposed. "Minor had just come back from the hospital when you jumped him. Now he's been workin' an' he's packin' a gun. An' if you down him you'll have old Laramie to tangle with an' I want no part of that old devil. He's bad."

Solemn nods ran around the circle.

"I think we can take care of Minor," Overman said. "We've got to. But we can't do it right away. Feeling is too high."

Again the circle nodded. "Then what are we goin' to do?" Mitchell asked.

"I'm goin' to talk to Ames," Powell Overman said. "I'll tell him that we'll get him a lawyer an' get him free. That's all we can do right now. We've got the brandin' to look after an' everybody's busy. We'll let the excitement die down an' then we'll take care of Minor."

Gloomy nods showed acceptance of the statement. Royce Mitchell got up. "I've got a crew at work," he announced. "I'm goin' out an' look after them. Hell, this is a mess!"

"I've got calves to brand, too," Neil said. "You talk to Ames, Powell. After all, we hired him. We can't let him down."

"I'll talk to Ames," Powell agreed.

And so the meeting broke up, the men filing out of the office and on out of the house. Alone in the office Powell Overman studied the wall opposite him. Mitchell had been right. It was a mess, and the chief ingredient, so far as Powell Overman could see, was Chet Minor. Chet Minor headed it all up. Without Minor, Barney Loveless would not take a hand, the Screwplate would not be against the other ranches and without Chet Minor the nesters would have no real leader. Overman knew that. He scowled at the wall. Chet Minor, damn him!

Just after dinner — a meal that he did not enjoy, for Kirkpatrick, as well as Maida, was present — Powell Overman went downtown. When he reached the jail Overman saw Laramie loitering near by. Laramie eyed the rancher sharply but said nothing and Overman went into the building. Honeyman, one of Overman's own riders, and the old jailor were in the office and they made no objection to Powell's talking with Ed Ames. The jailor took Overman on back to the cell, let him in, and retired.

Ed Ames had finished eating dinner; the tray containing his empty dishes was on the floor beside the door. Ames sat on the bunk in the cell, smoking, and when the jailor was gone Ames spoke to his visitor.

"It's about time you came around," he said, blowing smoke toward the ceiling.

"I've been fixin' things up," Overman answered. "We talked it over this mornin', Mitchell an' Neil an' some of the rest of us. There's bad feelin' in town, Ed."

"I know it," Ames answered surlily. "That's why I'm here. I was damn' glad to be put into jail yesterday."

"Now look, Ed," Powell Overman said, "you sit tight. We're goin' to get you a lawyer. The case against you is just circumstantial evidence. They can't make it stick. I don't think the grand jury will even find a true bill. You . . ."

"Yo're damned right they won't!" Ames snapped. "I'm not comin' before the grand jury. Yo're goin' to get me out of here, Overman."

The rancher shook his head. "Feelin' is too high," he objected. "If we tried to get you out we'd . . ."

"Listen" — Ames's voice was low and intent — "I laid out above Olson's place all the day that Laird was killed. I told you I wouldn't kill the doctor. I never saw Olson, but when I came back to camp I saw somethin'."

"What?" Overman demanded.

"I saw you ridin' in." Ames's voice was ominous. "I know where you'd been. I back-trailed you until it was too dark to see an' I know where you'd come from an' what you'd done. Yo're goin' to get me out of here, Overman. You don't want me standin' up before a grand jury an' tellin' what I know about you. It was you that killed Laird an' I can prove it!"

Under his tan Powell Overman's face turned pale. Ed Ames, pressing his advantage, spoke again. "Yo're goin' to get a gun in here to me," he stated. "Yo're goin' to have a horse outside where I can get him. Yo're goin' to be right there with the horse an' yo're goin' to help me out of the country. You think I'll lay here an' let you hang it on me? Not me! Yo're goin' to do those things tonight or I'll stand right up on my hind legs an' tell what I know!"

"Don't talk so loud, Ed," Powell Overman pleaded. "Somebody will hear you. I'll help you out. I'll do it."

"Yo're damned right you'll do it," Ames snapped. "Now listen to what I tell you."

He bent forward a little and Powell Overman, coming close, leaned down to listen, nodding his head at intervals.

202

It was mid-afternoon before Chet Minor came down to the jail. Laramie was still loitering in the vicinity but when he saw Chet he came over and spoke.

"Overman was in to see Ames," he announced. "Clarke's in there now."

Chet nodded. "You better go along," he observed. "I'll take the job on for a while."

"I'll get somethin' to eat," Laramie said. "Most of the nesters have left town an' I don't think the cowmen are goin' to start anything. I saw Mitchell an' Neil pull out awhile ago."

"Crow has gone too," Chet said. "I saw him leave. All right, Laramie."

Laramie strolled off and Chet leaned against the corner of the jail building. He was there when Clarke thrust his head out of the door and saw him.

"Ames wants to see you, Minor," he called. "He's been askin' for you."

Chet answered the summons, limping up the steps and into the office.

"You can't wear a gun back to see him," Clarke announced, eyeing the weapon at Chet's hip. "You ain't supposed to wear a gun in town at all."

Chet unlatched his belt and, folding it around the holster, dumped the bundle down on the desk. "Supposed to an' does are different," he said shortly. "I'll get that when I come back."

Clarke frowned but made no comment. "Come on, I'll take you back," he said.

Chet followed the officer through a door and down a short corridor to the cell. "Clarke said you wanted to see me," he said to Ames, who came to the cell door.

"I do," Ames answered.

From the office Vance Murray called to Clarke. The sheriff went to answer the summons and Ed Ames spoke again. "I don't just get you, Minor," he said. "I thought you was a man that tended to his own business."

"I do," Chet agreed.

"It wasn't your business to bring me in," Ames refuted. "If I'd killed a man it was the job of the officers to get me. You got clear out of line."

"I don't see it that way," Chet answered. "You'd killed a friend of mine. You . . ."

"I never killed the doctor!" Ames interrupted. "Believe it or not, it wasn't me."

There was the ring of utter sincerity in the man's voice and Chet looked at him questioningly. "I've done some things that maybe you wouldn't consider just right," Ames said, "but I didn't down Laird."

"Your tracks," Chet began.

"Not my tracks," Ames said. "You saw another trail besides that one, didn't you, Minor?"

Chet's thoughts flashed back to the trailing. He nodded. "We saw another trail," he agreed reluctantly.

"I thought so." There was satisfaction in Ed Ames's voice. "You find out who had a reason to kill Laird an' you'll find it wasn't me."

"But you were hired . . ." Chet began.

"You don't know why I was hired or who hired me, for sure," Ames said. "I got you back here, Minor, to tell you that I didn't kill Laird, an' to tell you somethin' else. They'll never make that charge stick. I'll be out of here an' when I get out I'm goin' to look you up. A man ought to stick to his own business an' you didn't stick to yours."

"It'll suit me for you to look me up," Chet assured. "You've tried it before. You took a shot at me up at the Rock Springs, didn't you?"

"An' you killed my horse," Ames answered. "He dropped on me when I'd got about five miles away. Bled to death. I laid out all night an' made it back an' you pulled me in. I'd have laid off you, Minor, but you wouldn't have it that way."

"You were lookin' for me when you came to the camp," Chet reminded.

"Suppose I was? That's business."

Chet nodded. "You won't get out, Ames," he said. "You killed Laird an' I know it. If you do get out you won't look for me any harder than I'll look for you. But you won't get out."

Ames grinned impudently. "Yes, I will," he boasted. "I'll be out of here. There's a man goin' to help me." The grin suddenly became hard. "I got too much on Overman for him to let me stay here. Overman an' some others. I'll be lookin' for you, Minor."

"An' I'll be lookin' for you," Chet replied.

"That's right," Ames agreed. "Now we know where we stand. So long, Minor. I'll see you." He left the cell door and walked back to the bed. Chet hesitated a moment and then turned and going to the office picked up his gun. Neither Clarke nor Murray, who were in the office, spoke to him, and Chet went on out.

A peculiar man, Ed Ames. A man with a different outlook on life. He was in a tight spot and knew it; still his anger against Chet Minor was not because of the position he was in but rather because he did not think that Chet had tended to his own business. A peculiar man and a peculiar outlook. Chet leaned against the jail wall. Ed Ames had said that he did not kill Laird, had pointed out that there was another trail. Suppose Ames was telling the truth? Suppose Ed Ames had not killed the doctor, then who? Chet shrugged. He was thinking needlessly. Ames had killed Dr. Laird and there was no more to it. Still the thoughts would not die down.

Chet stayed near by the jail the remainder of the afternoon. Burgess and another of the nesters came and talked with him before leaving town. The district attorney had not come in on the noon train but would be in that evening, Burgess thought. He was gruff and a little apologetic.

"I see how you figured it, Minor," he said before he left Chet. "You were right, too. If we'd gone ahead yesterday there'd have been big trouble an' we'd have been in the wrong. An' it wouldn't have done you any good this fall when the election came up."

"I wasn't thinkin' about the election exactly," Chet said. "I'd brought Ames in. I wanted him to have a square shake."

"That's more than he ever gave one of us," Burgess said. "An' we ain't forgot Ray Quick."

Burgess and his friend left and Chet wandered across the street and sat down on the porch of the store opposite the jail. Barney Loveless came and sat beside him and the two loafed comfortably, not talking, just letting the sun soak in.

But there were other places in Rifle Rock where no such peace prevailed. At Mark Scotia's house Powell Overman worked feverishly in the study. There was a shell belt and a holster on the desk before Overman and a little pile of sand and a pair of pliers. The dull blue gun for the holster lay on the corner of the desk.

With the pliers Powell worried out the lead bullets from the shells and dumped the glistening black powder down on a paper. He replaced the powder with a little sand, shoved the leads back into the brass cartridges and laid them aside. He worked rapidly, his hands trembling a little. When he finished he erased the plier marks as best he could, scraping the lead with his knife, and then, loading the gun, stuffed shells into the loops of the belt. Finished with the job he put gun and belt in a desk drawer and went out of the house. As he walked down the hall he heard Maida laugh at something that Kirkpatrick had said, and Powell's scowl deepened.

There were horses in the barn Mark Scotia had built behind his town house: the mounts that Overman and his men had used coming in from camp, and the buggy team. These latter were bays, matched and unmarked with the Triangle brand. Powell Overman hesitated and then shrugged. There was no need of taking a chance on any of the horses. He would leave them where they

207

were. He went back into the house and on to the office. There he sat down and waited, waited interminably, it seemed.

When dusk settled, Overman took gun and belt from the drawer, put it on, concealing it under his coat, and then, taking his hat, went out. He walked rapidly toward the town, reaching Idaho Street and traveling down it. At the supper hour Idaho Street was almost deserted and Powell Overman did not see Joe French, lurking in the shadows across the street from the jail.

Overman stopped at the jail and then, after a moment's hesitation, went in. Honeyman, who was there alone, did not hesitate about letting his boss go back to see the prisoner.

After a short time Powell Overman returned to the jail office and, sitting on the edge of the desk, engaged Honeyman in conversation.

"How is it going, Bill?" he asked.

Honeyman grinned. "Pretty good, Boss," he said. "It beats flankin' calves a mile. We been ribbin' ol' man Sykes all afternoon, tellin' him we're goin' to leave him alone with Ames tonight. The old man is about loco. He's got a shotgun loaded with buckshot over there in the corner an' he can't keep his hands off it."

"You aren't goin' to leave him, are you, Bill?" Overman asked.

Bill Honeyman laughed. "We may step out for a minute," he said. "We're goin' to send him back with Ames's supper. I'm waitin' for Shorty an' Vance to come back now. Sykes is scared to death."

208

Sykes was the jailor, a pensioner of the town being taken care of in his old age.

Overman frowned. "You know," he said, "I don't believe I'd do that, Bill. Ed Ames is dangerous. You can't tell what he'll do."

"He's got a fat chance of doin' anything," Honeyman retorted. "There'll be me an' Shorty an' Vance here all night, not to speak of Sykes an' his shotgun. An' besides that, there's either Minor or Laramie or Joe French hangin' around outside all the time. Ames wouldn't have a chance to make a break. If he did he'd be cut down right now."

"Don't fool with him," Overman warned. "If he starts to get out you shoot first an' shoot straight."

Honeyman looked at his boss. "Don't worry," he said. "Ed Ames has got too much sense to try a break. He knows that they ain't got much on him anyhow. I been talkin' to him some an' he ain't a bit worried."

Powell Overman was dissatisfied but he had done the best he could. With a casual "so long" to Bill Honeyman he went on out into the street.

At nine o'clock Rifle Rock looked like Rifle Rock always looked. Idaho Street was dark save for the lights in the saloons and in the jail. There were not many men on the street, nor was there any great number in the saloon. The men that passed along the street stopped and spoke to Chet Minor and Laramie who were across the street from the jail, loitering on the porch of the Bon Ton store, hidden in the darkness under the awnings. On the corners the street lamps burned, the pride of Rifle Rock, the one mark of civic advancement.

The lamp-lighter had made his rounds at dusk, placing his ladder against the lamp posts, climbing up to open the side of the lamps and touch his torch to their wicks. Rifle Rock was peaceful.

Across from Chet and Laramie, where the lamp in the jail office burned bright, there was the sound of sudden laughter and men's voices.

"Pretty happy over there," Chet said to his companion. "Somebody told a good one."

"Bill Honeyman," Laramie predicted. "Bill is always pullin' some sort of stunt. One time . . ." Laramie stopped abruptly. The laughter had ceased in the jail and it was very quiet. In the silence that followed Laramie's words a horse stamped somewhere down the street. Then, sudden as a stroke of the summer lightning that was flickering over the mesas to the west, there was an explosion in the jail. Red flashed before the window, and a shot roared. Following that sound voices broke out, high and excited. Chet Minor and Laramie were halfway across the street, running, guns in their hands, before the echoes of the shot died away.

Thrusting the door open Chet broke through it, then stopped stock still. Laramie, coming behind him could not check in time and his push sent Chet further into the room. Ed Ames lay on the floor, blood already trailing from his body. In one corner Old Man Sykes held his shotgun poised, and Shorty Thomas and Bill Honeyman stood, the surprise not yet wiped from their faces, and Vance Murray was just getting up from behind the desk.

"What happened?" Chet demanded.

"He was tryin' to make a break," Sykes shrilled. "I gonnies *I* stopped him!"

CHAPTER
FIFTEEN

The shot had brought Rifle Rock from its peacefulness. Men came running along Idaho Street, some of them with guns in their hands. Jim Clarke, arriving breathless from the hotel, took charge of the situation. It was Clarke who asked the questions and got the answers. Chet and Laramie, in the jail office, heard it all.

The story was simple enough. Honeyman and Shorty, with Vance Murray aiding and abetting them, had been riding Old Man Sykes. They had told Sykes that they were going to leave him alone with Ames, that there was no use of their all staying awake all night. Sykes had protested the plan vigorously and the deputies had been enjoying themselves. It was Sykes's protestations that had caused the bursts of laughter.

Ed Ames, from his cell, had called to Vance and Murray had told Sykes to answer. The old man refused and, still laughing, Murray had gone back to see what Ames wanted. Arriving at the cell he had been confronted by a gun in Ames's hand.

Murray had no choice. Under Ames's direction he had unlocked the cell and let the man out, preceding him to the office which afforded the one exit to the building. As they came into the office Ames had ordered the men to stand against the wall and keep their hands up. He would kill Vance, he said, if they did not obey him; and they believed him. Sykes, however, had taken a chance. Frightened, and with the memory of all the ribbing he had taken uppermost in his mind, the old man had dived for his shotgun and come up with it.

"Ames swung his gun on him an' pulled it off," Shorty said in concluding the story. "The gun just snapped an' Sykes up with the shotgun an' let her go. Lord! He just cut Ames in two!"

That statement was substantiated. Ames's body had been placed upon a bench and there was a pool of blood under it. Examination showed that all nine buckshot had taken effect in his chest and abdomen. The man had never known what hit him.

"You gi'me a shotgun loaded with buckshot every time!" Old Man Sykes shrilled in satisfaction. "You can keep yore ol' Winchesters an' yore ol' pistols. I'll take a shotgun every time," he repeated.

Clarke cleared the office after that, ordering the men out. They went reluctantly. Outside on the street, Laramie spoke to Chet.

"That's that," he said callously. "I reckon we can all go back to punchin' cows tomorrow."

Chet nodded. "I wonder where he got the gun," he said.

"Nobody'll ever know," Laramie stated. "There's been men in an' out of there all day. Sykes sure is ruin with a shotgun, ain't he? I guess that misfire saved the old man's life."

"I guess it did at that," Chet said. "We'd better hunt up Joe an' Mr. Loveless an' tell 'em what's happened."

"I guess we had," Laramie agreed.

Now there was truly nothing to hold Chet Minor in Rifle Rock. Chet realized that as he rode out of town the following morning, Joe French and Laramie on either side of him. Nothing now to keep him in Rifle Rock and suddenly he realized there was nothing to keep him in the Rifle Rock country. There was the claim, of course, but with Barney Loveless furnishing the money, he could pre-empt the claim and turn it over to Loveless. And when that was done he would have a little stake. There were other countries and other ranges. If Sally Laird had stayed in the valley . . . As Chet thought about Sally he could see the girl's face as he had seen it so often: happy and the brown eyes filled with laughter. He could see it again as it was when he had helped the girl into the car vestibule, sad and sorrowful. Had that been only yesterday?

"Thinkin' about how you'll run things when yo're sheriff?" Joe French gibed.

Chet grinned at Joe and shook his head. "No," he answered. "I won't run for sheriff, Joe."

He would not run for that office, he thought. There was no need of it now. Ed Ames was dead and it was not likely that the cattlemen would make such another attempt in the Rifle Rock. They had had their lesson and they had seen the power of the newcomers. And too, the cowmen had found that their own people, the townsmen of Rifle Rock, would rise up against them when matters came to bloodshed and killing.

"I don't think I'll be here," Chet amplified to Joe French. "Not after round-up is over."

Joe looked startled and started to say something. Laramie grunted. "There's other countries," Laramie said, as though he understood.

"There's other countries," Chet agreed.

Earl Keelin had moved the camp. It was further east now, at the Rock Springs cabin. Amador had the wagons parked in front of the cabin and he was glad to see Joe French return. Earl was a salty wagon boss, according to Amador, and hard to get along with. And Ben Revilla had pulled out, Amador told them, and they were short-handed as hell and weren't working much country. While he made coffee and cooked a meal, Amador told Joe French and Chet and Laramie all about the happenings at the camp during French's absence.

Before the meal was finished Pete McGrath came down from the mesa behind the cabin with a drive that he threw into the wire corral down below the horse corral and the shed. Another drive came in, and then another. Shortly the wagon crew was assembled. They were making short circles, bringing in only what they could brand and turn loose in a day, and that was not many cattle, short-handed as they were.

The remuda came in and went into the horse corral and while the crew ate dinner Joe French recounted the happenings in the town of Rifle Rock. There was silence about the camp-fire save only for the scrape of a fork or

215

spoon across a tin dish, but when Joe had finished there was talk and comment. It was inevitable that Chet was one of the subjects of that talk. He put his plate and utensils in the wreck pan and walked over to the cabin and went in. He did not want to listen. Inside, the cabin was dusty and a pack rat had been busy, as a littered corner testified. The familiar walls were unfamiliar. Chet looked about. Each small thing that he had done, each nail he had driven to make a convenient hook, the new rawhide hinge he had put on the cupboard door, the rag stuffed in the broken window, the post that he had cut and fitted to replace a broken leg on the table, reminded Chet of some happening. Each had a connection in his mind. Chet heard the men moving out by the wagons and went out, ready to take up the work just where he had dropped it so short a time ago.

"You'll rope, Chet," Joe French said. "Have at it, cowboy." And Chet followed Joe down to the corral and picked out the horse he wanted and waited while Joe snagged him out. The last few days and nights were an interlude, an unbelievable dream. Here was work. Here were the cattle and here was the crew, and the last few days were a nightmare that he had dreamed in the night.

They were done with the branding as the sun went down and the twilight came. Supper was ready: beef and potatoes and biscuits and syrup and canned corn, the hardy food that hard-working men need to stoke their muscles. They ate and lounged around the fire. Chet, isolating himself beside a wagon-wheel, let the others talk. The conversation, of course, pertained to

216

Ed Ames and Dr. Laird, and the things that had happened in Rifle Rock. For a long time men would talk of those things whenever they assembled. And then, gradually, that talk would die away and grass and water, cattle and horses, rains and news from town, the really important things of the range country, would supplant it. Away down below, in the creek bottom, rocks rattled and Joe French, getting to his feet said, "That'll be Loveless. He said that he would make the camp tonight."

It was Barney Loveless. He rode his horse into the camp, stopped and dismounted, and came stiffly over to the fire.

"Next time," Loveless said, "I'll take the buckboard, no matter what happens. I'm too old to ride so far."

From the wagon he got a plate and cup and loaded the plate with food. Then, from the coffee pot beside the blaze, he poured his coffee and squatted down companionably, beginning to eat.

"Olson's foot is better," Loveless said, between mouthfuls. "Doc Frawley says that he can come home tomorrow or the next day. I stopped at his place an' told the kids." The old man chewed and swallowed and then spoke again. "Them Olson kids are blame' good younguns," he said. "They're lookin' after things just like a man would. That oldest girl is ramroddin' the whole works. She sent up after Laird's cow an' she's got 'em all workin'."

"Did they find out who gave Ames that gun?" Laramie asked.

Loveless shook his head. "They ain't tryin' very hard," he said. "Clarke's kind of satisfied that he's got the matter off his hands. He's ready to call the deal closed. Ames killed Laird an' Ames is dead an' that winds up Jim's ball of yarn for him just right. He can go back to Conejos an' sit in his office an' let the deputies do the work."

The ranchman lifted his coffee cup, took a swallow and swore feelingly as he put the cup down. "Damn a tin cup anyhow! When the coffee's hot the cup's too hot to drink out of, an' when the cup cools off the coffee's cold. I never knew it to fail."

"Anything else new in town?" French asked.

"Ben Revilla came in to get a coffin for his sister," Loveless answered. "Murray had to go out there. You knew that Ben had a claim in the Amarilla Mesa canyon?"

Heads nodded, and Loveless, disposing of another mouthful of food, continued. "Ben had two of his sisters out at his place lookin' after it for him, Rosa an' that older Revilla girl, Petra. Rosa committed suicide yesterday."

"Suicide?" Several voices echoed the word.

Loveless nodded. "Ben went home when he left the wagon, an' told Rosa about Doc Laird. She took Ben's gun an' shot herself. She was goin' to have a baby an' she wasn't married."

The ranchman looked around the circle, eyeing each man, and then spoke again. "Nobody seems to know who had been foolin' with her. Ben came in an' bought the most expensive coffin Wolfbarger had. Paid cash for

218

it. Then he started to get drunk. I got hold of him an' found that other sister, Rufina, the one that's married to Julian Quintana. I took him over to her place an' she kept him there. Ben said that they'd bury Rosa out at his claim."

"I wonder why he camped in Amarilla Mesa canyon," Joe French said. "Ben never had any use for land. He was always there in town."

"I kind of wondered myself," Loveless agreed. "An' I wonder where he got the money to pay for the casket. It's a sure thing he didn't make it while he worked with the wagon."

"The Revillas are an old family here," Keelin said. "Didn't Ben's grandfather marry one of Alec Crow's wife's sisters?"

Loveless nodded and French said, "Maybe Alec is puttin' up the money for Ben."

Loveless shook his head. "Alec Crow wasn't in town," he countered. "They sent word out to him an' Gra'maw Crow. Wolfbarger didn't charge Ben with the coffin either. Ben paid cash for it." He changed the subject. "How many calves have you got in the last few days, Earl?"

Earl Keelin answered that question and the talk fell away from Ben Revilla and became the prosaic account of the round-up work. Chet Minor, thinking about Ben Revilla, scarcely listened to that talk. For those first few weeks following his return to Rifle Rock, Ben had been Chet's friend. The friendship had not gone very deep, that was true. Ben had stayed with Chet only as long as the money lasted, but still it had been a sort of friendship.

"When are they goin' to bury the girl?" Chet asked abruptly.

"They planned on doin' it today," Loveless answered. "Her bein' a suicide they couldn't have a priest, an' I guess they wanted to get it over with."

"Oh," Chet said, and walked back toward the wagon. He sat there, staring moodily at the fire while the talk went on. He would have liked to attend the funeral, just out of courtesy to Ben.

The fire died down and the talk waned. Men went to the bed wagon and pulled down their rolls. Presently Chet dragged his own bed from the wagon and unrolled it. He turned in, pulling off his boots and his clothing, sliding down between the blankets. They were damp and cold. He must air his bed tomorrow, Chet thought. Let the sun bake the body moisture from it. Flat on his back he stared up at the stars. Poor Ben. He had thought a lot of Rosa. She had been his favorite of the three girls. And someone had betrayed her and, desperate, she had killed herself. Life hadn't been worth living. Chet could appreciate that. He had seen the time when life was not worth living.

In the morning the work began once more, the never-ending work. Within two days the crew was augmented by the return of Sven Olson and the arrival of the nester, Hall. As the wagon moved north Pearl Suplan left to return to his own outfit, his place being taken by the rider that Stevens had sent as a representative with the Triangle wagon. Later Pete

McGrath also went back south and Jesse Lauder came back to ride with the Screwplate. Monotonously day followed day, circle followed circle, branding followed branding, and always at the end of the day's work Chet Minor felt as though he had left something undone, some task not accomplished. That feeling bothered him, hanging to him, clinging to his shoulders like an old man of the sea. And too, the emptiness remained, the hollow feeling in him that had come with the departure of Sally Laird. Chet Minor was a silent man in those days toward the end of the round-up, a man who did his work and did it well, who was pleasant and competent, and yet a little aloof.

They were past the Screwplate now and working the northern ranches of the Tramparas, the Bar O7 country. Rifle Rock town was miles away. The Rock Springs and Rock Creek lay far to the south. In the broken mesa country the work was harder and still it pressed on toward a close.

Clyde Stevens was often with the wagon now, a tall thin man with the stamp of the Texan hard upon him. Occasionally Barney Loveless came up from his headquarters to see how the work progressed. Stevens had but little to say and that little criticism, but Loveless brought the news of the lower country. The news was trivial.

With a week left before the end of June and with only a little over a week's work left for the wagon, Stevens came to camp. Chet was just bringing in a drive when the ranchman rode out to meet him. Stevens swung his horse in beside Chet, looking at the cattle, and asked a question. "You ride Block Mesa?"

Chet nodded.

"These all you get?"

"Yes," Chet said.

Stevens eyed the rider and then looked at the cattle again. "What did you pick up at that water hole on the south end?" he asked.

"I got that line-back cow an' a calf, an' those three two-year-old cows an' a dry cow," Chet answered.

"That all there was there?"

The question in itself impugned Chet's work and ability. For a bare instant he was angry. Then, seeing that Stevens meant no offense, he answered evenly. "Every one. I combed out that country under the rim."

"There was a curled-horn cow there with a mottle-face calf," Stevens said. "Right at that spring not a week ago. An' this ain't but about half the cattle that I saw on the mesa."

"Two of us went up there," Chet said. "Curly an' me. Curly thought that there was a bunch of cattle there but these were all we got an' he went on over west to see if he could find some more."

Stevens nodded and swung out from Chet to bring a cow and calf along. There was no more talk between them before they reached the round-up grounds.

When Curly, one of Stevens' riders, came in with a little drive, the ranchman went to talk with him. Presently Curly and Stevens came to where Chet sat his horse.

222

"Curly didn't see that crooked-horn either," Stevens said, "an' there's another marker or two missin'. Minor, somebody is throwin' cattle back into country that has been worked, or else they're takin' them clear out of the country. Curly saw some horse tracks over where he was."

"There were fresh tracks at the spring, too," Chet said. "I thought you'd been over there."

"Not since before it rained," Stevens said, referring to a rain that had fallen a week before.

"You better talk to Joe," Chet suggested. "He's comin' in now."

Stevens loped away to join French who was bringing a drive up from the south and Curly, cocking a leg over his saddle swell, began the fashioning of a cigarette.

"Somebody," said Curly, "is figurin' to steal some calves. The old man has been suspicious since these nesters hit the country. If I know him there's due to be some hell poppin'."

Chet shrugged. "The nesters might take a calf or two," he said. "They might butcher a beef, but that would be when the weather was cold an' they could keep the meat. I don't think the nesters are the rustlers. Why would they work way up here?"

"I don't know," Curly admitted. "If it ain't the nesters, then who?"

"Somebody who knows the country and would like to use the nesters for an excuse," Chet answered. "There's no use in blamin' everything that goes sour around here on the nesters."

French and Stevens were riding over toward Chet and his companions, talking as they rode. They were still talking when they arrived and French was pushing home a point.

". . . As good as Laramie," he was saying. "Better maybe. He's the best trailer I ever rode with."

"All right," Stevens agreed. "Send him then."

French looked at Chet. "You won't rope this evenin'," he announced. "I want you an' Curly to make a big swing over east of us. Cut sign all the way an' see what you find an' if you see any unbranded stuff let it alone. Just mark where it is."

Chet nodded and Curly grinned. "See?" he said to Chet when Stevens and French had departed. "I told you there'd be somethin' doin'. The old man's on the warpath."

Chet grunted.

They rode out as soon as they had eaten, mounted on fresh horses, the best circle horses that either had in his mount. Curly, because this was his country, took charge and indicated the direction they would follow. That was agreeable with Chet.

They went straight west and then angled toward the south, dropping into a rough, broken country that had been worked three days before. To Chet it looked as though this would be good country for the thing they sought, and he said so. Curly agreed and they worked the territory out carefully and patiently.

It was nearly sundown when that patience was rewarded. Chet was low in a draw and Curly half a mile away on a rise when Chet saw a crooked-horned cow and a calf beside her. There was quite a bunch of cattle near the crooked-horn. Chet lifted his arm, waving his hand to attract Curly's attention, and when he saw Curly coming down toward him, rode over to the cattle. He was riding through the bunch when Curly joined him.

"Is that the crooked-horn?" Chet asked.

"Yeah," Curly agreed.

"Her calf ain't branded," Chet said. "There's a dozen more cows with calves in here an' none of the calves have got a mark on 'em except an earmark."

"That's Julio Tidd's earmark," Curly stated. "Regular rustler's mark. He crops both ears."

"I reckon," Chet drawled, "he's a regular rustler. There's several dry cows an' some steers in here too, Curly."

"Yeah," Curly said again. "Looks like he wasn't satisfied with just the calves."

Chet shrugged. "We found what we were lookin' for," he announced. "Let's go back to camp."

For answer, Curly turned his horse.

They reached the camp late and finding Stevens there, reported to him. It was plain enough to Stevens, to Chet and Curly and to Joe French, the four that formed the consulting group. Julio Tidd, with or without companions but probably with several helpers, had picked up cattle in country that had not been covered by the round-up, and moved those animals into country that the wagon crew had worked. There Tidd had earmarked the calves to his marking. Later, when it was safer to do so, he would brand the calves, probably sometime after they were weaned, but more likely when the wagon had finished work and he could move the cattle to a safe spot. He would cut the calves away from their mothers, leave the cows and wean the calves.

"He's goin' to have quite a herd of cattle if he keeps that up," Joe French prophesied. "It's sure a start in the cow business."

Stevens was in no mood for humor. "Dry cows an' steers in the bunch too, was there?" he asked.

"More of them than wet cows," Curly answered.

"They were what he was after," Stevens said. "The calves were just a sideline."

"The sideline will likely get him in trouble," Chet commented, dryly. "Takin' that crooked-horn marker cow an' then earmarkin' those calves with his own earmark I'd say was a mistake. If I'd been doin' it I'd have used your earmark, Mr. Stevens. An earmark is easy changed later on. All a man needs is a knife. But then Julio never was very smart."

Stevens was scowling. "We got to catch him at it," he said. "He'd lie out of hell if he was found there. We got to catch him. When do you think he'll come for those drys an' steers?"

"If it was me I'd move 'em pretty quick," Chet said. "If he waits till the wagons are done he stands a chance of runnin' into some rider an' havin' trouble. When the wagon's workin' you pretty near know where the men are."

"They ain't goin' to be with the wagon this time," Stevens snapped. "Joe, I want you to let Minor come along with me. We're goin' to lay out an' watch them cattle day an' night."

Joe French glanced quickly at Chet. Chet made a rueful grimace.

"Wouldn't you ruther have one of yore own men?" French asked.

"I want Minor," Stevens answered. "Him or Laramie. I'd ruther have Minor. How about it?" He turned to Chet.

"Why, I'll go," Chet said. There was no way of backing out.

"When do you think they'll pick 'em up?" Stevens asked. "At night or . . . ?"

"I'd say early mornin' or late in the evenin'," Chet answered. "There's not a moon an' they could hardly be sure of what they had at night."

"An' they wouldn't move cattle in the daytime," Stevens said. "All right, we'll go out tomorrow. It's too late to do anything tonight."

Stevens strode away and Curly grinned at Chet. "I don't envy you none," he said. "I told you the old man was a heller!"

"See what you get for bein' such an outlaw-tamer?" Joe French echoed Curly's grin. "You'll lay out on the rocks tomorrow an' the next day an' maybe the next, or I don't know Stevens. He's out for meat."

"Well," Chet returned the grin, "it'll be better than workin' for a hard-hearted boss anyhow. I'm goin' to get some supper, Joe."

CHAPTER
SIXTEEN

Chet and Clyde Stevens left the wagons early the next morning, left before there was a hint of dawn in the sky. They carried cold food and two canteens with them, and Joe French, watching their departure, spoke to Chet.

"Looks like a regular war party," he jested. "All you need is the paint."

Chet was putting Joe's rifle into the scabbard on his saddle while Joe spoke. "An' we likely won't see a damned thing," he agreed. "I wonder how long this foolishness will last."

"There's no tellin'," Joe answered. "Stevens is hard-headed an' stubborn as a mule. Well, good luck, Chet. I hope you either see 'em or Stevens gets fed up today."

"So do I." Chet's answer was heartfelt. "So long, Joe."

With Stevens beside him they rode out into the blackness. By the time the east was light they were nearly to the rough country and before full daylight had come they were on a bench above the little park country where the crooked-horned cow and her calf grazed.

228

"There's a tank down below at the end of the park," Chet said as he tied his horse in the middle of a piñon thicket. "They water there. We can lay up here an' watch 'em."

Stevens agreed, and so, a good rifle's shot above the park, they bestowed themselves and settled down to wait.

It was foolishness, Chet thought, just a plain waste of time, and as the day wore along he was sure of it. Stevens had not much to say and Chet responded to the man's silent mood. But toward the middle of the afternoon, Stevens broke his silence.

"You think this is damned foolishness, don't you?" he asked abruptly. "It ain't. I've done this before. You wait long enough an' keep quiet enough an' things will happen. I hate to spend the time myself an' I hate to take you off the work an' leave Joe short-handed. But it's got to be done. One time in the Rangers, another fellow an' me laid out five days. We caught the man we were lookin' for. It just takes time an' patience."

"Suppose they don't come for these cattle?" Chet asked. "Suppose they get suspicious an' don't get here?"

"We'll try a while an' see," Stevens returned.

He relapsed into his silence after that and Chet lay watching the country below. The day lapsed into evening. Chet yawned. He was tired and sleepy. Evening stretched itself out to sundown and the afterglow.

"You want to go back to the wagon?" Stevens asked.

"Is there any use of stayin' here?" Chet answered.

"Go back an' bring some grub in the mornin'," Stevens said. "I'll stay here."

"There's still light," Chet began.

"They're comin' in below us!" Stevens rasped in a harsh whisper. "Get the horses!"

Down below in the dusk of the park, Chet saw movement. There was something afoot in the park. A man on horseback came through the trees at the edge. Two others joined him, pausing to look over the open ground before them.

"The horses!" Stevens whispered fiercely. Chet slipped back from the rim toward the clump of piñons.

He had the horses untied and out of the trees when Stevens joined him. "They're throwin' the cattle together," Stevens said. "We'll meet 'em at the lower end when they start to drive 'em out. Throw down on 'em, Minor, an' if they try to make a fight of it you better shoot first."

Chet felt a tingling all up and down his back. Stevens was climbing into his saddle. Chet also mounted. They rode off toward the east, circling the park, working down into the little neck that formed the exit from the opening.

They had almost reached the neck when something went wrong. In the park a horse nickered, long and shrill. Stevens' mount tossed his head to answer, and Stevens jerked the horse's head down. Chet had leaned forward, reaching for his horse's head to check any attempt at whinnying, when Stevens went past him. The rancher had spurred his horse when he jerked the reins, and the animal, a young horse, had lunged.

The lunge brought Stevens into the open where he could see. He yelled to Chet, "Come on," and spurred forward. Chet, coming into the opening, could see cattle bunched against the ridge, and beyond the cattle, riders making a hurried retreat. Chet too spurred forward.

Stevens' horse went down, stumbling for what seemed to Chet an immense distance and then falling. Stevens was thrown clear and Chet changed his course to reach the man. The riders beyond the cattle were going up the ridge now, mounting toward its top. Momentarily they were checked by the little rimrock of the ridge. Stevens had scrambled to his feet and he ran to his horse.

He caught the animal as it struggled up, but in place of trying to mount again, the ranchman tugged his rifle from its boot. Chet slid his horse to a stop beside Stevens' animal and as he did so the rifle in the ranchman's hands cracked, sharp as a whiplash.

It was poor shooting light, almost dark and impossible for a man to pull down his front sight into the notch of the rear. Perhaps that was an advantage, for the range was long. Stevens unloaded his gun, shot after shot spewing from its muzzle. The riders had found the way up the rim now and were taking it. One man, two men, went over the rim and disappeared. But the third man did not make it. Just as he reached the top, the third man lurched and fell heavily, trying to hold to his saddle horn. The horse lunged on up over the ridge and the man came sprawling down to lie like a discarded baby doll against the side of the rimrock.

"I got one of them!" Stevens' voice was shrill. Chet suddenly was cold. There was a knot at the pit of his belly and his mouth and tongue were dry. Stevens had lowered the rifle and now he walked toward his horse. Chet was surprised to find that he held the reins in his hand, that his own horse was trembling, ready to buck or run.

"One of the bastards," Stevens said as he came up. "I dropped him. Let's go up an' see who he is."

Stevens mounted and the two rode through, scattering the cattle. Up under the rim of the ridge they stopped and both dismounted. Ben Revilla lay there, sprawled out. He was not trying to move, not trying to get away. His eyes were open and he smiled as he recognized Chet.

Chet bent down over the man, opening his shirt and exposing his chest. There was a hole there, just under the heart. It was no question of doing anything for Ben Revilla; it was simply a question of time before all things were done.

Chet looked up at Stevens. The man's face was hard and implacable. "He's a cow-thief," Stevens said, as though answering something he saw in Chet's eyes. "You'd have done the same."

Chet knew that it was true and looked back at Ben. Revilla was still trying to smile. "Hallo, Chet," he said, his voice a whisper. "Pretty bad, *que no?*"

"Pretty bad, Ben," Chet answered soberly. He stood up then and spoke to Stevens. "One of us better make a swing an' see if we can find his horse before it's clear dark. We're goin' to have to take him in."

232

"I'll go," Stevens said shortly.

The ranchman mounted and took the slope to the break in the rimrock. Searching for that break had stopped Ben Revilla. Chet bent down over the man again while, from above, rocks rattled as Stevens' horse scrambled up.

"Not long," Ben Revilla said. "I don't care, Chet."

There was no use in kidding Revilla. He might live an hour. He might go immediately. He was bleeding internally; there was but little blood from the wound.

"I'll build a fire," Chet said. "There ain't much I can do, Ben, but I can see with a fire." He moved away, his horse, ground tied, watching him as he moved.

Chet came back carrying dry cedar, dragging a big cedar limb in his free hand. He broke the limb against a rock, the smaller branches between his hands. A match flamed, the cedar crackled, and then a little blaze shot skyward.

"Chet!" Ben Revilla's voice was faint.

"Yes, Ben." Instantly Chet was at the man's side.

"You didn't shoot, did you, Chet?"

"No, Ben. I didn't have time."

"I'm . . . kinda glad . . . it wasn't you."

"So am I." Chet's voice was honest.

"Tidd an' Frank Oakes an' me been stealin' 'em," Ben said. "We sold to Runkle. That's why I had the place at Amarilla Mesa. That's why Rosa was there."

"I'm sorry, Ben," Chet said.

"About me? Why? I don't care."

"About you, and about Rosa."

"Rosa was goin' to have a baby." Revilla's voice had sunk to a whisper. His eyes were closed as though that would conserve his strength. "She told Doc Laird when he came to see her. Told him whose baby it was, I mean. Doc said he'd make the baby's father take care of Rosa. He was a married man."

"When was that, Ben?" Chet asked.

"Before round-up started. Before I came with the wagon. Doc was killed right after Rosa told him. He came to see her an' he told her that the man would send some money. Doc was killed on his way home."

For a time only Revilla's hard breathing broke the silence, that and the snap of the cedar in the fire. Then Ben Revilla spoke again.

"Chet?"

"Yes, Ben."

"One time I told you about that horse you were ridin' the day you got hurt?"

"Yes, Ben."

"I . . . told you about those rope marks on his *rump?*"

Faintly into Chet's mind came the recollection of that conversation so many months ago. "About there bein' a rope mark across the horse's rump?" he asked. "I remember."

"An' when you roped that bull, Powell Overman follow you too close. You yell at heem, you say."

"I did," Chet agreed. "He was too close."

"Powell hit your horse with a rope," Revilla whispered. "That make the horse *jomp* an' he was jerk . . . down. I been thinkin' . . . 'bout that."

234

"Take it easy," Chet warned. "Take it easy, Ben. You . . ."

"I don't . . . care," Ben Revilla whispered. "I . . . don't care . . . Chet."

It was quiet then, with only Ben Revilla's harsh breathing breaking the stillness. Chet sat thinking. How badly Powell Overman must have wanted that place! How badly he must have wanted to succeed Eades Druerson. He had been willing to maim and to kill for a chance at the job. Why — Chet shook his head — he and Powell had been friends, had worked together, shared their blankets, borrowed money from each other, taken the rough and the smooth side by side; and because of a job, of money and a girl, Powell had thrown all that overboard, tossed it away. And now Powell had the job, and he had the girl and the job and the girl had pushed him on and on, into hiring murder, into committing murder. Once more Chet Minor shook his head. The things that are in a man and the things that press him along upon a path!

In Ben Revilla's throat a breath caught. The man choked it out, gasped it away, his last breath. The rasping was stilled and only silence remained.

Chet Minor put his hand on Ben's chest. There was no movement, no heart beat there. Up above, the rocks rattled and Clyde Stevens' voice called, "How about it, Minor? I found his horse. Do you think we can get him in?"

Chet stood up. "Easy," he called, and his voice was hard. "All we got to do is pack him. He's dead!"

Stevens came down the trail leading two horses. He stopped, looked at the man on the ground, and then at Chet Minor. "Well," he said uncertainly.

"Let's go," Chet said. "There's nothin' more that we can do here. It was Tidd an' Oakes with him. Let's go."

Later, when they were out of the roughs, when Ben Revilla's horse, with Ben across the saddle, was following along behind, pulling back because he was hard to lead, Stevens broke the silence once more.

"He wasn't much good," said Clyde Stevens. "Never was."

"No," Chet agreed, "Ben wasn't much good." He paused then, and after a brief wait concluded, "But he was a friend to me."

It was necessary that Chet Minor accompany Clyde Stevens to Rifle Rock the next day. It meant a full six hours' trip on horseback, for they were fifty miles from Rifle Rock going across country and more than that by road. To lessen the distance they chose to go on horseback, packing the tarpaulin-wrapped body of Ben Revilla. It was further agreed that they would pick up fresh horses at the Screwplate.

By doing so Chet would lessen by twenty miles the distance his horse would travel.

"I'll go in with him," Chet told Joe French, "an' stay in town as long as I have to. Then I'll pull out an' head back. I'll likely make the Rock Springs camp by tonight an' come on in the mornin'."

Joe French agreed and so Chet joined the waiting Stevens.

236

In a little less than three hours they were at the Screwplate where they ran in fresh horses from the pasture and changed saddles. Loveless was at home and he talked to Chet while Chet took his saddle from his horse and put it on a fresh mount.

"The round-up will be done in another week," Loveless said. "I want you to go back to Rock Springs after that, Chet."

"I've been there long enough for you to pre-empt that now," Chet said. "I don't want to go back to the Rock Springs, Barney."

"I've got to put a hay crew down there right away," Loveless announced. "You'd do me a favor if you'd go down an' look after things. I'm goin' to loan you the money to pre-empt that place anyhow, Chet. You could stay there through the hayin'."

"An' then next winter an' then go on round-up again next spring an' then hay next summer, I suppose," Chet said.

"Well, what's the matter with that?" Loveless asked. "Chet, you could borrow some money from Claypool an' run some stock out of the Rock Springs. You're goin' to be elected sheriff in November, sure as shootin'. Claypool has got that fixed up. All Rifle Rock is for you an' so are the nesters. Conejos is willin' to trade if we'll support . . ."

"I won't be runnin'," Chet said shortly. "I won't be here next fall. I've got to go on now, Barney. I'll stop on the way back. I've got somethin' to tell you."

"Go on then," Loveless said. "Stevens is waitin'."

237

Chet mounted his fresh horse and joined Stevens and they rode away. From the Screwplate to Rifle Rock neither of the men spoke.

In Rifle Rock the two went directly to the jail. Vance Murray hurried over from the Staghorn in time to help carry Ben Revilla's body into the office. He went out again to get a coroner's jury and the justice of the peace, and, Sykes being away at the time, Chet and Stevens were left alone. Stevens sat down on the bench that had held Ed Ames's body. There were still stains on the floor under the bench. Chet went to the arms cabinet in one corner and made a cursory inspection of the firearms there.

He was interested mildly in a gun and belt, and picking it up, pulled a shell from one of the belt loops and toyed with it. The shell was a forty-five. Chet carried a thirty-two twenty. He took out one of his own shells and made a comparison, put his shell back in his belt, and idly tugged at the lead in the forty-five. It gave under his pull, resisted a little, and then the cartridge came apart. Chet, thinking to gauge the powder charge, dumped the contents of the shell in his hand. It was sand. He put it back in the shell and reset the bullet. At that moment Murray came in.

"J. P. will be here in a minute," he said. "I've got a jury comin'. What you got there, Chet?"

"I don't know," Chet said.

Murray came over to him. "That's the gun Ames had when he tried to make his break," he announced. "We're keepin' it. Sort of a curiosity."

238

"It is at that," Chet agreed. "It missed fire when Ames tried to use it, didn't it?"

"Yeah," Vance Murray agreed. "It . . . here comes the J.P."

The inquest was brief. Stevens and Chet gave their evidence and the jury, without leaving the room, returned a verdict. The foreman and his colleagues were agreed that Ben Revilla came to his death at the hands of Clyde Stevens while attempting to steal Stevens' property.

"I'll talk to the prosecutor," the justice said. "He won't want to do anything about this, I know Clyde, but I'll have to talk to him anyhow. In the meantime I'll release you under your own recognizance."

Stevens grunted at that and murmured something about a hell of a fuss over killing a half-breed. Chet talked to Vance Murray and exacted Murray's promise to look after Ben Revilla. He would inform Alec Crow of Revilla's death and also see that Ben's sister, now in town, was informed. Stevens had gone with the justice down to his real estate office to swear out warrants against Julio Tidd and Frank Oakes and Runkle.

"There's nothing to keep me then," Chet said to Vance Murray. "I'll head back to the wagon. Joe's short-handed with me gone, an' we want to finish up. We just got a shirt-tail of country to work before we're done."

He left Murray and going across to the Bon Ton, bought a half pound of coffee and a box of crackers; then mounting, he rode out of town.

Chet had plenty of time to make the Rock Springs before dark. He did not hurry but let his horse walk, breaking occasionally into a trot and then falling back again to the walk. The horse was a fast traveler and covered ground. Chet paid only enough attention to stay on the road to Rock Creek. He turned facts and happenings over and over in his mind, adding them up and always arriving at the same answer. The sun was well toward the top of the western mesas when Chet struck Rock Creek. He smiled grimly to himself. He would twist the knife that was in him; he would ride past the Lairds'. And so, instead of continuing the long tangent that would bring him to the cabin, he turned a little north. He had gone a mile and was dropping back toward the creek again when he saw smoke. It came from what must be Laird's claim and the first thing that Chet thought was that some vandal had fired the house. He put spurs to his horse and shook out into a dead run. Then he slowed to a lope, to a trot, and to a walk, and stopped. There, before him, was the well-remembered house. Chet sent his horse along. As he reached the house the kitchen door opened and Sally Laird walked out and stood on the stoop, looking at him.

Chet could think of no words. "Hello, Sally," he almost stammered, at long last.

The girl was composed. It is probable that she had been planning this meeting for some time. "Won't you come in?" she asked.

240

Chet got down from his horse. He led his mount up to the stoop and stood looking at the girl. "You came back," he said inanely.

Sally smiled. "I came back," she said.

"Are you goin' to stay?" Chet asked.

The smile left the girl's face. "I don't know," she answered. "I thought . . . I heard what happened, Chet."

Chet had regained some part of his composure. He nodded, his face troubled. "About Ed Ames?" he asked.

"Yes." Sally Laird looked away and then back to Chet again. "Perhaps now they won't . . . perhaps there will be peace in this country, Chet."

The man's face became suddenly stern. "Sally," he said brusquely, "Ed Ames didn't kill your father. I thought he did an' I took him in, but Ames didn't do it."

Sally's eyes were wide. "Then . . . ?" she questioned.

"I know who did," Chet said.

The girl stepped down from the stoop and came up to Chet. She put her hand on his arm, almost timidly. "They wanted me to stay in Ohio," she said. "Chet, couldn't you let it go? Couldn't you . . . couldn't we go somewhere and try to forget these terrible things? Couldn't we, Chet?"

Chet released the reins he held and covered the girl's hand with his own. "Sally," he said miserably, "why did you come back?"

The girl's honest eyes met Chet's. "Because . . ." she began and then hastily, "Don't make me tell you why I came back, Chet."

"Did you come back because of me?" Chet's voice was hoarse.

Sally Laird lowered her eyes. It was answer enough.

"I ain't worth it," Chet said. "I'm no good, Sally. I thought, one time, maybe I could amount to somethin'. I never will. I've got a job to finish, Sally, an' when I get it done you wouldn't want to look at me."

"Chet," the girl looked at him steadily in the face, and now it was Chet's turn to avert his eyes, "couldn't you let it go? For me, Chet?"

Chet's face showed the strain under which he labored. It was in his voice when he answered. "I've thought an' thought," he said. "All last night an' today I've thought. There can't be peace in the country . . . Sally, it isn't just that. Your father was my friend — that's part of it — but there's things between me an' this fellow that I can't lay down. I'm human, Sally. Don't you see?"

"And you would rather have your revenge on this man than to be with me?" the girl asked slowly. "You mean to kill him, don't you, Chet?"

"I meant to," Chet answered honestly. "I meant to kill him."

"I can't stop you, Chet." Sally's voice was sorrowful. "But you were so fine, you stood for what was right; how can you take justice into your own hands, Chet?"

"I don't know," Chet answered. "I don't know what I'll do. Why did you come back, Sally?" It was a plaint, almost a cry of pain. "Why didn't you stay back there where you were, an' let me alone?"

242

Suddenly the girl was close to Chet, her arms about his neck, her cheek pressed against his chest. "I'm afraid for you," she whispered. "You're all I have. Dad is dead, killed in this awful country. Promise me, Chet. Promise that you'll let it go. We'll go away. We'll go somewhere and be together. There will be peace and . . ."

She stopped. Chet's arms had gone around her to hold her close. Now the arms relaxed and the girl stepped back out of them. "You won't," she said. "It's no use, is it?"

"I've got to think," Chet said hoarsely.

The girl stepped further away. "I haven't any right to interfere," she said slowly. "That's it, isn't it? You were right: I shouldn't have come back. I should have stayed away. You were right, Chet."

Chet Minor almost groaned. "You don't understand it, Sally," he said. "It isn't just to me. That's part of it. If a man had kicked you down into the alley you'd want to get even; but that isn't all of it."

Sally looked at him with wide, unbelieving eyes.

"This fellow killed your father," Chet continued. "He's the man that's behind all of it. If I let this go there'll never be peace in the country as long as he's alive. All the folks, all the little men, will have it hangin' over them, death an' bein' scared and hidin' around, never able to walk out into the open. Don't you understand, Sally? Can't you see it?"

"I can understand that what I offered you wasn't enough," the girl said. "You'll do what you think you must do. Good-bye, Chet. I won't see you again."

She turned abruptly, mounted the stoop and went into the house. The door closed. Chet Minor stood staring at the blank wood of the door. He shook his head as though to clear it. He would call her back. He would tell her that it was all right; he would do whatever she wanted him to do. He took a breath to make that call and then let it go again. He could not call. Some things a man stood for. Some things a man must do regardless of what was offered him or of what happened after he had done them. Chet turned away from the closed door and, slowly, as though he were an old man, mounted his horse. The horse turned, took a tentative step and then, more briskly, moved toward the west, toward the Rock Springs camp.

In the Rock Springs cabin Chet put his saddle blanket down on the dusty mattress of the bunk. That was his bed. A fire in the stove and coffee boiling in the pot; that and crackers from the box, made his supper. Down in the corral the horse munched hay and drank from the trough. Up in the cabin, while the moonless night grew black, Chet watched the light of the fire, showing through the cracks of the stove. The fire died away and still Chet Minor sat, looking at the empty blackness, thinking, thinking, thinking.

In the morning he went on, riding north. It was still early when he pulled his horse to a stop at the Screwplate headquarters, dismounted, and with his spurs jingling, walked to the door. Before Chet reached it Barney Loveless opened the door and came out.

244

"Come down off yore high horse, did you?" Barney asked testily. "Got a minute to spare for the old man this mornin'?"

"I've got to talk to you, Barney," Chet answered.

"Come in an' talk then," Loveless invited.

Inside the headquarters, Chet sat on a bench. Barney, finding a chair, pulled it around and sat down across it, his arms on the chair back. "Well," he commanded, "break down an' talk. Get it off yore chest."

"Barney," Chet said, "I know who killed Doc Laird."

"Ames killed him," Loveless stated. "Everybody knows that."

"No," Chet shook his head. "Powell Overman killed him."

"Overman?" Loveless came up from the chair with the exclamation.

"Powell Overman," Chet agreed. "Sit down, Barney."

Loveless sat down again, staring at Chet as though some monster from Mars occupied the bench. Chet continued, his voice calm.

"It was Powell Overman. I'll tell you how I know. Overman had been foolin' around with Rosa Revilla. Rosa went out with Ben to the claim he took. She was goin' to have a baby. Doc Laird looked after her. Yesterday, before he died, Ben told me that Rosa had told the doctor who the father of her baby was an' the doctor had promised to see the man an' make him look after her an' the kid. The doctor went to the Triangle to see Powell. I know he did. Sally told me, an' she said her father was worried about somethin'.

Laird went to Powell an' told him that he'd have to take care of Rosa an' the kid. Likely the doctor threatened Powell some. Anyhow, Powell was afraid of Laird. He had to get him out of the way. When Doc Laird was killed we went out, Laramie an' Joe an' me, an' cut sign. We followed along the tracks we'd found, an' there was a place where another trail came in. Both horses was shod the same an' both had a number two shoe. Both tracks went right to the Triangle wagon. We found Ames there an' we knew he was a killer, so we took him in.

"The afternoon before Ames made his break, I talked with him. He told me that he wasn't goin' to stay in jail. He said that he'd get out, that he had too much on Overman for Overman to let him stay there. I thought he meant that Powell an' them had hired him, but it wasn't that. Ames had trailed Powell back to the Triangle wagons. He knew that Powell had killed Laird an' he just kept his mouth shut, knowin' that Powell would get him out.

"Yesterday, when I was in the jail, I was foolin' around with the gun Ames had when he tried to make his break. I pulled the lead out of a shell. I thought maybe it was a reloaded shell an' that the bullet hadn't been seated good, an' I went to dump the powder charge in my hand. There was sand in the shell in place of powder. The night Ames tried to break out, when Laramie an' me went down to let Joe go to supper, Joe told us that Powell had been into the jail. It's a safe bet that when he was there he gave Ames that gun with sand in the shells in place of powder. He knew that Ames would be killed when he tried to make his break. You see how it hangs together, Barney?"

"Yo're guessin'," Loveless said hoarsely. "You'll never make that stick in a court, Chet."

"But I'm right," Chet insisted. "It's got to be that way. Ames an' me had quite a talk. He was sore at me for bringin' him in, but he said that he didn't kill Laird. Then he made that break about havin' somethin' on Powell that would get him out of jail."

"But the girl," Loveless expostulated. "She knew who the father of her baby was. She could have spoke up an' . . ."

"Powell would have killed her too," Chet said with assurance. "He wasn't takin' chances. But he figured that Laird was the most dangerous. He could send a little money over to Rosa an' keep her mouth shut. Likely she was in love with him an' didn't want to hurt him. When she found out that Laird was dead she got desperate an' couldn't see a way out, so she killed herself."

Chet paused and Barney Loveless said nothing. Chet could almost see the thoughts working in the older man's head. "Powell crippled me, too," Chet said casually, almost as an afterthought. "Ben Revilla told me how he did it. Powell was right behind me when I roped that bull an' he hit my horse with his rope just as the bull took the slack out. The horse jumped an' was jerked over. Ben saw the rope marks on my horse when he brought the horse in."

"Powell Overman," Loveless said slowly. "You can't prove a thing, Chet, but yo're right. What do you think you'll do?"

"I meant to kill him," Chet said, his voice hard. "Now I don't know."

"Why not?"

"Sally Laird is back," Chet answered. "I talked with her. I don't know what I'll do, Barney, but I can't let Overman get away with it. If he does, the next thing we know there'll be another like Ed Ames in here. The whole country will be stirred up. Overman is at the bottom of all the trouble, Barney."

Loveless nodded agreement and again asked his question. "So what are you goin' to do, Chet?"

"I think," Chet said slowly, "that I'm goin' to lay it on the line to Powell. I'm goin' to tell him what I know. Then what I do depends on what he does. Sally says . . . Sally don't want it to go any further than that. If Powell drops the whole thing, if he pulls out an' doesn't come back, it won't go no further. I'll do that because Sally wants it that way."

"But if Powell don't?" Loveless questioned.

"Then I don't know," Chet admitted. "I'm goin' to lay it out for him though."

"You think a lot of Sally, don't you?" Loveless probed. "You think she's about right."

Chet took a deep breath. "Sally," he said. "Sally . . . well, they broke the mold when they made her, Barney."

"Are you an' Sally goin' to hook up?" Loveless asked bluntly.

"I won't see her again," Chet answered. "She's done with me. She said so. But I've got to go through with this, Barney. Hell, I'm human! Powell Overman kicked me into the gutter an' I'd be there yet if it wasn't for you an' Joe an' Doc Laird an' Sally. I owe him for that. But I could let that go if it wasn't for this other thing. You see how it is, Barney?"

"I can see better than a woman," Barney Loveless said. "When are you goin' to see Powell, Chet?"

Chet shrugged. "There's no hurry," he answered. "I'm goin' back an' help Joe with the round-up. Powell won't leave the country. He'll be here. After we get through will be time enough."

"I'll be along when you tell him," Loveless said suddenly. "You won't be alone."

Chet got up from the bench. "Now you see why I ain't goin' back to Rock Springs," he said. "I'd like to accommodate you, Barney, but I don't think I will."

"We'll see," Loveless drawled. "You goin' on to camp now, Chet?"

"Right away," Chet agreed.

"You goin' to tell Joe an' Laramie about this?"

"No. I'll not talk to anybody till I talk to Powell."

Loveless nodded approval. "Tell Joe I'll be up to camp tomorrow or the next day," he said. "An' Chet, you think this over. You size it up all the way around, an' remember I'll side you when the showdown comes."

"Thanks, Barney," Chet said. "I'll remember. But I've already thought it over."

He went out of the house, the old man following him. Mounting, Chet said good-bye to Loveless and rode away toward the north. Barney Loveless watched him go. When Chet had disappeared, the old man brought out a plug of tobacco from his pocket, bit off a chew, and when he had the cud under control, spat into the dust of the yard.

"A woman is always raisin' hell with a man," Barney Loveless said. "Always! Now there's a right good boy. Just a pretty fair sort of hand. Damn it! I guess I'd better . . ."

Loveless did not say what he had better do. He went to the corral, caught and saddled his wrangling horse and rode out into the horse pasture. Half an hour later he returned with the horses. From these he singled out his buckboard team and, roping them out, put on their harness. An hour after Chet Minor's departure from the Screwplate, Barney Loveless also left the ranch. Barney Loveless drove south, toward Rifle Rock but, more immediately, toward Rock Creek and the Laird claim.

CHAPTER
SEVENTEEN

At the end of June the Screwplate wagons pulled into the ranch. They were done with the branding. Now came the season when the Rifle Rock made hay and then would follow the beef round-up. The wagons would go out again when that time came, but until then there was an interlude.

Chet Minor, unsaddling beside the corral, did not join in the hilarity the completion of the work had caused in the rest of the crew. All through the last of the work he had been silent and sober. Now he turned his horse loose, put his saddle in the shed and went to the house. The Bar O7 riders had dropped out at Stevens' ranch and this was only the Screwplate that had come in. Sven Olson and Hall were going to stay at the ranch that night and then go on home. Jesse Lauder, Earl Keelin, Laramie, Joe French, Chet, these were the real Screwplate men. Chet could not account for the way he felt about the Screwplate. He belonged there, it seemed to him.

The morning after the wagons had come in, Loveless paid off. He gave the riders their checks and he did a kind thing: he hired Hall and Sven to go on the hay work. The money that would bring would be a godsend to the nester families down on Rock Creek.

Chet was the last man that Loveless paid, and he held Chet a while, talking to him, after the rest had gone out. "I fixed things up in Rifle Rock for you, Chet," Loveless said. "When you go to town you'll find some money in your name at the bank. That's for you to use to pay your pre-emption."

Chet nodded abstractedly. "I'll get a deed made out to you as soon as I get a patent," he said.

"All right," Loveless agreed. "Now about that other thing, Chet?" Loveless eyed him steadily. "Are you goin' through with it?"

"I said I was," Chet answered.

"But are you?"

"Yes."

"Are you goin' to town today?" Loveless persisted.

"I thought I would," Chet said. "Barney, I'd like to buy two horses. I'd like to buy that buckskin horse I broke, down at Rock Springs, an' I'd like to buy old Jug. Will you put a price on them?"

"I want forty dollars for the buckskin," Loveless answered. "I'll take twenty for Jug. I wouldn't let him go at all except that I know you'll look after him. Jug don't owe the Screwplate a cent. He's paid for himself."

"That's good," Chet said. "I'll pay that. You can take it out of this check, or I'll pay you in town."

"Make it in town," Barney answered. "We'll settle the whole thing up in town, what I owe you for the claim, an' all."

Chet nodded agreement. "I'll have to ride this saddle you loaned me, goin' in," he said. "I'll get a saddle in Rifle Rock. I hocked one with Wayt Higlow."

Joe French thrust his head in through the door. "Are you goin' in, Chet?" he demanded. "We're about ready."

"Coming," Chet answered. "Are you goin' to town, Barney?"

"I think I will," Loveless said. "Tell Amador to hitch up my team."

Chet went out and Barney Loveless sat behind his desk a while, looking far away and tapping the desk top with his gnarled old fingers. Then, stiffly, he got up, started toward the door, stopped, and returning to the desk got a blue-barreled gun from a drawer, checked the loads in the cylinder and put the gun in his waistband, settling his vest over it.

When he went out, Amador had the team ready and the riders were saddled and waiting. Chet had the old saddle on the buckskin colt and was leading Jug. Loveless climbed up into the buckboard, took the lines from Amador and grinned wryly at his men.

"Let's go, boys," he said. "Sorry I kept you waitin'."

Out of deference to their boss the Screwplate hands did not push on to Rifle Rock. They followed behind the buckboard, Laramie riding with Chet and Joe French, Keelin and Lauder behind them.

Laramie looked at Chet's bed, lashed to Jug's back, and asked a question. "Goin' to pull clear out of the country?"

"Maybe," Chet said.

Laramie grunted. "I left a country once," he announced. "I wouldn't go back there."

"I won't be back here," Chet said.

Loveless kept the buckboard team moving right along. He drove good horses and they covered country. Indeed, the buckboard made as fast time as a saddle horse, the only difference being that the buckboard had to follow the road.

It was midafternoon when the Screwplate men reached Rifle Rock. Other outfits had preceded them. Rifle Rock was teeming with activity. This was the end of the spring round-up; extra hands had been paid off and the regular crews from the ranches were in town spending their money. The Fourth of July was near and Rifle Rock always staged a celebration on the Fourth. On the flat outside the town, preparations were under way for the festivities. As they rode past, the Screwplate men eyed the platform that was going up.

"Big time on the Fourth," Joe French called. "We'll just stay in an' see it."

Riding down Idaho Street, having passed the depot, Chet saw many acquaintances. There were riders from the Triangle, from the AC, from the Gunhammer. There were men in from Neil's Rocking Chair and from Bob Jumper's JAK. Nesters, too, were in town, and Chet saw Stevens of the Bar O7 standing on a corner talking with Jim Clarke, the sheriff, and Martin Gardner, the district attorney. Stevens called to Chet and came out into the street. Chet rode over to the ranchman.

254

"We've just got hold of Julio Tidd an' Frank Oakes," Stevens said. "They were brought in this mornin'. Gardner wants to talk to you about what Revilla told you. You goin' to be loose pretty soon?"

"Sure," Chet agreed. "Any time. I'd like to put my horses up first."

"We'll meet you down at the Staghorn," Stevens said. "In about twenty minutes. Will that be all right?"

Chet nodded his agreement and Stevens stepped back up on the sidewalk while Chet rode on to rejoin his friends. He caught up with them and they went to the livery barn. There, turning their horses over to the hostler, they separated, Chet to go to the Staghorn and the others to spread out over Rifle Rock, renew acquaintances, take a drink, spend their money.

In the saloon Chet met Stevens and the two officials. Clarke had nothing to say to Chet, but Gardner asked him questions concerning the statements Ben Revilla had made implicating the rustlers. Chet answered these and Gardner, satisfied, asked another question.

"We're going to hold a preliminary hearing in the morning," he said. "You'll be there?"

"I'll be in town," Chet answered.

"At the justice office," Gardner amplified. "All right, Mr. Minor, we'll expect you."

Chet excused himself and went on out. He had to meet Barney Loveless at the bank.

He spent an hour or more at the bank in consultation with Loveless and Claypool. There was the matter of the claim to settle. Claypool drew up the necessary papers and accompanied Chet to the United

States Commissioner's office where Chet paid the pre-emption price and proved that he had resided at the Rock Springs claim for the prescribed length of time. Laramie and Joe French were called in off the street to act as witnesses in that proof.

Back at the bank again, Loveless and Chet reached a fair agreement as to the value of Chet's time and his homestead right. Barney would pay Chet as soon as the land patent came through. And then the business was finished and Chet went out on the street. He had not seen Powell Overman since his arrival, but he knew that Powell was in town. Otto Hahn, at the Staghorn, had told Chet that the Triangle was finished with the spring work and that Overman was at the town house. He had been about to tell Chet something else, but Stevens had come up then to claim Chet's attention and Otto left to attend the wants of other customers.

The thing Otto Hahn had begun to tell Chet when he was interrupted was a rumor that had spread over Rifle Rock. It was being talked in the houses, whispered when two women came together, mentioned, low-voiced, in the stores: the rumor that Maida Overman had left her husband.

To Rifle Rock it was only a rumor, but to Powell Overman it was grim reality. He had come in from the round-up work, tired, worried, and with guilt hanging heavily upon him. It is one thing to kill a man in desperation; it is quite another to continue living after having committed murder. Not that Powell Overman regretted having killed Dr. Laird, nor did he regret the fact that, as truly as though he had pulled the trigger of

Old Man Sykes' shotgun, he had killed Ed Ames. The murders bothered Overman no more than the suicide of Rosa Revilla bothered him. Relief was his principal reaction when he thought of Rosa and Laird and Ames. The thing that preyed heavily upon his mind was the fear that he would be found out. That was the thing that made him lie awake at night, that put the haunted, worried look in his eyes. And when he returned from the ranch, the spring work completed, he found his wife gone and with her, Kirkpatrick.

There was a note in his bedroom, short and pointed. Powell read the note and, carrying it, went downstairs and questioned the woman who cooked and kept house, the woman that Maida had hired to replace Rosa Revilla.

The housekeeper knew but little. Mr. Kirkpatrick and Mrs. Overman had been gone two days, she said. Mr. Kirkpatrick had taken his luggage and Mrs. Overman had taken a grip. The drayman had come for Mrs. Overman's trunk. Aside from that, the housekeeper knew nothing, even though she suspected a great deal. She did not mention her suspicions. Powell Overman, with the note still in his hand, went into the office, the old office where Mark Scotia had once directed the affairs of the Triangle, where the cattlemen had met, where Powell had pulled the leads from .45 shells. Seated at the desk, he put the note down before him and stared at the wall. After a time he picked up the note again and read it through once more.

"Powell," Maida had written, "I am going to Kansas City with Norville. I will divorce you there. You have nothing to offer me and I am tired of living like a savage. Norville promises me everything I want and I intend to take it. If you do not contest the divorce you may remain as manager of the Triangle. That should please your vanity. If you choose to contest my divorce there are many things that I can bring up. You must use your own best judgment in the matter, *my dear*," — the "*my dear*" was heavily underscored as though Maida wished to inflict a still deeper wound — "but I believe that you will see the wisdom of keeping quiet. You will hear from me through my lawyers very soon. Maida."

There it was, bald and bare-faced as a Hereford calf. Powell Overman crushed the note in his big, blunt-fingered hand and threw it from him.

Powell did not leave the house that day; he did not go out until late in the evening of the second day. He could not go out. He knew that Maida's departure had been noted and that it was being talked about. How could he go out on the streets of Rifle Rock and face the curious stares of the people that he knew? It was an impossibility. He drank a little while he stayed in the house, not a great deal but enough to build up a fine, keen edge to his anger. When he did leave the house late in the afternoon of that second day, he was not drunk but he was red-eyed as an angry rattlesnake and, like the snake, dangerous to the first living thing that blocked his path.

There was a certain bravado in Powell Overman that finally sent him to the heart of Rifle Rock. He had hidden his hurt and shame (it could not be called sorrow), but now he was ready to appear and challenge anyone that dared to comment. For months, all through the round-up Overman had worn a gun strapped about his middle. He put on the weapon before he left the house.

On Idaho Street Powell Overman strode along, his head up, haughty and contemptuous. He walked past Wolfbarger's, nodding to Tom Neil who stood there, but ignoring the lesser lights, the riders that spoke to him. On down the street he went until, before the Bon Ton store, he stopped. Royce Mitchell was leaning against one of the posts that supported the awning in front of the Bon Ton, and Powell engaged in conversation with Mitchell.

Chet Minor and Barney Loveless, emerging from the Staghorn with Laramie and Joe French following them, were on their way to supper. The pleasant evening light that follows sundown in June was on the street, clear and sweet as spring water. Chet Minor saw Powell Overman pass by, and stepped forward, but Barney Loveless restrained him.

"Not on the street," Barney said.

"Where else then?" Chet demanded, and pulling free from Barney, limped hastily along. Across the street Overman, long-legged and unblemished, distanced the limping Chet. It was not until Overman stopped to speak to Mitchell that Chet came abreast. Laramie and Joe, sensing that something was afoot, hurried after Chet. Barney Loveless, stopping when Chet started across the street, spoke to his men.

"Don't come over," he said sharply, "but watch close."

Laramie and Joe stopped on the sidewalk, exchanging glances that spoke eloquently of their curiosity. Loveless hastened across the street after Chet.

When Chet reached the porch of the Bon Ton, his head came about level with Overman's waist. Chet was on the board sidewalk and Powell Overman, on the porch of the store, was elevated. Chet stepped around the end of the hitchrail where a drowsy cow horse dozed and coming up beside Powell spoke abruptly.

"Can I speak to you a minute, Overman?"

Overman looked down, saw Chet's set, earnest face, and turned back to Mitchell. "As I was sayin' . . ." he began, ignoring Chet.

"If you want Mitchell to hear what I'm goin' to say, all right," Chet interrupted, his voice low but very distinct. "I'm goin' to say it anyhow."

Royce Mitchell looked at Chet and then back to Overman. "I'll be inside the store when you're finished, Powell," he said. Overman did not answer and Mitchell walked away.

"Well," Powell Overman rasped, looking down at Chet, "what have you got to say to me?"

"Just this." There was no hesitation in Chet's low voice. "I know that you killed Doc Laird, Powell. I know all about it. I'm layin' it on the line for you."

Barney Loveless had come up and stood, perhaps five feet behind Chet and to his right. Across the street Joe French and Laramie were watching intently and others of the men on Idaho Street, seeing Chet Minor talking to Powell Overman, stopped the things they were doing, to watch.

For half a minute, following Chet's statement, Overman made no move, did nothing. Simply he was quiet, staring down at Chet Minor. As he stared Powell Overman's long face changed color slowly, at first suffused and then the blood fading from it, leaving a pallor beneath the tan. His eyes, wide when Chet said the first words, gradually narrowed until they were slits in the mask of his face.

"I know it," Chet said again. "I'll tell you . . ."

Powell Overman's voice was hoarse as he interrupted Chet. It was as though Powell and Chet were alone on the street without Laramie and Joe, without the curious onlookers, without old Barney Loveless, craning his neck to listen.

"I wish I'd killed you," Overman grated. "I tried to, an' all I did was cripple you. I wish I'd killed you!"

"I know that, too," Chet began. "You . . ."

"You know about me an' you know I killed Laird," Overman rasped the words. "Do you know that Maida's left me, Minor? You know so damned much . . ."

The words broke then, changing suddenly into action. Powell Overman's big hand lifted and went back swiftly and surely to the gun at his hip. The Colt cleared leather, swept up and a shot crashed in Rifle Rock's quiet, as a red ring blossomed from the muzzle of the gun.

Chet had half expected this. Still he did not move to defend himself. "Powell!" he said again, his voice raised now. "Powell . . ."

Barney Loveless had leaped to the right, away from Chet. Barney was tugging at his waist, the hammer of his gun caught in his vest. Across the street Laramie had dived a hand into his shirt, and was pulling the gun he wore there. Once more Powell Overman dropped his gun in line, his thumb pulling back the hammer. Madness blazed in the man's eyes and Chet, moving to his left, knowing murder when he saw it, pulled his gun.

The crash of the 32-20 was sharper, more whip-like than the roar of Overman's .45. They blended, mingling their reverberations. Dust whipped up from the street behind Chet Minor. A man yelled, high and shrill, on the sidewalk, frightened by the whine of the ricochet that whimpered past his head. On the porch of the Bon Ton store Powell Overman stood bolt upright; he teetered there just at the edge, precariously for an instant, and then with all his long body rigid, came falling, crashing down into the dust of Idaho Street.

Across the street Laramie came running. Barney Loveless stopped the useless struggle with his fouled weapon. From the jail office, directly opposite the Bon Ton, Jim Clarke burst out, a gun in his hand.

They took Chet Minor into the jail office, Jim Clarke with the 32-20 he had wrested from Chet's lax hand, Barney Loveless and Joe French and Laramie, a compact bodyguard about Chet. They kept him there while out in Idaho Street a crowd boiled and eddied, while Vance Murray dealt with the crowd, while Martin Gardner, brought from the hotel, fought his way through the congestion. They kept Chet there for a long time, kept him until the crowd outside had quieted, until the light was gone from the streets of Rifle Rock, until Barney Loveless, fierce as an old eagle, shouted down Jim Clarke and Gardner and forced them to listen.

It was Barney who told the story, Barney who followed out, piece by piece, detail by detail, the events that had led to Powell Overman's death, to the sudden flaring of lead and powder in Idaho Street, Barney that stamped home in the minds of sheriff and attorney the fact that Powell Overman had killed Laird, had, in a way, killed Ed Ames.

"You can't make nothin' of it but self-defense," Loveless concluded. "Overman pulled his gun an' shot. He was ready for a second try at the boy. I'd have shot him myself if my damned gun hadn't got the hammer caught. Hell! I wasn't goin' to have Chet killed. It was self-defense an' that's all there is to it; but if you want to try to make somethin' else out of it Chet will go on the stand an' tell the whole story. You ain't goin' to look very good if he does that, Jim, an' there's goin' to be some cowmen around here explainin' how they came to hire a killer like Ed Ames. I'll leave it to you an' Gardner. You do what you want, but Chet'll have the best lawyer in the state if it comes to a trial, an' when we get done hell will look like a summer holiday compared to Rifle Rock."

Gardner turned from fierce old Barney Loveless and called Jim Clarke aside. They talked in the little corridor that led back to the cell, while Vance Murray stood beside the window and looked out into Idaho Street.

Clarke and Gardner came back. "We've decided," he said. "It was self-defense, pure and simple. We'll present the evidence to the coroner's jury in the morning. Jim is going to talk to Mitchell and some of the others and I don't think there will be any trouble." There was a significance in the last sentence that made old Barney and Laramie and Joe French smile grimly.

"And there is no need of airing this before the public," Gardner concluded. "Do you think so, Mr. Minor?" He looked at Chet, standing motionless beside the office desk. A smooth man, Gardner; a politician and a man that could sense the direction of the wind.

"I told Barney," Chet said, his voice flat and expressionless. "Barney an' me an' the ones that are here are all that know."

Gardner looked at the men in the room. He smiled oddly, as though asking their approbation for the thing he was doing. "The Scotias are an old family here," he said. "There is no need of airing soiled linen. Can't we drop it here and forget about it? Mr. Minor will come free on a self-defense verdict, and we can let it rest."

Laramie nodded his grim head. Joe French's black beard bobbed. Old Barney Loveless looked like a pleased old eagle and even Jim Clarke's sullen face lighted a trifle.

"We're all agreed," Gardner said. "Mr. Loveless, I'll release Mr. Minor in your custody. You'll be at the inquest in the morning. I think it's perfectly all right for you to go now."

Barney Loveless collected his forces with his eyes. Joe French and Laramie stood up. Barney put his hand on Chet's arm. "We'll go to the hotel," he said. "Come on, Chet."

And Chet Minor allowed the old man to lead him out of the office.

CHAPTER
EIGHTEEN

Barney Loveless passed up the Fourth of July celebration in Rifle Rock. The festivities went ahead, despite the death of a prominent citizen, for Rifle Rock did not mourn Powell Overman particularly. Somewhere a rumor had leaked out, a grim rumor concerning Powell Overman and the deaths of Laird and Ed Ames. Rifle Rock buzzed with the talk and looked slant-eyed at Tom Neil and Royce Mitchell and the other cowmen. The cowmen acted as though nothing had happened.

Barney Loveless, in passing up the celebration, had to talk to Chet. Chet was all for leaving town. Chet, with his saddle reclaimed from Wayt Higlow, his two horses and a bed roll, was ready to leave the country. He wanted to leave. A jury, skilfully led by Martin Gardner's questioning of witnesses, had exonerated him in the matter of Powell Overman's death, but still that thing hung heavily upon Chet Minor. It was not a thing to throw off with a shrug. Barney did considerable talking, invented excuses, and as a last resort explained to the silent, limping man that he must go with him to the Rock Springs and there point out the exact corner stakes of the claim. Barney Loveless who knew every foot of the country from Rifle Rock to the Tramparas, asking for help in locating corner stakes! It was plain stalling and Chet knew it. But Barney had been a friend, was a friend, and even when a friend was obstinately dumb, Chet would not let him down.

So, on the morning of the Fourth, with Rifle Rock already getting a little high on liquor, with the bunting draped over the store fronts and with the flags flying, Chet rode out with Barney Loveless in the Screwplate buckboard, rode north and west.

Because Chet did not want to talk, Barney respected his wish. He drove his team along, humming a little tuneless song, looking at the good green grass and the good blue sky and the plump backs and rumps of the good bay horses. The buckboard rolled along and the wheels sang on the soft dirt of the road, even as Barney sang in his throat. Where the road forked, Barney turned north and Chet broke his silence.

"You can take that other road and go straight across," he suggested. "The creek isn't up an' you can make the Rock Springs ford."

"I know it," Barney answered, and kept on driving north.

The road turned west again, dropped into the creek bottom, climbed out and crowned a rise. Down to the creek bottom again the road went and down to the creek bottom went the Screwplate buckboard. And then the road came around a bend and the buckboard came around the bend and Dr. Laird's house with the barn and the fence and the cowpen and the pile of hay that was left from winter, was spread out before them. Barney drove the buckboard to the fence, stopped, and climbed down over a cramped wheel. Chet sat in the seat, unmoving.

"Better get down, Chet," Barney suggested. "I've got to stop here a minute."

"I'll wait here," Chet said dully.

Barney Loveless grunted and walked off in the direction of the barn while Chet sat in the seat of the buckboard, his eyes fixed straight ahead of him so that he did not see the door of the house open.

There was the sound of a small foot crunching on gravel and Sally Laird said, "Chet."

Chet turned at that and looked down at the girl standing beside the rig. He stepped out of the buckboard and Sally Laird moved back to give him room to alight.

"Sally," Chet said hoarsely, "you've got to know. I killed Powell Overman."

The girl's face was white, but her eyes were clear and steady. "I knew that, Chet," she said.

"You knew . . . ?" Chet blurted, unbelief written plainly in his eyes. "You knew and still you come to me like this? Sally . . ."

"Won't you come in the house, Chet?" Sally Laird asked and, not waiting for an answer, walked slowly toward the stoop.

Chet stood stock still. The girl reached the entrance, stepped up and turned, and Chet Minor, limping, scrambling in his haste, went to her. The door of Dr. Laird's house closed behind him.

Barney Loveless came out from the barn where he had been standing, and walked to the house.

Shamelessly he peered through the window. Then, shaking his head, he squatted down beside the house, his back against the wall.

There were plans in Barney Loveless's shrewd old head, plans for the future. The country was settling. There would be difficulties in that process. The cowmen would faunch and rare back and raise hell, but without Powell Overman, without a leader like Overman, there would be no trouble that could not be ironed out.

It would be fine to have a neighbor like Chet at the Rock Springs. Barney had plans for that. Fall was just a month or so away and with the fall an election would be held. Barney Loveless had plans for the election. He was an old man and he had no child. He needed a strong young shoulder on which to rest his weight, a strong young back on which to unload the burden of the Screwplate, a keen young mind to train in the mysteries of buying and handling cull cattle so that a profit was derived therefrom.

With a heave and a grunt and a scowl on his weathered face, Barney Loveless got up. Once more he peered through the window, long and steadily. When he turned around he was grinning with satisfaction. There was no danger, from what he had seen, of Chet Minor's leaving the Rifle Rock. No danger at all. A woman's arms would hold him there, just as they were holding him now. Barney Loveless squatted down beside the wall and went right on with his planning.

About the author

Bennett Foster was born in Omaha, Nebraska, and came to live in New Mexico in 1916 to attend the State Agricultural College and remained there the rest of his life. He served in the U.S. Navy during the Great War and was stationed in the Far East during the Second World War, where he attained the rank of captain in the U.S. Air Corps. He was working as the principal of the high school in Springer, New Mexico, when he sold his first short story, "Brockleface", to *West Magazine* in 1930 and proceeded to produce hundreds of short stories and short novels for pulp magazines as well as *The Country Gentleman* and *Cosmopolitan* over the next three decades. In the 1950s his stories regularly appeared in *Collier*'s. In the late 1930s and early 1940s Foster wrote a consistently fine and critically praised series of Western novels, serialized in *Argosy* and *Street & Smith's Western Story Magazine*, that were subsequently issued in hardcover book editions by William Morrow and Company and Doubleday, Doran and Company in the Double D series. It is worth noting that Foster's early Double D Westerns were published under the pseudonym John Trace, although some time later these same titles, such as TRIGGER

VENGEANCE and RANGE OF GOLDEN HOOFS, appeared in the British market under his own name. Foster knew the terrain and the people of the West first-hand from a lifetime of living there. His stories are invariably authentic in detail and color, from the region of fabulous mesas, jagged peaks, and sun-scorched deserts. Among the most outstanding of his published Western novels are BADLANDS (1938), RIDER OF THE RIFLE ROCK (1939), and WINTER QUARTERS (1942), this last a murder mystery within the setting of a Wild West Show touring the western United States. THE MEXICAN SADDLE (Five Star Westerns, 1999) and GILA CITY (Five Star Westerns, 2003) are Bennett Foster's most recent books. As a storyteller he was always a master of suspenseful and unusual narratives.